Soft Targets

There are two kinds of targets:

HARD: Arrogant in its security, surrounded by armed guards, bullet-proof glass, and every conceivable electronic defense.

SOFT: A hard target plucked quivering from its shell...

Ace Science Fiction books by Dean Ing

ANASAZI
PULLING THROUGH
SOFT TARGETS
SYSTEMIC SHOCK

SOFT TARGETS

DEAN ING

ACE SCIENCE FICTION BOOKS
NEW YORK

All characters in this book are fictitious.
Any resemblance to actual persons,
living or dead, is purely coincidental.

A portion of this novel was published as "Very Proper Charlies"
in the October 1978 issue of *Destinies,* copyright © 1978
by Charter Communications, Inc.

SOFT TARGETS

An Ace Science Fiction Book / published by arrangement with
the author

PRINTING HISTORY
Ace original / October 1979
Ace Science Fiction edition / May 1980
Second printing / July 1986

ISBN: 0-441-77407-5

Ace Science Fiction Books are published by The Berkley Publishing Group,
200 Madison Avenue, New York, New York 10016.
PRINTED IN THE UNITED STATES OF AMERICA

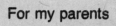
For my parents

". . . I found fear a mean, overrated motive; no deterrent and, though a stimulant, a poisonous stimulant whose every injection served to consume more of the system . . ."

—T. E. Lawrence,
Seven Pillars of Wisdom

FRIDAY, 19 SEPTEMBER, 1980:

Still naked and sleep-fogged after his morning coffee, the wire-muscled little man retrieved his attaché case from his pillowslip and placed it with reverence on the apartment's sleazy table. He touched the case in a necessary spot, then traded regal glances with Elizabeth II of England, whose likeness faced him from predominantly brown engravings. As an eye-opener, he reflected, caffeine was no match for cash.

The twenty-five thousand was in hundreds, all Canadian money. There would be more soon, if his sources were sufficiently pleased with his Buffalo broadcast of the previous night. Next to the money was his Hewlett-Packard hand calculator; American, modified in France. His German passport, tucked into a flap, had been faked in Italy. The Spanish automatic with its armpit holster took up most of the remaining space; he had obtained the piece in Quebec

while killing time—among other things. He
flicked his great dark eyes to the note pad flanking his passport, deciphering his personal
shorthand which was by Arabic out of Gregg.
Altogether, he thought contentedly, a cosmo-
politan survival kit.

He grasped the little HP calculator and
queried it. 9:37 A FRI, the alphanumeric display
read. He could easily have programmed it to add,
19 SEP 80 TORONTO; or perhaps 6 DAYS TO
BORDER. Even among HP units, it was a very
special gadget. He winked—a signal Americans
usually misread as harmless duplicity—at the
stacks of Elizabeths, closed the case, and stood.
There would be time for calisthenics before making the buy.

He began with simple hand and foot exercises,
progressed to ritual defensive maneuvers, then
dervished through a repertoire of offensive
moves, breathing easily in marvelous silence as
he negotiated the furniture. No surplus flesh
masked the tendons that slid just beneath the
skin. The knee was solid again, so he covertly
eyed the pencil mark he had made chin-high on
the door moulding. He took one bare-footed step
as if to flee but rebounded, the other leg sweeping up flexed, then extended in a vicious slanting blur.

The ball of the foot gently swept within centimeters of his target, then thrust away. He
landed quietly and rolled, to freeze into a
crouch, mouth open to quiet his breathing. His
weaknesses in martial arts were philosophical
ones. He knew few peers in the prime requisites
for unarmed combat: speed, silence, ferocity.

Not once had he made enough noise to excite comment from the next apartment. He was pleased with himself but he was not smiling. In his apparatus of deceit, the smile was a favored tool. He essayed two more flying side kicks, testing his eyes, his precision, his right shin's *peroneus longus* muscle that really made the move so murderous, and stopped only because of a creaky board in the floor. Satisfied, he tapered off with mild arm and leg flexures before his shower. The cold water sent blades of pain twisting up his limbs. Now he smiled, and turned the water on full force.

His scrub disturbed the flexible cobbler's cement on his fingertips and he applied a fresh coating. When dry, its sheen was unseen as it filled the tiny whorls of flesh. Now his touch was anonymous, matching the prosthetic tip of his left small finger.

He dressed quickly, choosing the ice-blue silk dress shirt and the deeper blue conservative jacket above dove-gray trousers. He shrugged into the harness, placed his piece carefully in the holster against spring pressure, and decided he would have time to find chemicals at supply houses enroute to the big buy. He flipped through the thick yellow-page Toronto directory, made several notations, and checked the window telltales. Then, taking the attaché case, he paused to emplace a telltale on the bottom door hinge before sliding out to the hall.

The garage attendant wheeled his rented Toyota to him, proof that no unfriendly hands had dallied under the car. Then he drove down Bathurst on his shopping foray. At the paint store, paying for the aluminum powder, he asked to use a telephone.

A young woman's voice tinned through the earpiece, "Salon du Nord," making it sound like a beauty parlor.

"Monsieur Pelletier, s'il vous plaît," he replied. His accent gave away less in French than in English. There were advantages to operating in a bilingual country.

Pelletier was in, Pelletier was oozing charm. Pelletier had the stuff. "But of course," he said, "packaged as you requested, Mr. Trnka."

"Quality assurance tests?"

"Of course. I believe your appointment was this morning."

"Precisely," said the little man, pronouncing his favorite English word. Though fluent in English, he had chosen the name 'Trnka' because so few people could say whether his accent was truly Czech. Once he had preferred the Turkish 'Jemil,' but no longer. Turkish was too close. He reaffirmed the appointment and minutes later drove into an area of new light industry.

Salon du Nord occupied half of a two-story building. Its logo phrase, "Electronique— Recherche et Perfectionnement" had its English equivalent below: "Electronic R & D." He had dealt with the firm only through an intermediary, but Pelletier was known as a useful source.

He was immediately shown to Pelletier's office. Pelletier was short, scarcely taller than his visitor but heavier by a good twenty kilos, all smiles and reeking of bonhomie. 'Trnka' smiled, detesting him on sight. "I trust you're enjoying your stay in Toronto, Mr. Trnka," Pelletier began.

"Very much; but I am pressed for time," the little man replied, placing the attaché case in his lap.

Pelletier sighed. "Of course." His soft hands reached into his desk, reappeared with a plastic belt. Aligned like cartridges along the belt were twenty black oblongs, somewhat more slender than dominoes. "Unusual packaging," Pelletier said, offering the belt. "But, ah, very practical." Again the smile like an oil slick, bright and wide. And thin.

The visitor nodded and detached one of the black oblongs. The tiny microprocessor boasted eighteen gold-plated prongs down its length on each side, giving it the look of a centipede by Mondrian. "Certified for all functions, you say," he prompted.

"Yes indeed. But there's an exceedingly smart little computer in each one, Mr. Trnka. We can't test every one for every function although I personally supervised random sampling of the entire lot."

"Random? You are telling me that most of the microprocessors are untested," the visitor replied softly.

"On such short notice, and for such a price . . ." Pelletier displayed his palms.

"Fortunately," said 'Trnka,' "I can test them myself." He took the HP unit from his case, withdrew a tiny circuit board with a flimsy cable and IC socket. Pelletier gaped in silence as the HP, the test circuit board, and the microprocessor were assembled. Lastly, 'Trnka' energized the HP and fed it a slender tongue of ferrite tape. They watched the alphanumeric display flicker for perhaps twenty seconds.

Pelletier smiled engagingly. "Forgive my curiosity," he wheedled. "It occurred to me that your circuitry could have—unusual applications."

"Games," was the reply. "We hope to give the Atari people a rude shock."

"I see," said Pelletier, unconvinced. "Something like war games." He flinched at the responding glance. It softened in a flash, but for one harrowing instant Pelletier felt that he gazed into the eyes of a Comanche warrior.

At length the HP display stabilized on CONFORME. Silently, 'Trnka' substituted another microprocessor. "Sixty-three seconds," he said to the restive Pelletier. "It would have taken you just twenty-one minutes to run exhaustive function checks on this group." He was not pleased.

"Mr. Trnka, it will take you seven hours to check them all. May I suggest you simply return any you find faulty?"

"Like this one?" The HP display read OP AMP X.

"It is not easy or conventional to include that operational amplifier in a unit of that size," Pelletier reminded.

He was answered by a grunt. The faulty centipede was pocketed while another took its place. Pelletier fidgeted as two more microprocessors were tucked away. At last the belt was reassembled with its seventeen conforming units. 'Trnka' snorted softly. "It will be necessary to use your telephone."

Pelletier indicated his desk phone and wad-
dled out to give the illusion of privacy. 'Trnka'
was certain his call would be recorded. He had
no other reason for the call.

He reached McEvoy with the phone's third
buzz. Mr. Trnka was unavoidably detained. No,
nothing serious. Yes, he was still interested but
must delay his trip a few days. Still, they might
meet today as planned. Two o'clock? Fine; Slip
Three.

Pelletier, in his photoreduction lab, listened to
the call while querying his own system at his lab
computer terminal. The detectors built into his
entryway insisted that Mr. Trnka carried
roughly a kilogram of some dense metallic article near his left armpit. Pelletier was not surprised, but he was perspiring lightly now. How
could he have known the *salaud* would have
such a test rig? He considered the alarm button,
then the money, which Trnka had promised
would be in cash. If Trnka paid fifty cents on the
dollar for such faulty units, Pelletier and his
partner would lose little. If Pelletier got more, he
could still claim it *was* fifty, and then Pelletier
alone would profit very well indeed.

And the damned Czech expected to be in Toronto a few more days. Pelletier wondered why,
and then heard the conversation end. He allowed the little foreigner, still grafted to his attaché case, to find him slurping coffee from a
foam cup in the hall. Then—insultingly—he was
ushered back into his own office.

"I am prepared to discount the entire lot of
four hundred microprocessors, Mr. Trnka, by
fifteen per cent," Pelletier said blandly.

"I need four hundred units, twenty of the belts. And I shall take delivery of four hundred," the smaller man lied. "With such a high failure rate we must test them all. Do you agree?" A glum nod from the fat man. "It is my intention to pay you in cash for half of them now, discounted as you suggest, and to test them. You, meanwhile, will test the rest—*all* of them—and manufacture a sufficient number that I will have," he paused, closed his eyes and said as though to a child, "four hundred microprocessors."

Pelletier's mental circuits flickered. Eighty-five hundred dollars in the raw, today, and an equal amount to come later. He debated the ways in which he could profit from this frightening little Czech. "I could have them in a week," he offered.

"Tuesday," the man said. Pelletier did not like even a little piece of the smile that accompanied the ultimatum.

"I will do what I can." *To see the last of you,* he added to himself.

The attaché case opened and the visitor counted out eighty-five brown Elizabeths. He pushed them across the desk. "You will want to count them."

"I trust you," said Pelletier, his voice quavering as he stroked the cash. He watched the swarthy little man walk to a small sedan, the attaché case burdened with nearly two hundred microprocessors. Then Pelletier counted the money. Next he replayed the telephone call. The number was that of a fly-for-hire outfit located at Island Airport just south of Toronto. McEvoy did not seem to know Trnka well, and Slip Three suggested a boat rather than an aircraft. Pelletier knew little of such things and did not much care. It was enough to know that Trnka would be good for another eighty-five hundred, after which Pelletier could pay his respects to the police in return for a certain latitude they allowed him in business. Trnka was a fool, thought Pelletier, to deal directly in cash. Even though his microprocessors were very, very smart.

'Trnka' did not assume that Pelletier was a fool. He drove directly to the new bridge over the Western Gap and onto the seaplane slips on Toronto Island. At one o'clock he found the decrepit old Republic Seabee wallowing in its slip, its high wing seesawing gently. The amiable curmudgeon pumping water from the fuselage bilge turned out to be Ian McEvoy, and soon they were sharing lunch at a counter with a view. The little man could spot anyone approaching the aircraft, the better to learn if Pelletier really wanted his anonymous cash more than he wanted to inform. He had seen Pelletier tremble like a pointer while raking the money in; but he had not come this far by trusting nuances.

McEvoy accepted the stranger at face value: a sinewy little Czech given to expensive clothes, on the long side of thirty and able to pay for eccentric notions. Between bites of his sandwich, McEvoy said, "Sure she'll get you and the lady to Lake Chautauqua, Mr. Trnka. It's maybe an hour's flight time, but there isn't much to do when you get there." He brightened. "For a little more I could take you to the Finger Lakes. They're in New York State too. A little more action."

A pause, as though genuinely pondering the idea; as though there really was a woman. Then, "She humors me, Mr. McEvoy, and I shall humor her. She tells me that Lake Chautauqua is a good location for the film and I need to take some footage along the shoreline for study. You are familiar with cine cameras?"

"Just home movie stuff." McEvoy held a hunk of bread to his face. "Clickety-click, and off to be developed. Nothin' like an honest-to-God movie. You mean you aren't interested in landing at all?"

"We hadn't considered it. Why?"

A shrug of the narrow shoulders. "Just makes it simpler. If we land, I hafta notify Customs when I file my flight plan. They say it's reciprocal clearance, I say it's a hassle." A twinkle in the moist blue eyes as McEvoy studied his client's tailoring. "But you don't look like a shit-runner to me." He took another mouthful of his monte cristo.

'Trnka' assembled a smile for the pilot. "I am merely combining business with pleasure, Mr. McEvoy." He watched two people stroll toward the seaplane in the distance, spied the cameras, noted that the woman was stout, the man clumsy. He continued talking with McEvoy, discussing fees and weather, increasingly sure that the pair at the slip were only tourists. The couple continued their stroll and presently passed beyond the slips. Pressed for a time estimate by McEvoy, he said, "Wednesday or Thursday. We may pay you a visit before that." He left the buried implication that he would be somewhere in Toronto.

"Speaking of pay," McEvoy put in slyly. The little man's blue jacket yielded a slender envelope which McEvoy inspected. He withdrew the three hundred dollars, then absently stuffed the bank notes into his oil-stained leather jacket. "Half of that would've done it, Mr. Tee," he grinned. "This retainer just bought me a fathometer."

"And your silence," said the smaller man. "Film companies have their little secrets. There is one more thing . . ."

"I thought there might be," McEvoy mumbled. He seemed ready to give back the retainer.

"You can stow some equipment for me until then. Just a piece of luggage; camera, film, clothing. But my car is very small and the suitcase is both a bother and a temptation to thieves." He saw strain lines disappearing from McEvoy's face and continued, "A pilot of your years must be a careful man. I think the cine camera equipment may be safer in your care than in mine. I have a tendency to forget things." He delivered this last phrase sadly, tentatively, the confession of one ill-equipped to deal with details.

McEvoy sealed his agreement by paying for lunch, then walked with his client to the Toyota. If he had any lingering worry, it evaporated when 'Trnka' opened the suitcase, poked among the clothing and equipment. These were not the actions of a guy running heavy shit, McEvoy thought; the thing wasn't even locked. He hefted the suitcase and shook the small man's hand. "What you need is a bigger car," he joked.

"And struggle to fuel and steer and park it?

How I loathe the American product," said
'Trnka,' frowning, pleased to wedge more mis-
direction in as he climbed into the Toyota.

Ian McEvoy trudged back to his Seabee,
pleased with an honest negotiation, cudgeling
his memory to recall where he had seen Trnka
before. Movies? He had heard that voice somewhere, for sure. Maybe on the TV . . .

The telltales in the apartment were undis-
turbed, the weather report optimistic. He left the
clothes on their hangers but applied more cement to his fingertips, scrubbing glassware and
fingers meticulously as he had the Toyota's interior. Then he turned his attention to the telephones. First there was the microprocessor,
which passed an on-the-spot function check before he installed it on a circuit board and patched
the tiny rig into the automatic answering device.
He disconnected the smoke alarm in his kitchen,
then placed the answering device, connected to
both telephones, in the sink. He dumped his
small potted plant on the floor, cleared the hole
in the pot's bottom only to cover the hole with
tape, and twisted coat hangers into a sling that
suspended the empty clay pot over the circuit
board.

Next he mixed a cupful of magnetite and
aluminum powder, pouring the potent stuff into
the clay pot. He used squibs and an igniter common to model rocketry though he always, always employed them in threes, wired in parallel
for reliability. Finally, though its crudeness irri-
tated him, he deployed the twenty-meter extension cord and connected its bared wires directly
to the squib circuit. He knotted the free end of the

extension cord around a chair leg near a wall
socket and spent several minutes taping the
mousetrap firmly to the chair. Adhesive tape
was so damnably adhesive it could take a faint
impression of a fingerprint even through the
protective cement. He had plenty of time, and he
knew how to use it.

After he wired one leg of the extension cord to
the trap, arranging it to complete the circuit
when triggered, he deformed another coat
hanger and taped it, centered vertically, to the
inside door knob. He measured a length of cord
with great care, tying a loop in its exact center
and securing the loop over the mousetrap's trigger. Each end of the cord was then loop-knotted
to an extremity of the coat hanger. The cord was
very slightly slack. He turned the door knob several times. Either way the knob turned, the
lengthened arm of the coat hanger would assure
triggering, completed circuit, squib ignition—
and a few more gray hairs for the apartment
manager.

At last he was ready, going through his prep-
arations again, checking every connection. It
was rush hour by now on a Friday afternoon, and
he would be all the more anonymous. He took up
the attaché case, studied the entry rig again, and
then plugged the extension cord into the wall.
That moment always set him on edge: you never
knew.

Then he slid one loop knot loose and opened
the door, peering casually into the empty hall
before he swiftly secured the loop again and
tightened it. He set the lock on the inside, picked
up the attaché case, and stepped into the hall,

pulling the door closed. He did not test the knob. If the lock was faulty the knob would turn, and if the knob turned much *he* would get the gray hairs. He strode from the building and down the street to another parking complex where an attendant brought all six meters of his dun-brown Pontiac Parisienne, the Canadian version of a Catalina. Moments later he turned north on Route Eleven toward Lake Simcoe, chafing at the need to drive around Lake Huron en route to Winnipeg. But, *"To regain the initiative we must ignore the main body of the enemy and concentrate far off,"* he quoted silently. El Aurans had known.

He held the big Pontiac at the legal maximum, unmoved by the occasional view of sunset over inlets from Georgian Bay. At Parry Sound he fed seventeen imperial gallons to his brute, nagged himself into checking the equipment in its trunk, and made a toll call to one of his two Toronto numbers. His own voice said, "Mr. Trnka regrets that he is unable to take your call at the moment. At the tone, please leave your name and number." The response tape was blank. More important, his communication center was still functioning, which meant that no one had traced him to the apartment. Yet.

He drove nearly to Marathon before he entered a rest stop, evacuated himself, and fluffed out the slender goosedown mummy bag. It was not optimal, but neither was confrontation in a motel by some red-suited lackey of the Royal Canadian Mounted Police. He slept.

On Saturday he passed Winnipeg ahead of schedule, crossed Manitoba, stopped well into

Saskatchewan. Hunger, as he knew, kept a healthy animal poised for the hunt—whichever end of the hunt it was on. He nibbled at fruit, then, in the mornings and feasted at the end of each day's travel.

Sunday he was immersed in listening to a mysterious noise in the Parisienne's luxurious vee-eight and nearly failed to hear a news item on the radio. Government sources had disarmed two charges of high explosive hidden in the structure of the Cap Rouge Bridge north of Quebec City. The massive charges would have rendered the bridge useless for weeks. On undisclosed evidence, both metropolitan police and the RCMP sought one Jean Bonin, known as a violent Quebecois separatist.

He snorted to himself, certain that the evidence was as simple as fingerprint impressions in the plastique. Bonin was an excellent provider, but an idiot with explosives. He would wind up in Archambault Penitentiary yet. The Cap Rouge fiasco, at least, explained why Bonin had refused him even a kilo of plastique. And now it belonged to the government! *C'est la guerre*; another toll call assured him that in Toronto, Mr. Trnka still regretted . . .

The terrain was a distinct drawback as the Parisienne labored into the Canadian Rockies, its malaise now more pronounced. He skirted Banff, stopped near Lake Louise, and nestled into the mummy bag at midnight. The cold was one thing he had never mastered, and anger at this failure in himself kept him awake too long.

Monday he flogged the car through Kamloops and past Ashcroft, unwilling to admit that the

Parisienne was no vehicle for mountain driving.
He found a turnoff with a downhill slope leading
to the highway, nearly backing the big machine
over a precipice. He was grimy, he was hungry,
he was in no mood to appreciate the cataclysmic
rush of the Thompson River that boiled south-
ward below him in the moonlight.

He was in the same mood at dawn on Tuesday
and feared for long minutes that, even after gliding down onto the highway and building up to
cruising speed, the Parisienne might not start. It
guzzled fuel at an infuriating rate but, once past
Chilliwack, he knew he would make it to the
ferry south of Vancouver.

Thirty-three hundred kilometers to the east in
the offices of Salon du Nord, Pelletier gnawed a
cuticle and waited for a call which, he was increasingly sure, would not come. If Trnka was
buying the remaining microprocessors, he was
infernally slow about it. If Trnka was buying
time, Pelletier himself was dilatory. He thought
about the anonymous cash again. He would wait
one more day.

TUESDAY, 23 SEPTEMBER, 1980:

During the long ferry ride across the Strait of Georgia to Sidney on Vancouver Island, the little man poked at the vast pig-iron innards of the Parisienne as long as light permitted. Unknowingly he moved two frayed plug leads apart and, at Sidney, was intensely relieved to hear the engine splutter to something like a willingness to move the two thousand-kilo machine. He drove to Victoria, found the upper harbor, and left the car near the small boat flotilla off Wharf Street. It might never start again, but this possibility did not disturb him.

Wednesday morning he contacted Bonin's man, Charles Graham, identifying himself as Domingo Baztan. The Basques, too, had a separatist movement and unusual accents.

He stood some distance from the boathouse at first, pleased that the long individual boathouse was in good repair. The man who unlocked the

door was a tall windburned specimen dressed in
ducking to his shoes. The beret said he was
Graham. The accent suggested he was a New
Jersey transplant. They met inside the boathouse
and traded ritual handclasps, Graham standing
so near he seemed to loom.

"Hope you didn't want me to pick up your
man today, Baztan," the larger man said. "I've
got to put her in tune first." He indicated a
powerboat that lurked beyond.

Forgetting himself, 'Baztan' cursed in Arabic.
The boat was fifteen meters long, eel-slender, its
lines promising great speed and minimal radar
echo. Though no sailor he knew instantly that
some rational alternative must be found. "It
looks very fast," he said.

"Runs like a striped-assed ape," Graham
chuckled, motioning 'Baztan' alongside the
craft. "Twin turbocharged chevy four-fifty-
fours, sixteen hundred shaft horses between 'em.
A Cigarette will cross Juan De Fuca Strait in
fifteen minutes with weather like this."

"Cigarette?"

"That's what they call this breed. Designed for
ocean racing; the only thing that'll catch it is a
bullet. They're sots for fuel, though. That's part
of the three thousand you're paying."

The little man studied the boat, realizing that
it would have to reach one hundred forty
kilometers per hour to cross the treacherous
ocean strait as Graham boasted. Anyone lying
under its hull would be pounded to marmalade
at that speed. No, the Cigarette would not do.
Well enough for Bonin's uses, perhaps. He
cleared his throat, choosing to sound vulnerable.

"Is it a smooth crossing? The man is very old, very frail."

Graham thought about it. "Maybe I could strap him in foam cushions, when we clear Port Angeles on the way back." He jerked a thumb at the sleek craft. "This thing is the Can-Am car of powerboats, Baztan, at eighty knots she'll rearrange his guts. There's nothing I can do about that," he smiled.

"His heart is very bad," was the response.

"Then he'd need a transplant in ten seconds. Do you care?"

The little man brightened. Graham had given him another idea in his cover story. "After I cross over tonight and bring him to meet you at Port Angeles tomorrow, my responsibility is discharged. If he arrives with you here in Victoria, well and good. If he should happen to fall overboard and you arrive back here alone—again, well and good." A brief smile for Graham. "But he is not a fool, and I think he would refuse to accept your trick Cigarette. And then I would not be paid."

"I'm not the dumbest jack-off in the world either. If you can't drive him across the border he must be pretty hot."

A shrug. "What we need is a craft that is docile and looks it."

Graham led him along creaking planks until they stood at the mouth of the boathouse, blinking in the strong light. He pointed toward the nearest of the sloops that nodded at moorings. "The *Bitch* is the only other boat I have, a refitted Islander Thirty-Four. She'll do all of six knots with the big jib, friend; she wouldn't outrun a

pissant with waterwings." He eyed the little man
with shrewd good humor: "But I won't have to
be fast on the south crossing, and maybe not on
the return trip. If you really don't care whether
the old geezer makes it all the way," he added.

'Baztan's' smile was bland. "I believe the sail-
boat will do. How long will you need for the
crossing?"

"Four hours, maybe five; I have to run close-
hauled a lot with the fuckin' winds in the strait.
What do you care, so long as I make Port Angeles
tomorrow?"

"My client asks such things. When should we
rendezvous?"

"High noon, with a brass band?" Graham
laughed. "I'll start from here about noon tomorrow. That way we'll have your guy on deck
without too much light. I want it dark before I'm
back in the strait if I'm gonna, like, dump some
ballast."

There was no need to ask about that ballast.
The smaller man produced an envelope from his
wrinkled but very expensive jacket. Moving
back into the shadow he allowed Graham to
watch him peel fifteen bills from the stack and
tuck them into a pocket. The other fifteen he
handed to the Canadian, who counted them
without apology. "You will have the rest in Port
Angeles."

"Why not right now," asked Graham, stepping
closer, and a trifle too quickly.

"Because that is as it must be," he heard, seeing for the first time how a spring-loaded
armpit holster works. The little man's right hand
did not actually disappear into the jacket but

only seemed to flicker at its lapel, and then Graham was dividing his time between staring into the barrel of a Llama automatic and into the still darker barrels of the little man's eyes. Given the choice, he found he honestly preferred staring at the pistol. The death it suggested would at least be swift and clean. Taking two backward paces, 'Baztan' moved against the boathouse wall. "You will understand if I ask you to precede me."

Graham was still protesting as he stepped through the doorway. "I never meant to spook you, fella," he said, turning to see 'Baztan' who now stood relaxed with empty hands. They were small hands, carefully groomed, and he noticed that they were not shaking as his were. He thrust his hands into his pockets, feeling the money again. He had thought it would be interesting, though no contest, to take the entire three thousand just to see what would happen. Now, standing a head taller than the innocently smiling 'Baztan,' he felt like a tame bullock beside a wolverine. "No hard feelings, Baztan. I should've moved slower." He thrust out his hand, feeling the limp dry fingers in his own. "See you in the States tomorrow about five," he said. "I'll have to go to diesel and switch mains'ls, so look for a dark red sail on the *Bitch*." He strolled toward the sloop. The back of his neck itched. He let it itch.

'Baztan' walked back to the business district, choosing a hotel at random. In the telephone booth he extracted the HP from a pocket, punching a simple program into it before dialing his second Toronto number. After a moment he

placed the HP to the mouthpiece and punched
the Memory Return key. A series of tones came to
him faintly. It would be lunchtime in Toronto,
he mused; perhaps McEvoy was consuming
another sandwich.

Then the relay connection fulfilled its task as
he heard McEvoy answer. The filters masked the
background which might otherwise suggest a
long-distance call. "This is Jan Trnka, Mr.
McEvoy," he said. "I seem to have overlooked
another detail."

"Anything I can help with?"

"No, regrettably. Business compels me to
delay our flight. And yet I need the film. You
don't suppose," he began quickly, then laughed.
"No, I don't suppose you could fly your aircraft
and use a camera simultaneously." He spoke as
if asking for some rare feat of valor.

McEvoy could, of course. Changing film
might be a chore but he was, after all, his own
mechanic. "But jeez, Mr. Tee, how do I know
what you want to shoot?"

An excellent reply crossed his mind but was
throttled. "As much shoreline as you can on the
lake," he said, "a cross-section of everything that
is—the word?—photogenic? I myself could do
no more. And," he lowered his voice, "I shall be
very grateful."

McEvoy squirmed between rocks and hard
places. "You think you could pay me the balance
before I take off, Mr. Tee? I could drive over and
pick it up now."

A pause to simulate weighing the idea. "That
may not be necessary, Mr. McEvoy. Where is my
suitcase?"

"Stowed in the Seabee."

"Would you mind bringing it to the telephone? You can call me here when you have it." He gave a number. What could be more innocent? It was obviously a Toronto prefix.

He heard McEvoy hang up, waited seven minutes, then heard the connection come to life again. "Mr. Tee? Ian McEvoy. I got it here." He was puffing from exertion.

"Open it, please, and check the coat pockets. My damnable memory may have done us a favor for once."

There ensued a long pause, then a faint raucous chuckle. Clearly, then: "Jesus Christ, man, there's twelve hundred dollars here!"

"Two hundred more than we bargained for. It is yours, Mr. McEvoy, if you will allow me to pick up cartridges of exposed film on Friday. Will you be going today?"

"Don't see how. It'd be dark before I could get over to Lake Chautauqua. Would tomorrow be good enough?"

It was perfect. He let McEvoy twit him about leaving hard cash lying around in unlocked luggage, then mentioned being late for an appointment.

He stepped from the booth, checked the time, and walked to the bus depot where he took his attaché case from a storage locker. He found a restaurant with two entrances, expecting no surveillance but taking the usual precautions, and ordered filet of sole. Awaiting his early lunch, he pondered the likelihood that Ian McEvoy was working with Canadian authorities by now. Yet it took time to check the location of a telephone;

still more time to secure a large apartment building. It was unlikely that police would cut power
to the apartment, or to the telephone. But it was
possible.

At the moment when the little man started
toward the pay telephone in the restaurant, Pelletier was scanning a collection of photographs
maintained by the Royal Canadian Mounted
Police. Pelletier drew a blank with the Quebecois, another with known elements of Meyer
Cohane's people in the Jewish Defense League.
He had basked in virtue when complimented on
his ability to remember a telephone number; Pelletier would have been unwise to admit indis-
criminate bugging of a client's calls because
police saw such criminal activity as their own
particular vice.

RCMP plainclothesmen had already checked
on Ian McEvoy. He had no previous record and
eked out a precarious presence by flying sports-
men into wilderness lakes. To a business-suited
gentleman of endless curiosity he said yes, the
Seabee was for hire but he was already booked
for the following day. Yep, he had plenty of hull
storage, even for a moose head. Tomorrow? Oh,
just a photorecon job for some movie people.
Nope, he would be carrying no passengers.

The RCMP left a staff sergeant in plain clothes
with field glasses in an unmarked car, unwilling
to confide in McEvoy. Their job might have been
simpler had they simply asked him about his
client. But McEvoy was under suspicion.

While Pelletier's eyes grew red-rimmed in his
search for a make on Mr. Trnka, the little man in
Victoria reached his Toronto number. With a

casual glance around him, he brought the HP
from his pocket, punched an instruction into it,
then let his machines confer. A poignant three-
second tone from the HP was identified in the
sink of the Toronto apartment and its instruction
executed. The little man fidgeted for another
fifteen seconds before the line went dead. He
nodded to himself, replaced the receiver, and
ambled back to his table.

In the Toronto apartment, beads of light had
grown in the clay pot over the sink as the squibs
energized pyrotechnic igniters. The beads began
to sink from sight into the silvery mixture before,
reluctantly, the thermite caught fire and pros-
pered.

Thermite is a simple composition of great utility when it becomes necessary to weld, say, the
frames of locomotives. Because one of its com-
bustion products is pure liquid iron. The other
product is aluminum oxide, also common in
solid rocket exhaust.

A tiny ravening sun radiated from the top of
the clay pot as its temperature rose to approxi-
mately twenty-five hundred degrees celsius.
Since thermite is hot enough to melt concrete
there was a considerable quantity of smoke,
which boiled above the starlike glare and
crawled across the ceiling.

An observer with protective goggles might
have seen the thin trickle of brilliant yellow-
white molten iron that began to drip through the
hole in the pot. It instantly destroyed the microprocessor, consumed the circuit board, and
proceeded to fry the answering device into
bubbling junk while smoke thickened in the

two-room apartment. Tiny particles of
aluminum oxide began to fall as snow on the
carpet while the sink enamel pinged and spat
under incandescent metal soup. The stream of
iron dwindled, slag already congealing as the
clay pot disintegrated to add its thermal content
to the mass in the sink. The cast-iron sink began
to char the wooden counter at its lip, then slowly
cooled. At that point, tendrils of smoke found
their way through ceiling moldings into the
apartment above.

In Victoria, the little man dallied at his lunch,
which was evidently filet of shoe sole, but abandoned it after a few minutes. He walked to his
own hotel, tossed a pillow on the floor of his
room, and lay with his bare feet touching the
locked door. He would need sleep now, to assure
alertness that night.

While the sleeper husbanded his strength, an
apartment dweller in Toronto arrived to find her
smoke alarm whining in panic. Fire marshals
traced the problem, took one look through the
door they forced in the apartment below, and
radioed the Toronto Metropolitan Police. Within
an hour they had conferred with the RCMP
which, unlike the generally similar Federal
Bureau of Investigation to the south, has more
sweeping powers in domestic matters.

A thorough description of the apartment's
contents reached Ottawa early in the evening,
and shortly afterward Ottawa sent five new
photographs by wire to Toronto. None of the
new pictures were from passports or mug shots;
all were of a special category of people whose
expertise in communication devices fitted the

Toronto pattern. Neither the three men nor the two women were thought to be in Canada—until now. Pelletier took the group of new photofaxes, spread them irritably—and howled with delight.

Pelletier brandished a 'known photograph,' distinguished neither by clarity nor recency, and handed it to the RCMP sergeant, who flinched. It was 'Trnka,' beyond any shred of doubt. At that moment, there were five men on the case. A few minutes later, after RCMP/Ottawa contacted FBI/Washington, there were over thirty.

The HP tintinnabulated in the sleeper's ear at ten o'clock, Pacific Standard Time. Presently the little man strolled from the hotel to a dust-covered Pontiac off Wharf Street, and then moved on to the Inner Harbour. He watched a tall figure move across the lights from the cabin of an Islander Thirty-Four, continued his walk, and stopped again as the lights went out. He cursed softly, realizing that Graham intended to sleep aboard the damned boat. He found a coffee shop, wasted an hour, then returned to the Pontiac.

He dressed inside the car, beginning with the wetsuit, struggling into the zippered black turtleneck and charcoal denims more by feel than by sight. The deck shoes were new, stiff, and uncomfortable. He stuck the Llama automatic into his waistband and locked the car, taking one of his three B-four bags with him from the trunk. He sank the bag in shallows, two moorages from the Islander, and brought the other bags.

The water was cold only on his hands and feet, but he had trouble with the microbubbler in the darkness. Exhalations from SCUBA gear had

been a clear signature of manfish since the early
Cousteau aqualungs, and a trained ear could
identify this signature through a fiberglass hull.
The microbubbler changed both pitch and
rhythm of exhalations. It was an absolute necessity for the job.

He adjusted flotation on a B-four bag, tugged
on his flippers, carefully made his way under
two hulls by touch and emerged silently at the
third hull. A quick surveillance assured him that
he had the right boat; then he submerged again
in the friendly blackness. His flashlight played
across the great weighted keel and, seeing rings
set into the keel, he let fate smile for him. It
would be necessary to bond only one ring to
have a triangulated lashing. The work went
quickly. To be on the safe side he emplaced a
second ring with the thermoset adhesive. He did
not risk testing the rings too much, but lashed
the sodden bag in place and took his bearing
again before dousing the flashlight. Then he returned for the second bag.

It was two in the morning before he eased
aching muscles from layers of cloth and rubber.
He wiped the Pontiac's interior with a cloth
wherever some stray print might have clung,
scrubbed his skin with the blue jacket to warm
himself. What had he forgotten? Nothing.

Fool! The HP and the Llama both. The cold
had made him stupid. He shoved the pistol into a
rubber bag, leaving the zipper open for instant
recovery, and set the HP alarm for a three-hour
delay.

First light proved the Parisienne abandoned,
strewn with expensive clothing and an empty

attaché case under a mummy bag. Charles Graham spent most of the morning belowdecks with his spare mains'l, applying spurious United States Registration. He was tempted to abandon this business; it was one thing to snuff someone you actively disliked or who—you suspected—might be setting you up. But it was something else to kill some poor old helpless stranger. It would be a pleasure to put little Baztan over the side into Juan De Fuca—but Baztan, he thought, might not be the one who went over. Baztan might also become downright unpleasant if Graham did not show up at Port Angeles in the State of Washington. Sighing, Graham scanned the wharf for loiterers while he brewed tea in the galley. He did not think about the Pontiac, or about nearby boathouses.

At half-past eleven Graham cast off, easing the hull back on her inboard diesel. He was too busy to notice the splop and swirl from a neighboring boathouse, and got underway without the sails. He could crowd on plenty of sail once away from the Inner Harbour and into Victoria Harbour proper, but proceeded slowly until he could get some leeway. The diesel made a scant wake, but enough to hide the myriad of tiny bubbles that closed the gap toward his rudder, then disappeared torpedolike beneath his portside rail as he lounged at the tiller.

The Islander's sleek hull was designed to slip easily through the water and Graham assumed that some vagrant current was responsible for her sluggish performance. He would have reconsidered if he had seen the excrescences that rode her keel. A fathom below her waterline, rock-climber's carabiners snapped into place one by one as the manfish struggled to place himself in such a way that he felt minimal force from the water. He was fairly warm in his wetsuit under cotton clothing, but he had not yet felt the currents of Juan De Fuca, cold and treacherous as a spider's bride.

He felt more vulnerable as the sloop forged ahead. It might have been better to risk a border crossing afoot into Montana or Washington, he thought, but increased border patrols and sensing devices had made that chancy, even for Quebecois, who had provoked those precautions. He fumbled for a spare tank in the nearest B-four bag, letting the sling straps bite under his shoulders. It might not be such a bad trip, this way—unless his suit heater batteries failed.

The sloop coursed out from the city, under sail now, on a sou'easterly heading. Near the corner of St. Lawrence and Dallas streets a man watched her progress as he spoke into a telephone. "Yessir, no mistake, it's Graham's *Bitch*. Well, that's her name, Inspector, can I help it? Nossir, she could be on a tack toward Port Townsend or just on a pleasure cruise. Right, sir; not very likely for Charles Graham. All right, I have twenty-power glasses; I'll let you know if he heads for Dungeness or Port Angeles." He replaced the receiver, took up the glasses again. For an hour he watched the sloop. Then he made another call.

Near Buffalo, New York, a tiny craft plunged upward from the concrete airstrip, its pusher engine shrilling eagerly. Small by normal standards, the single-place Bede Five was also ridiculously fast. Its thin airfoils carried the ad-

ditional burden of a long-range tank cupped flat
against its belly. The Bede arrowed westward
over Lake Erie, soon overtaking the ancient Republic Seabee amphibian that galumphed along
on VFR at one thousand meters altitude. The
Bede's pilot throttled back, lazing several kilometers in arrears, radioing his position as he
passed the New York State shoreline and Route
Ninety. He turned back only after learning that
the big float-equipped Cessna from Erie, Pennsylvania was closing from the West and had the
Seabee on radar.

Moments after the Bede had curved away on
its homeward leg, the Cessna surged ahead. Its
quarry was sinking toward the northern end of
Lake Chautauqua, making no effort to pretend
otherwise. The Cessna swept over the lake high
enough for maneuvering advantage, yet low
enough to land quickly. All three men in the
Cessna were equipped with chutes and
government-issue automatic weapons befitting
agents of the FBI. The attaché in Ottawa had
forwarded an RCMP sergeant's opinion that
only a pilot was aboard the Seabee, but it was a
capacious craft and might hide a stowaway for
days. The pilot had filed a flight plan but had not
contacted Customs. The Cessna hung back, waiting for the amphib to flare out for its controlled
bellyflop.

And hung back. And hung back. The old Seabee droned down the narrow lake, swooping
near the shore at picturesque spots and banking
out again from time to time. At the southeast end
of the lake, the Seabee began its sluggish return,
and eventually passed northward back toward

Lake Erie. In the Cessna, the three agents traded shrugs; for all its suspicious behavior, the Seabee had broken no law.

In Juan De Fuca Strait, Charles Graham waited until he was fifteen kilometers from the Canadian shore, then started the diesel again and changed mains'ls. Directly below, the manfish fought to free a spare tank from its lashings. Switching tanks under such conditions was a peril he had not fully appreciated and, his hands numb even with the heating elements, he was clumsy. The empty tank, moved by vagaries of the current, bumped hard against the keel and was gone, bobbing in the wake of the *Bitch*, a perfectly obvious sign to anyone who saw it. Graham was grunting over his halyards and saw nothing else; the huge dacron sail lay flaccid along the mains'l boom and required all his concentration. The manfish nearly lost his fresh tank as well but finally lashed it to his chest and hung in his straps, hands tucked under his armpits for warmth.

The crossing took nearly five hours. At one point the manfish saw, with a terror he denied, a great gray mass that levitated toward him from below. He fingered the Sharkill. No fish, he hoped, could possibly be so vast—and then he saw that it was a sand bar, the *Bitch* gliding so near it she could have run aground. He debated cutting loose to swim for shore which, he felt, must be very near. He waited for surer signs; a wise decision. He was two kilometers from land.

Port Angeles, huddled in the protecting arm of Angeles Point, sprawls along the Washington State side of Juan De Fuca Strait with its back to

the rain-sodden Olympic Mountains. Charles
Graham rounded the point in a subtle riptide to
see the town, coming about expertly despite the
odd sluggishness of the *Bitch*. He scanned the
wharves for 'Baztan,' who was much nearer than
he knew, and offered a line to a friendly idler
who caught it and made it fast. When he had
secured the *Bitch* fore and aft, Graham stepped
up to resecure the idler's clumsy work, then
strolled away alert for a frail old man with a
tough little man.

The friendly idler waited for a few moments,
then shifted the toothpick in his mouth and dallied behind Graham. The FBI was better at tails
than at knot-tying.

Fifty meters from the *Bitch*, a burly man under
a long-billed cap nodded to another man, who
adjusted his face plate, clamped his mouthpiece,
and slid from his boat into the water. Once they
bonded their transmitter just under the waterline near the stern of the *Bitch*, they could fix her
location whenever they liked for as long as the
battery lasted. The transmitter was disguised as
marine growth. If Graham noticed it he would, at
worst, only remove it. Customs and Immigration
fretted about Graham on both sides of the border.
The burgundy mains'l had almost fooled the
watchers in Port Angeles but hull lettering and
Graham's features had not changed. His mains'l
could be explained as borrowed; a minor viola-
tion. Better to give him a long leash and, while
they were at it, to check his hull. It would not be
the first time a man had run contraband in his
keel.

The manfish had lashed one of the B-four bags

to a distant piling and was wrestling with the
second bag when he saw, impending above him
in the sunlit murk, the second manfish. He
quickly released the bag which tumbled slowly
out of sight below, fumbled for carabiners on the
third bag, saw that he would be too late. He
unzipped the third bag, heedless of the masses
that cascaded lazily downward, and armed the
Sharkill.

The stubby Sharkill, no larger than a baseball
bat with handles, had been an afterthought
purchased chiefly for study. It was also said to be
effective on even the largest *carcharadon*, firing
a single salvo of small concussion warheads
rocket-propelled in a conic pattern. It was a di-
rectional pattern, designed to implode flesh, a
great hammerwave of water to surround and
pulverize a shark's gristle without releasing
blood in the water. The Sharkill was an almost-
perfect weapon, but its warheads were stupid:
they had to be set for the quarry's distance or
they would streak away, quicker than bar-
racudas, to explode at maximum range. For
once, the little man had skipped a detail.

He kicked backward, shielded by the keel, and
aimed the weapon as the new arrival spotted
him. It did not matter who the intruder was;
better a mysterious underwater explosion now,
than an excited SCUBA enthusiast on the wharf
in moments. If all but known friends are
enemies, then all strangers are enemies. He
triggered the Sharkill.

The young agent saw a silver-gray gleam in
the other swimmer's hands. It did not look like a
weapon until it fired. Six petals unfurled into

streamers that sizzled past him, one passing between his knees, but before he could wheel to escape he felt the distant shocks.

The warheads continued for thirty meters in the water, two exploding far below, the others slanting outward. Two more broke the surface and, unencumbered by water, detonated in air bursts well beyond the boat that contained the agent in the baseball cap. The last two warheads flanked the FBI boat before triphammering its shallow-draft hull.

The fleeing FBI agent in SCUBA gear found his own boat settling as he boarded it, nearby tourists too stunned by the air bursts to find his predicament funny. The burly agent in the cap, clambering to the wharf, shook his head to clear the ringing from his ears. In moments he realized the situation, and the wetsuited agent found canisters in his boat before it was completely awash. He tossed the canisters to the wharf. The third agent raced to the *Bitch* and, arming the canisters, hurled them into the water on both sides of the sloop.

The manfish saw the canisters fall, saw silent puffs as each discharged several liters of chemical. He knew the chemical was intended for him and did not wait to discover its function. As the material spread, it thickened into a colloidal gel that turned many cubic meters of sea water into salt treacle. It would have immobilized him had he not fled. He swam to the pilings, found his one secured bag, and used churning flipper-strokes to put him as far down the wharf as possible before he turned to proceed along the shoreline a few meters below the surface.

He continued until his breathing supply was
exhausted, the light beginning to fail as shallows
forced him near the surface. He lay still then, the
bag his anchor in the shallows, gasping the salt
air and awaiting his ally, darkness.

Charles Graham went through predictable
stages for the federal agents: anger, innocence,
astonishment. He did not believe he had carried a human parasite across Juan De Fuca
("He'd freeze his balls off!") until a wetsuited
agent recovered damning evidence from below
the *Bitch*.

They let him reconsider his innocence overnight and began afresh the next morning with a
rough-smooth treatment. Chilton, the husky
agent, was rough. Polsky, the tier of inferior
knots, was smooth. In the cell with Graham,
Polsky leaned against the wall. Chilton stood
with one foot on Graham's bunk, furry forearms
crossed over his knee. "The very least that's
going to happen is impoundment of your boat,"
Chilton finally said with poisonous relish.

Polsky withdrew the toothpick from his
mouth. "Unless you can show good faith," he
murmured.

"At worst," Chilton continued, "you'll end up
playing rock hockey with a sixteen-pound
hammer in British Columbia Penitentiary."

Graham looked from one to the other. "I'm
clean! Take the *Bitch* apart, you won't find a
thing." He glared at Chilton. "I think it's a frame;
you bunch of pussies planned this whole thing!"

"Somebody sure did," Polsky agreed. He let
Graham chew on that for a moment while he
chewed the wooden splinter. "It wasn't us,

Graham. Chilton thinks it was you." He seemed about to go on, then gave a quick headshake. "Doesn't matter what I think."

Suddenly it mattered very much to Graham. "What, *what*? Your guess is as good as mine..."

"My guess? Somebody knew you were coming. Somebody used you. Somebody wanted to make you look like an asshole."

Graham was silent long enough to fumigate a few details for inspection. The deal with Baztan was dead, now. The Basque could have set him up for somebody, all right. Not Baztan himself, he was already in Port Angeles. Or was he? A glaze washed over Graham's face. "There was one guy I mentioned it to," he hazarded, and soon found himself checking photographs in a room without bars. Graham had met a few men whose photographs graced the stack, but nobody looked like his client.

With Graham's help, the agents forwarded a report that included 'Baztan's' habits of packing heat and heavy cash. Graham was released with orders to drop in for a chat with the RCMP in Victoria. As Graham was casting off, young Polsky sprinted down the wharf with a sheaf of fresh photographs from Washington. The wirephotos covered a cross-category of diminutive men who had used Basque cover, met the other criteria, and were hoped to be almost anywhere but in the United States. Graham identified the same man Pelletier had, instantly, without doubt. It was an eight-year-old alien registry photo.

"Arif?" Graham studied the data with the photo. "Who's Hakim Arif?"

Polsky sat down heavily on the *Bitch*'s transom. After a moment he looked up. "Well, there was Abd-El Kadr; his boys used to stuff testicles into empty eye-sockets after a raid," said Polsky, very matter-of-fact. "Then there was General Qassem, who liked to have his enemies tossed to his troops a piece at a time. All's fair in a jehad—holy war.

"Dr. George Habash was a pediatrician who bazookaed a schoolbus," he continued, staring evenly at Graham, "all in the name of freedom and equality, naturally. And Carlos Ilich Ramirez-Sanchez. Carlos is your up-to-date terrorist, Graham; he can work with electronics or old gelignite, and he can make the explosive himself if he has to. Carlos planned the Entebbe hijacking back in seventy-six, but he's not above tossing antipersonnel hand-grenades into a crowded movie theatre. They say he's dickering with the Libyans for plutonium now. Or his heirs are."

Graham watched gooseflesh crawl on his arms. "Sanchez I heard about. On TV, I guess."

"No doubt. And every time he gets TV coverage, some sheikh sends him a care package to pay for another spectacular."

"Arif's one of that bunch?"

Polsky stood up, straightened the photographs in a neat stack and stepped to the wharf. "From it. Not *of* it. Hakim Arif is a fanatic Carlos expelled from his group because he was out of control," he said softly. "He likes a free press because it publicizes his atrocities. He only recruits fanatics. You want a summary, Graham? He is a one-man jehad. He is also the guy you were going to meet right here," he said, pointing toward his feet.

"And you think he was in the wetsuit?"

"I hope not. He'd feed on our media like botulism on tuna salad. You'd better hope he was, because now maybe he won't be looking for you again."

"Who's he looking for now?"

The agent sighed, snapped the photographs against his thigh. "Soft targets," he said.

"You mean he's not particular."

"Oh, yes. Yes, he's very particular, Graham. Sleep well," Polsky said, and hurried away.

The identification of Hakim Arif came twelve hours too late for Mary Kellam, who had given a lift on Thursday night to the damp little fellow with the canvas bag so she would not have to fight sleep while driving to Bremerton. The sleep that overtook her was endless. Hakim mutilated the pathetic old corpse before dumping it because the knife lent authenticity to the appearance of a bizarre sex crime.

By dawn he had abandoned the Kellam car. While awaiting a connection at the Tacoma bus terminal, he idly watched television. He considered calling Talith, but chose to wait until he was better equipped. He must not erode his leadership of Fat'ah with signs of vulnerability.

The hour was equally early in Anaheim, fifteen hundred kilometers to the south, where television's regulators, the Federal Communications Commission, had convened—fittingly, one

newspaper quipped, adjoining Disneyland.
Maurice Everett stared out his window in the
hotel to the small bogus Matterhorn that stood
several hundred meters from his suite in the
Marine Tower. If he squinted enough he could
almost imagine it was a massif in the Rockies.
Born a hundred and fifty years too late to be a
mountain man, Maury Everett had movod from
Iowa to Colorado as soon as he had a choice of
terrain. His executive career with Oracle Microelectronics in Colorado Springs was all but
inevitable, once his college and military re-
quirements were behind him. The endless com-
pacting of communication devices made it clear
that Oracle would either get into television or
make way for some company that could. By
1980, Everett had years of liaison with ENG
newsmen who used Oracle's Electronic News
Gathering equipment, and good connections
with conservative democrats. How this qualified
him to be appointed a Commissioner, one of the
FCC's famed seven dwarfs, was a mystery solved
only in Washington. But mavericks had settled
the west, and someone evidently felt that they
might settle the electromagnetic spectrum.
Maury Everett was not disposed to argue. At the
moment, he was strongly disposed to chuck the
damned agenda in favor of Frontierland. He
squashed his whimsy with a faint sigh, shrugged
the big sloping shoulders, and ordered enough
breakfast for two smaller men.

Everett noted that the recent appointees
tended to arrive promptly; the older hands took
their time. He filled the conference room door-

way punctually at nine to find Barbara Costigan
hiding her plain features under counterculture
beads and poncho, sharing coffee with Dave Engels. Everett slid into a seat across from Engels,
nodded into the merry hyperthyroid eyes of the
'retired' FBI man. Engels was a terror on the
handball court but that nervous energy did not
meld easily with sedentary work. At the moment, he was swirling his coffee to see how close
he could come to spilling it.

Costigan tore her eyes from the Engels coffee
and smiled her relief at Everett. "We were wondering where everybody's going to stand on the
religious broadcast thing," she said.

"I thought it was pretty clear yesterday,"
Everett rumbled softly, tugging at his tie. He
frowned at the ceiling, trying to recall the quote:
"Stance of neutrality, acting neither to promote
nor inhibit—same old wording, Barb. I think it'll
carry."

Engels's head jerked up to glance beyond
Everett. The new arrival was John Rooker; tiny,
bald, tweedy, the professor of political philosophy. Rooker sat down with Leon Cole, a
snappy dresser who understood political cam-
paigns better than any other member because he
had managed so many, so well.

Last to arrive was the attorney and Chairman,
Thomas Wills. Powell, they all knew, would not
be coming. Thick and slowmoving, Wills eased
down into his seat and bestowed a Santa Claus
smile at the assembly. "With apologies for the
time," said the reedy old voice, "I can tell you we
have those videotapes now."

Everett cursed to himself. Most videotapes at these conferences were dull affairs. The religious broadcast controversy went as Everett had guessed, and more quickly than usual.

Moving to the next items, Wills studied his notes. "We have tapes of the Texas courtroom ENG problem, the Conklin kidnapping in Phoenix, and that outrageous thing in Buffalo. Do I hear a motion?"

"I move we see the last one," said David Engels quickly. "For one thing, I've always wondered what this guy Arif looks like in person."

A faint smile from Wills. "I take it you've dealt with him professionally, Mr. Engels. Well, he's managed to disappoint you again. He wore a hood, you know."

"But it's a landmark in political campaign stupidity," said Cole. "I second David's motion."

The videotape rolled, the bay-window-sized screen lit in full color. The Federal Communications Commission stored a bushel of mail from the event they watched now, a five-minute political broadcast aired the previous week over an NBN affiliate in Buffalo, New York. Cromwell Cawthorn was a local candidate of the anti-Semite Purification Party, which had somehow gained a toehold in Buffalo. Cawthorn demanded and got air time from a reluctant WGRT-TV, citing the FCC's Section 315, paying the regular fee for his right. The tape began with a closeup of Cawthorn, well-fed and unctuous in his male Anglo-Saxon Protestant self-assurance. He was an abominable speaker.

"Some of my friends and neighbors," Cawthorn brayed, "say the Purification Party is not forward-seeking. I tell you, the Purification Party is the wave of the future. It has friends beyond the borders of our fair country, and today I want to prove it."

The camera pulled back to show that Cawthorn was not alone. A small figure sat near Cawthorn, one leg crossed over the other in casual elegance, a black hood completely hiding his head in contrast with the dazzling white double-breasted suit. "Folks, I want you to meet my friend and fellow freedom fighter, Hakim Arif." Twenty-two seconds of air time had elapsed.

In the tower in Anaheim, chuckles met Cawthorn's inept performance and Leon Cole vented a low whistle, perhaps envious of the clothing worn by Hakim Arif. But there was nothing risible in the hooded man's voice. They fell silent at its soft sibilance, the gently rolled r, the cautious effort to correctly render the th.

"Greetings from Fat'ah," the hood nodded slightly, "to all of the victims of Jewish oppression wherever they may be." Everett, glaring at the screen, found himself clenching and spreading his big hands, surprised at his own first reaction. It was the same cold sick breathlessness he felt whenever he saw a small animal beneath the wheels of a truck. Then the blood began to sing in Everett's veins as Hakim Arif, gesturing with languid ease, proceeded to promise aid to the foes of the Israeli conspiracy. "All over the world, victims of Zionism are rising to demonstrate a single will. The will to live in a free Quebec, a free South Molucca, a free Ireland," he paused expertly, then lowered his chin and voice, "—a free Palestine." The hood jerked up. "The Jew is the very symbol of oppression. He wants only his own land—and all of the land adjoining it. Ah, and the Coming of his Messiah, always the Coming."

Arif's was an astonishing presence that survived faulty reasoning and transition through videotape. It invested the conference room with the ambience of a cobra pit. The calm precise voice spat and crooned, stroked, stung, the slender hands moving in concert. To a few lunatics the message would be gospel swathed in flame. To most viewers in Buffalo, it had been icy horror.

"To those who ask whether the military operations of Fat'ah are truly necessary, Fat'ah replies: *they are precisely that.* To those who have known some Jew who showed a spark of human decency, Fat'ah reminds you that in war, there is nothing personal. Each operation is a military operation, and must be supported by those who love freedom.

"The friends of world Jewry are the enemies of peace and freedom. The friends of Fat'ah—like Mr. Cawthorn—are the friends of final peace. The Jew wants the Coming of his Messiah?" A two-beat pause before, "Fat'ah will see that he goes to meet it."

Everett did not remember the fatuous mouthings Cawthorn had made afterward. Cawthorn did not matter: he was only the envelope in

which this reeking turd had been handed to the
voters of Buffalo, and in their own homes.

As the lights brightened in the conference
room, Everett met the stunned gaze of Barb Costigan. She had been an investigative reporter
herself and could usually be expected to stand
fast against government interference with a free
press, but: "Utterly unconscionable," she said
into the silence.

Professor Rooker nodded gravely. "Of course,
Ms. Costigan. But it is different from a few other
incidents only in its degree."

"Not true," Leon Cole said. "For one thing, it
wasn't even to the point of Cawthorn's candi-
dacy. It was a global message, a—a hymn to
hatred," he finished, hoping he had found a useful phrase.

"Why the hell did Cawthorn do it," asked Engels. "It must've queered his chances at the
polls."

"Cawthorn never had a chance anyway," said
Cole, cynical with his campaign experience. "I
suspect Cawthorn did it for more money than the
cost of his entire campaign. He made a profit on
the Purification Party; it's that simple. What I'd
like to know is, where that interview was done."

"I can tell you that much," David Engels said,
stretching his long legs restively. "Consider it
restricted data. The tape was made in Quebec
two weeks ago with private equipment and a
CBC man, moonlighting the job. The Mounties
just pieced that together in the past couple of
days. They had assumed Arif was already in the
States when that videotape was shown on a Buf-

falo station. Arif made a smart move choosing Buffalo. He got coverage in Toronto, too, with the new cable channels."

"They must be turning the whole province upside down for him," Everett said.

"They would've, but they got a strong fresh lead in Toronto yesterday," Engels grimaced. "Turned out to be a very cute diversion, apparently a solo effort using telephone links, a blind lead with a rented aircraft, and so help me God, a thermite bomb to delay tracing him."

"So he's in Toronto?" Rooker's face was hopeful.

"No such luck. Hakim Arif got clear across to Victoria, while the RCMP had its thumb in its ass, pardon me Barb."

"Either he's several people," Everett mused, "or he's mighty spry."

"Spry enough," from Engels. "He made it into Washington State under a little sloop, we think, and the Canadians are damned glad he isn't loose up there anymore. I leave it to your imagination how the Bureau feels. They almost stumbled over him. Well—they'll nail him." Engels's tone suggested an inaudible, *maybe*.

Thomas Wills coughed politely for attention. "If we can return to the present," he said drily, "I suggest we separately consider drafting statements at your earliest conveniences, to further elaborate existing policy on political messages."

The members scribbled notes, Costigan doodled nervously with her pen. "Could you help with a legal opinion, Mr. Wills?"

The gray brows elevated into a vee in the stolid

face. "Not really; it isn't an attorney's problem at
this stage. A philosopher's, perhaps. Dr.
Rooker?"

A courtly smile from the educator. "You do me
honor, Mr. Wills. I think the problem resolves
itself, if Mr. Cawthorn fails to achieve public
office and uses his terrorist money to buy something besides bullets."

Engels: "But it's inflammatory material! This
little Arab isn't just threatening violence, he's
promising."

"Just as the Jewish Defense League does,
whenever the American Nazi Party schedules a
parade. Our system is designed to withstand ex-
tremism of many stripes, Mr. Engels," said
Rooker, with patient scholastic phrasing.

"Are you forgetting that we are part of that
system? If we do nothing, are we delinquent?"

"Over-response is repression, Mr. Engels.
Sometimes the best thing to do is—nothing. I
think our system can absorb extremist rhetoric."

"So long as it stays purely rhetorical," Everett
growled, louder than he intended. He flushed
uneasily.

David Engels, the only other member who
knew Everett well, snapped his fingers. Costigan
jumped. "That's right, you're Jewish, Maury. I'd
forgotten."

Everett ran a hand through his bush of graying
brown hair. "So do I generally," he said. "It's my
mother who's really Jewish, my dad was a goy;
she claims I am too." He grinned suddenly, a
boyish cast on the ruddy fortyish features: "But
don't you say it to her."

"Drown me in chicken soup, most likely," Engels muttered, getting his small laugh.

"It'd put you out of your misery," Everett snarled good-naturedly; "you're already dying in Charlie's old jokes." The riposte was not quite fair: NBN's star comedian, Charlie George, had used the idea in a TV sketch only days before. Charlie was a favorite among the Commissioners, most of whom had met him at some media fete. Carefully awkward in his slapstick, but with overtones of Sahl and Cavett, Charlie George brought to television a sense of the absurd that was layered like veal parmesan, with peppercorns of logic and political truths to sting the unwary palate. Engels was not the first government figure to steal Charlie's material.

Wills coughed again. "The agenda, gentlemen? The other videotapes may constitute new business."

"I'd like to view the Phoenix kidnapping," Barb Costigan said. "I know some of the people involved, and that injunction was granted on what seems like awfully shaky grounds. But again, isn't that a legal matter?"

Wills leaned back, nodding, patting his paunch reflectively. He took his good time with an answer. The Commission had already taken complaints from all three of Phoenix's major network stations on an injunction which, within hours of a banner news event, had prevented television newsmen from using parts of their on-the-spot ENG coverage. The event was unprecedented in media terms, and in a highly public place. Yet the kidnapping of CBS corres-

pondent Wally Conklin had begun in a room of
the Phoenix Convention Center, and that room
had been rented for a private gathering of news-
papermen. The private element was at issue: was
it reasonable to prohibit results of electronic
news gathering after ENG equipment had been
allowed in the room?

"The ENG reporters claimed implied con-
sent," Wills said slowly, "when they carried
their ENG equipment in. But not one of them
bothered to ask for a release beforehand. They
were newsmen covering an event of other
newsmen—a family affair, as it were. But the
family doesn't always pull together. I tend to
stand with the private group—really only one
member of it, and a member from another
medium, at that. It gets a little complex," he
admitted. "Hadn't we better show the tape and
then discuss it?"

No one disagreed, partly due to curiosity over
footage that had been forbidden to the public.

The videotape began as ranking members of
the Investigative Reporters and Editors sat with
Wally Conklin, the famed CBS anchorman, in a
half-acre room of the Convention Center in
Phoenix, Arizona. The correspondent had been
perspiring in the August heat despite air condi-
tioning, and minced no words in his assess-
ments. "Frankly, some network people are afraid
to use your findings," he was saying to the IRE
members, "because they feel your work has too
much emotional carryover from the Don Bolles
bombing. We realize it was the Bolles incident
that caused the IRE to be formed—but perhaps

with too much zeal in your efforts to do what is really police work."

"You just don't put out hard contracts on reporters, Mr. Conklin," one newsman rapped out. "Every thug in the world knows that."

"They forgot it with Bolles," Conklin replied, as two young men shoved in front of the cameras. One was dark and bearded, the other clean-shaven.

The men marched quickly toward Conklin. A seated reporter, reacting more quickly than the rest, stood to face them, only to back away as he saw what the cameras did not reveal at first: a heavy .45 automatic leveled at Conklin. The bearded intruder produced a museum piece, a long-barrelled naval Luger with a small drum clip. Over angry shouts could be heard the man with the Colt automatic: "They did not forget, you reactionary scum! Nor did they forget in Turin when *La Stampa*'s editor was executed." The accent was German, the features fiercely handsome above a strongly built frame. The camera zoomed in for an extreme closeup, the ENG man holding his camera steady despite frantic efforts by the assembled men to flee. The German turned a wolfish smile on Conklin who was slowly rising, face leaden with apprehension. "And we have not forgotten this man's efforts to seduce Egyptians into a fool's paradise with the *dammt* Israelis," the German continued, obviously intending to be heard by microphones over the turmoil. He wrenched Conklin's collar, twisted hard. The correspondent's mouth trembled but he did not respond. There was no

point in crying, 'why me'; a media man who
dabbled in Middle-East diplomacy assumed new
risks. Conklin knew why him.

"This man must be re-educated," cried the
bearded man, waving the Luger to clear a path
through the ranks of journalists. Some IRE members were shouting, some lying prone, one actually taking notes as he stared at the unfolding
drama. A lithe young woman with long honey-
red hair, her ENG equipment shoulder bag
emblazoned with the letters of an independent
station, backed away, stumbling toward the door
at the rear of the room. Her face registered terror.

A second camera angle showed why the room
had not emptied quickly: a dozen reporters faced
a swarthy young man who guarded the doorway.
He held a Schmeisser machine pistol, his lips
stretched away from bad teeth in a rictus that
could be pleasure or wild hatred.

"Weitergehn, Chaim," the German barked,
and the youth at the door whirled, moving into
the rotunda beyond the room. A man across the
rotunda glanced around, saw the Schmeisser
and screamed like a woman. He ran for the glass
doors toward the outside. He never made it, as a
burst of gunfire from the Schmeisser cut his legs
almost in two. At this point the camera angle
plummeted; the cameraman had dived for cover.

Another ENG man was of sterner stuff, record-
ing the scene as he followed the two men who
herded Conklin. They hustled the correspondent toward exit doors, the German pressing his
Colt against Conklin. The honey blonde stumbled again, fell to her knees near the youth with

the Schmeisser as his companions urged Conklin through the exit and into bright sunlight.
There the cameraman had stopped, his view
momentarily obscured by others.

The blonde woman seemed dazed, reeling up
without her equipment bag as the youth waved
his gun barrel in obvious warning against any
newsman foolish enough to try following the
German outside.

Then the woman pivoted, her right elbow
ramming deep into the youth's midriff as she
forced the weapon muzzle down with her left
hand. The Schmeisser loosed a brief hail of
slugs, some smashing into a meter-thick bronze
cuboid sculpture nearby. The blonde continued
her move, the youth holding onto his weapon,
providing her with a lever as she spun him
crashing against the metal cube. Her own mass
added to the impact as the youth faltered face-
forward into sharp-edged bronze.

The woman was a flailing, snarling puma,
clutching the Schmeisser as she kicked the
youth repeatedly in the groin, her free hand a
hatchet against his face and neck. She ham-
mered him until he slumped, leaving a sticky
splotch crimson against the golden sheen of
bronze.

She leaped away with the weapon, kicked her
shoes off, fumbled with her prize before scud-
ding it across the floor. "Take him," she cried,
snatched up her bag, and sprinted down the
rotunda away from the exit.

The screen went blank in the FCC chamber.
Wills cut through the excited murmur of his

colleagues with, "Those were the segments pro-
hibited by the injunction."

"Je-zus, who's the Amazon," breathed David
Engels. "I know some people who could use
her."

"So does she, Mr. Engels," was Wills's
amused reply.

Then Engels fingers popped again, and this
time everyone jumped. "Vercours? *That* was
Vercours?" He was grinning incredulously at
the chairman.

A single stately nod.

"Now that Mr. Engels has identified our mystery challenger," said John Rooker with malici-
ous humor, "perhaps he can inform the audience."

"The tapes that were made public are on this
reel, if I may go on," Wills put in.

Engels nodded to Rooker. "Then you'll see."

"Roll the tape, *roll the tape*," Everett demanded, irked.

Wills complied. The new scene was from near
ground level, just outside the rotunda in the
open air. A half-dozen men had taken up positions behind outcroppings of the adobe brown
walls of the Convention Center. All were peering
down the broad walk. Fifty meters away a uni-
formed policeman sprawled unmoving, his service revolver glinting just beyond him. The
bearded man writhed some distance further, his
Luger forgotten. He knelt on the paving, tearing
at his belly, then rolled onto his back and tried to
stand erect again. The policeman's fragmenting
Glaser slug had gut-shot the man. Effectively, he

was dead when the slug burst in his peritoneum; but this death was merciless. "Fri-i-itz," the man screamed, thrusting bloody hands aloft.

A second policeman risked a shot: dust spanged from the concrete lip of a shallow pool beyond the dying man. The German, protected by his hostage, reached the pool and tumbled with Conklin into the water. Even at maximum zoom the details were fuzzy, but it seemed that the German hoped for protection in the pool. The water was too near the lip, but slowly whirring near one end of the pool were elements of a monumental sculpture in steel and aluminum.

Jerome Kirk's "Tiered Orbits" was already a noted piece of mobile sculpture, its concentric metal circles glittering red on stainless steel axes as they turned. The piece would have fresh celebrity now. The German wrestled his hostage to the two-story mobile, seemed to be arguing. A faint, "Schnell! Schnell!" sounded among the shouts that punctuated the scene.

The Colt now in his stomach, Wallace Conklin reached up to grasp the outermost of the great metal circles. The German, head twisting furiously around to check the terrain, followed. At the edge of the screen, then, a honey-gold flash heralded the young woman from the rotunda, who had doubled back through the building in a flanking maneuver.

She dived crabwise and rolled twice, cradling her shoulder bag, coming to rest behind a concrete tube that surrounded a small tree near the pool. The earth-filled concrete tube was easily a meter high and two broad; the woman, evidently shaken from impact against the concrete, lay for a moment on her back. Then she pulled the bag onto her abdomen and peered inside it.

The policeman began to curse the crazy reporter, waving helplessly until he saw the German aim in his direction. The .45 is not one of your quicker slugs, but it hits like Reggie Jackson. The cop sought cover.

The bearded man lay flopping and twitching, a fleshy sackful of aimless synapses. Conklin, at gestured orders from the German, managed to climb astride the great metal arc, then hugged it and lay horizontal. The German, too, straddled the metal, the Colt again only centimeters from Conklin's expensive head. For moments the scene appeared frozen, the kidnapper vulnerable to a sniper yet with a peculiar advantage: the slowly rotating sculpture constantly changed his position and his cover while he scanned the area, working out some new strategy. He seemed intent on the busy street beyond.

The blonde kept down, rummaging in her equipment. A pocket mirror gleamed in the sun before she slid it upward, a makeshift periscope trained on tiered orbits. The German shouted threats, intent on the men who had taken cover in his wake. At that instant the mobile began to shift, its metal circles now moving at varying speeds in accord with some preprogrammed sequence. Very soon, now, it would scissor its occupants in a blind embrace.

The blonde began to search her equipment bag, working quickly as she lay on her side. Presently she slid the bag out to provide a rest for the mirror, then eased up into a squat, her feet a full unladylike pace apart. She held several loops of power cord in her left hand, and something that bulked larger than a microphone in her right. The German craned his neck to study the street again, and apparently caught sight of the woman. But as he swung the .45 to this new menace, he could not see that his perch was closing the gap on the next concentric circle.

The metal scissors closed inexorably, nudging nearer, pressing the German's shoulder so that his shot went wide. Conklin, his hair in the German's grip, slid lower as he saw the scissors closing. Then the thick metal circles swung into the same ecliptic. The German, his thigh pinioned, screamed and swept his gun arm back toward Conklin who stared helplessly upward.

The blonde was five meters from the pool, ten from the German, and one second from an assassination.

She spurted up from her cover, vaulted to the pool lip, and sprang toward the German, hurling the battery pack she had tied to the power cord. The heavy battery pack sailed overhead but she passed beneath to splash barefooted into the pool, yanking the cord like a lariat. The cord passed across the German's extended arm, taut from the battery pack's mass, snapping the arm hard enough to wrest the heavy automatic from any normal man.

The German was not a normal man. Fighting free of the cord, he swung the Colt again toward Conklin, now single-minded on killing. The blonde shouted and flung the cord at his face, so that the German missed Conklin's head at one-meter range.

A heavy Conklin fist swung upward then in a roundhouse right to match any monument. The German's head flicked up and back, rebounding from the metal sculpture. His arms went limp, Conklin tumbling into the knee-deep water as the German slumped half conscious. Now both Conklin and the blonde were beyond arm's reach. A fusillade from the building wrenched and shook the German's torso, and a ragged cheer spread across the plaza.

Faintly, above the cheering, there came a shriek of tires on pavement from somewhere beyond the camera's view. Wally Conklin was not cheering. He was embracing the blonde.

The screen went blank in Anaheim. "Now," David Engels breathed in awe, "you've met Gina Vercours."

It took the Commission a few moments to recover from the videotape; a thousand Hollywood scenarios and ten thousand stage killings were poor preparation for the shuddering, flopping reality of violent death.

Everett saw that John Rooker cradled his face behind hands that shook. Costigan was pale, rubbing her arms to banish gooseflesh. "Pretty strong stuff, Thomas," Everett said to Wills. "You might have warned us."

"My apologies. The Phoenix stations, I'm told, showed only brief clips. For obvious reasons."

Leon Cole waved his hands, mystified. "But why no injunction on this? The footage outside in the plaza was much more horrifying. Why prohibit only the inside footage?"

Wills let one eyebrow rise. "Because, Mr. Cole, the inside footage included closeups."

Everett: "But that wasn't the stated reason."

Wills: "No. But it was Ms. Vercours's real reason. I have this orally from Conklin."

"Ah; so the Vercours woman got the injunction," Cole said. "But that doesn't make sense. I'd think that, as an ENG reporter herself, she'd enjoy all that coverage. It could have made her reputation overnight—and she's, um, a strikingly handsome lady."

"Her status changed appreciably between her sack lunch that day, and her dinner in the Hyatt House with Wally Conklin," said Thomas Wills. "Conklin had her on a retainer within ten minutes. The next time you see Wally in a place where it's tough to maintain tight security, take a close look around. You'll probably find Vercours among the ENG people roaming around him."

"She was my tennis instructor, you know," Costigan chirped.

"In Chicago?"

"No, a vacation in Phoenix. Gina had ideas of making it on the Phoenix Racquets, but she wasn't quite *that* good. I got her interested in ENG. God, I'm glad I did."

"We're moving off the point, I'm afraid," Wills murmured.

"I see the woman's angle," said David Engels. "Vercours realized she'd be compromised if everybody in the country saw her in closeups. With a new job as bodyguard, she wouldn't want those tapes aired. But how'd the little independent station that hired her get so much clout with a judge, so fast?"

"It didn't, Mr. Engels. Wally Conklin did."

Everett laughed, "Wheels within wheels. Conklin asked for the injunction on her behalf then? Conklin is CBS, but Ms. Vercours is strictly a private individual."

"You can say that again," Barb Costigan giggled.

Rooker, more composed now, put in: "I take it that CBS knows of Wallace Conklin's part in this."

"To be sure," Wills replied, "but they felt it politic to make their protest along with NBN and ABC. What if the Vercours injunction becomes a common ploy by many people who find themselves in the news in some quasi-private capacity?"

The Commission took up this sobering thought, wrangling through a coffee break toward a solution; perhaps a test case. As always, such gritty questions would take time to resolve and as always, media men would tiptoe over rotten eggs until the FCC, in good time, set out fresh guidelines. The meeting broke up in time for Everett to grab a quick lunch with David Engels before taking the copter shuttle to catch his Denver flight.

Engels studied his colleague as their order arrived. "Why so subdued, Maury? Still thinking about Phoenix?"

A brief nod. "Not just the violence, Dave. I saw worse in 'Nam." He paused as Engels forked a bite of his entree, then continued slowly. "Do you realize we've spent the better part of the morning, and much of the conference, grappling with a wave of problems brought on by a bunch of shit-gargling terrorists?''

Engels stopped chewing, met Everett's glance. He tried twice before he could swallow. "Did you have to say that while I have a mouthful of chicken a la king?"

"*Mea maxima culpa,*" Everett said in mock contrition.

"Your mother'll love hearing you've turned Catholic."

"What I've turned is chicken. This link between terrorism and the media, especially TV, has me worried, Dave." Everett gestured with his spoon, searching for a simile. "It's like—not a link at all. More like an intertwining," he muttered.

Engels tore into a buttered roll, "Emigrate to China," he cracked. "Either China. They don't fuck around with terrorists in police states, ol' buddy."

"I hear you," said Everett, picking through his Crab Louis. "A free press means freedom to sell time to some murderous little nit with his head in a sack. At least we bagged that bunch down in Phoenix," he finished.

"Not all of 'em. Jeez," at Everett's startled glance, "you must spend a lot of time noodling around in the Rockies, Dan'l. The German with the gee-eye forty-five was Fritz Valken; one of the Baader-Meinhoff gang—and I wish we'd taken him alive. The beard was some guy named Hashem, an Algerian national who was supposed to be in class at M.I.T. A grad student in nuclear engineering." He saw Everett blink at the significance of terrorists being trained in nuclear technology. "Yeah," he answered the unspoken comment; "but now he's building bombs in hell. It was the kid with the Schmeisser machine pistol who got away."

"Christ, after getting smeared by that hysterical miz?"

"Fanatics take a lot of killing," Engels shrugged. "He apparently ran out while a gaggle of reporters were trying to learn how to pull a trigger, and he had some woman waiting in a getaway car. By the way, the Vercours woman was anything but hysterical. Maybe you haven't seen a *tai kwando* offense used in anger, but I have. Vercours is foxy."

"Damn' right," Everett grinned, remembering the way those long legs moved, the strawberry sheen in the honey-blonde hair. "But she's just a trifle butch for my taste."

"Not foxy looking; foxy smart," Engels said, corraling a speck of chicken. "A pretty hard target. And she'd better be, leaving that Chaim character loose somewhere with his nuts in a splint."

"I thought that's what I heard." Everett frowned. "Chaim isn't Arabic, it's about as Hebraic as you can get. I mean, what the hell?"

"Some Jew you turned out to be," Engels chuckled, glancing at his watch. "Immigration photo and prints on the weapon checked perfectly. The young guy was one Chaim Mardor. He's Israeli, all right, from some religious order so strict it doesn't even believe there is an Israel. Even though he was born there. Don't ask me to justify it, pal; I can't."

Everett watched Engels signal the waitress, reviewing old tales his mother had spun with friends from Tel Aviv. Natural? Something to do with nature? "Neturay Karta," he blurted; "right?"

"Something like that," Engels agreed, then switched to his frail imitation of Yiddischer speech: "God forbid I should have to keep all those momzers straight."

"One of these days you're gonna give offense," Everett beamed at his departing friend. "But not this time."

"Because I let you beat me at handball," Engels guessed.

"Let me's rickety ass. No, because you bought lunch." They exchanged grins, like most middle-aged American males unable to say what they felt: our competition is trivial; our affection is not. Everett watched Engels filch mints near the cash register, then let his smile slowly fade as Engels walked out.

He lingered at his table, reflecting on the irony of an orthodox Jewish sect so conservative it could find common cause with Third-World radicals. 'Neturay Karta,' his sabra mother had said, meant 'guardians of the city.' In the orthodox quarters of some Israeli cities lay houses and attitudes musty with a hundred generations of tradition. Old Testament Hebrew scriptures insisted that ha-messiach, the Messiah, would come one day—but at a time when He was most needed; a time when there was no Israel.

The strict fundamentalist Neturay Karta sect argued that, since the scriptures were scrupulously exact, the Messiah would not come so long as Israel existed. Therefore, they reasoned, they must abet the Coming of *ha-messiach* by destroying the State of Israel. If young *kibbutz* women strayed into Neturay Karta haunts in short sleeves or worse, shorts, they risked being stoned by fundamentalists who would rather have a dog carcass putrefying in the street than have it removed by a girl in such scandalous garb. Everett had heard of retaliatory raids by *kibbutzim* to break a few heads in the old quarter. Until now it had seemed a joke to Everett, albeit a bad one. But Chaim Mardor was no joke; he had shot down a passerby as if eradicating vermin. To Mardor it had to be a sort of holy war; an Arab's jehad. And there could be no greater glory for some than to die in a jehad.

To a true believer it all made sense. Everett finished his coffee and headed for the heliport, wondering.

He wondered just how retired David Engels was.

He wondered how much money Gina Vercours made—assuming that money was her motive.

He wondered if he would ever have time to visit Frontierland.

Deplaning at Denver, Everett went immediately to the Hertz people. His own Mini-Cooper 'S,' a tiny British racing sedan with the look of an unsanforized golf cart, was undergoing an operation. In his enthusiasm Everett had permitted a specialist to shave the head too far. Now it was being replaced for reliability. The Mini was a rolling joke, but the laugh was on the other fellow. Despite their boxy shapes the Minis had thrashed Porsches in Alpine road-racing. Like Everett, his Mini was getting older; and like him it had attained scruffiness without losing much stamina.

Hertz had the compact Zephyrs; nothing smaller. While he waited, Everett idly took note of the little man in the dark jeans and zippered turtleneck who stood nearby. The man's identification did not suit the Hertz girl too well, but she would let him take a big Mercury if he could provide cash plus deposit in advance. The little man paid in Canadian currency and made a notation in his Hewlett-Packard calculator. Everett took the Zephyr's key and his credit card, nodded to the man, and walked away wondering.

He wondered where he had met the little man's combination of accent and gesture before; the face was wholly unfamiliar.

MONDAY, 6 OCTOBER, 1980:

Late on a Monday afternoon, Talith swooped past her mail slot en route from the experimental psych lab to a seminar. Graduate students did not rate locked boxes, but at least they did not have to sort through a stack. She glanced at the cubbyhole above her name, passed on, then abruptly checked her progress and fished out the small perfumed envelope. From a woman? Probably the letter had been placed in the wrong slot. It was addressed to Leah Talith, Department of Psychology, California State University, San Jose, CA 95101. The letter bore a Denver postmark.

Her slender calves aching from several flights of stairs, Talith hurried to the seminar, pausing only at the coffee machine. The class was popular and eighteen students were too many for a seminar, but after Talith slit the envelope with a razor-edged fingernail, she was glad to be one among many. The letter purported to be a partial

listing of towns containing Friends of the Kibbutz members. It was a long list.

Talith knew her fingers trembled on the coffee
cup, knew young Jamie Hilborn was watching
her. He did that a lot. She folded the letter away,
inched her left hand downward, began to stroke
the flesh of her thigh just above the knee as
though unconscious that Hilborn's gaze had followed her hand. Presently she stretched her legs,
exercising the calf muscles. Jamie Hilborn
would not be taking many notes this day, or
thinking about her letter.

Talith did not return to the seminar after its
intermission, but hurried to her apartment near
the park on South Sixteenth. It was typical of
Fat'ah to disguise even the envelope, and as she
locked her doors she was giddy with anticipa-
tion. She drew the massive zip-code book from
a shelf and started to scribble numbers next to
the towns listed.

Grand Rapids, North Dakota did not matter
except that it provided its five-digit number:
58446. Virgin, Utah and Maryville, Missouri
were equally insignificant. The numbers were
all that counted.

Leah Talith felt hunger pangs before she had
all two hundred and thirty numbers. It was a
long message, the longest she had ever received.
Her instructions in July, before the Phoenix attempt, had been much more succinct. She ignored the growl in her belly and, from her tam-
pon cassette, took the one-time pad.

The one-time pad is not the only unbreakable
code system, but it is easily the simplest to use.
Talith's pad was written in washable ink on the

backs of postage stamps in a stamp roll, and had
to be kept absolutely dry. Each stamp carried
twenty of the five-digit numbers, and somewhere one of Hakim Arif's Fat'ah men had an
identical grouping of numbers. The groupings
they coded and sent were not precisely the same;
indeed, the difference between a given zip-code
and the next number on Talith's one-time pad
varied between one and twenty-six. The
twenty-six variations made letters in English,
the language used because it employed many
terms that ill-suited Arabic. Despite the bril-
liance of cryptanalysis techniques, they fail before the one-time pad. In the message to Talith,
the vowel e occurred seventeen times. It occurred as seventeen different five-digit numbers,
so that a frequency count was not possible—or,
at any event, nonproductive. The one-time pad
was not as sophisticated as indeterminate qua-
dratics. It did not have to be. Talith licked twelve
stamps that evening, erasing the sequences after
their one-time use. Then, for the first time, she
read the message for its content.

   The message left her little room for improvisa-
tion; it even specified the model numbers of the
necessary equipment to be purchased. But that
would be Rashid's problem, since he controlled
the funds. She could improvise in site selection,
at least, before signaling readiness of their Fat'ah
cell for its distinguished visitor. She felt certain
that the Pueblo telephone number was that of a
public telephone booth. She would either call at
the proper time or not at all.

   Trained by Fat'ah lieutenants after her re-
cruitment from Neturay Karta, she had never

seen Hakim Arif, had seen only half of his other
followers. But Talith knew that the demands of
Fat'ah in communication skills were refractory,
as Hakim was refractory. If Hakim was sending
an aide to prepare for his coming, the contact
number would be no private one.

Hakim Arif's man would arrive on Saturday,
25 October, expecting videotapes of the day's
news as well as a cell meeting. Rashid would be
glad to abandon his studies in California State
University at Northridge, several hundred kilometers away. She could only guess at the
willingness of the motorcycle mechanic, Bernal
Guerrero; but while he occasionally questioned
an order, he was a complete professional. She
was not so sure about Chaim.

Talith frowned as she sought the address near
the village of Felton where Chaim Mardor might,
or might not, be found. He had always been
mercurial, a temperamental link in Fat'ah's be-
havioral chain-mail. After she had driven him
bleeding and frenzied from the center of Pheonix
on that disastrous day in August, he had become
more reclusive. Talith told herself she would
cover for any cell member with emotional
lapses, and knew that she lied. Chaim would
have been eliminated by now, were it not for her.
Chaim was a problem that must be faced; but
Chaim was also, with Talith, Neturay Karta. She
would give him time to recover, to realize his full
potential.

As a weaver among counterculture people in
California's Santa Cruz mountain communes,
Chaim was accepted. His gentle fingers teased
lovely portraits from yarn, driftwood and feath-

ers; and occasionally they squeezed a trigger. He lived with a brace of young women who found in his quiet intensity a strangeness enough for two. Chaim found himself a capable respondent because, apart from their camouflage value, their combined significance was zero. Talith had begun to suspect that he was impotent with her because she was significant. This, she felt, was a great pity: one of the pleasant articles of her new Fat'ah faith was its demands on her body.

Talith put the apartment in order before driving her small van into the southern mountains toward Felton. Chaim might not be roused by the visit of a Fat'ah lieutenant, but the message had suggested something that would. Chaim could always be galvanized by the verbal trigger, Hakim Arif. Though the fact had not emerged clearly enough for her to deny it, the same was true of Leah Talith.

SATURDAY, 25 OCTOBER, 1980:

At the first buzz of his phone, Everett decided to ignore it. He had planned his selfish Saturday since the Anaheim trip, determined that official business would positively not deflect him from one last October day in the high country. Everett lived his fantasy whenever he could—briefly by necessity, alone by choice. It was not until the third buzz, as he struggled into a forest green pullover, that he recognized the buzzer tone of his unlisted number. Only his informants, and probably a few old colleagues of David Engels, had access to that number, a tenuous link between newsmen and the federal government.

Everett spoke briefly, listened long, and promptly forgot the Rockies that stretched in sere majesty across his horizon near Colorado Springs. "You're already there, are you," he said, thrusting the earpiece between head and shoulder as he tugged on heavy socks. "But why the Shoshone-Beardsley intersection? Doesn't the parade go through the center of Pueblo?" A pause. "Sure; handy for you and me, and for the tactical squads too. Those mothers must be awfully confident. You have any idea at all what kind of trouble's brewing?" A final pause. "So we'll have to wing it. I'll make it in maybe fifty minutes if I take the superskate, but I haven't a CB rig in it. My problem anyhow. And thanks, Leo—really."

Once before he hit U.S. Route Eighty-seven and twice after, Everett was noticed by Colorado Highway Patrol cruisers. The Mini was in racing tune again, though he rarely had time for his infatuation with the little freeway raptor. The big cruisers invariably saw his honorary highway patrol decals, fell back to check his plates, then let him continue fleeing south at nearly three kilometers a minute. A Commissioner was supposed to be circumspect, but Everett used this special privilege only in the line of duty.

He took the second off-ramp at Pueblo as if the curve were a personal affront, then eased off as he entered boulevard traffic. According to the newsman's tip, he would have time to find the intersection before the terrorist demonstration. Briefly, Everett was reminded of Charlie George, who had sat near him at—what was it, the Associated Press convention? The comedian had opined in his laconic drawl, "TV will still play whore to any pimp with a machine pistol. We're the tush of terrorism." Everett had laughed at the remedy Charlie had proposed. But then, you were supposed to laugh at Charlie.

He spotted vehicles of two different networks as he neared the target area, and forgot about comedy. The van, he overtook; the big Honda bike overtook them both, more by maneuverability than speed. *The van gets you status, the bike gets you there first,* he mused. Newspeople could do ENG with two-wheeled vehicles though the Honda did not carry powerful transmission equipment. Everett kept the van in his rearview and when it stopped, he found a niche for the Mini. From that point on, he was in enemy country.

One of the most disturbing things was that the enemy, while promising a news event to media people, had not identified itself. That could mean a hoax by some amateurich crank—or it could mean the precise opposite.

Everett hesitated a moment in choosing decoy emblems. His was a camouflage problem: he wanted to avoid a make by newsmen, and a few knew Maury Everett on sight. But he also wanted to avoid getting himself killed. He donned wraparound dark glasses for the first criterion, and an armband over his rough leather jacket to meet the second. Terrorists generally knew who their friends were: the armband said simply, PRESS.

Following a National Broadcasting Network cameraman on foot, Everett wished he too had a lightweight videotape rig—even a dummy Oracle Micam would do. It was rare for a terrorist to deliberately down a media man and when it happened, it was usually a revenge killing. But Everett's informant could not predict details. Everett remembered the videotapes he had seen in Anaheim; it was prudent to suspect gunfire.

The boulevard was lined with spectators en-

joying that foolish marvel of autumn anach-
ronism, a homecoming parade. Everett could
not pause to enjoy the brassy polychrome of assembled high school bands that high-stepped, a
bit wearily by now, between wheeled floats. He
focused instead on the ENG people. One, a bulky
Portacam slung over his back, clambered atop a
marquee for a better view. Two others from competing stations took up positions nearer the intersection, almost a block from Everett. The com-
forting mass of a stone pillar drew Maury Everett
into its shadow. He could see a thousand care-
free people laughing, pointing, children darting
after stray float decorations, cheering at discor-
dances in the music of these devoted amateurs.
Was the tip a false alarm? If not, Everett thought,
this happy setting might be shattered within
minutes. And he was powerless. He smiled
without mirth: *Bureaucracy giveth, and bureaucracy taketh away. Blessed be the
name* . . .

Watching nubile majorettes cavort despite a
chill breeze on their naked arms and legs, Maury
Everett faced his personal dilemma for the hun-
dredth time since his appointment. Newsmen
dubbed their solution 'disinvolvement.' You
have a job and you assume its risks. If you are
government, you stay in your own bailiwick and
off the toes of other bureaucrats. If you are business, and most explicitly media business, you
rise or fall chiefly on informal contacts—and in
newsgathering, you do not interfere with the
news event. You do not divulge sources for two
reasons. The legal reason is backed by the Su-

preme Court, and the selfish reason is that fingering a contact is professional suicide.

If Everett somehow interrupted the impending show after its careful leakage to ENG people by some unknown malcontent, his sources would evaporate instantly, permanently. Freedom of reportage, even when irresponsible, was a fundamental function of American media. John Rooker called it surveillance. Everett called it hellish.

The Portacam man had shifted position to a second-landing fire escape next to the synagogue. A thorough pro, he was taking footage of the parade so that, whatever happened, he would be able to salvage some sort of story. Everett saw that all of the floats featured the same general theme: athletics. Lumbering beyond him was a float honoring the 1980 Olympics winners, a crudely animated statue labeled 'Uri' waving three gold medals. That would be Yossuf Uri, Israel's surprise middle-distance runner. The hulking mannikin beside it represented the Soviet weights man, whose heart had later failed under the demands placed upon it by too many kilos of steroid-induced muscle tissue.

The casual connection of death with the float display goaded Everett's mind toward a casual inference, but he froze for too many seconds while the details linked in his head. A synagogue on the corner, an Israeli hero approaching it, and a vague tipoff by a terrorist naming the intersection. No matter how little the ENG people knew, Maurice Everett clawed his way to a terrible conclusion.

Later, he could regain an uneasy sleep whenever he awoke streaming with the perspiration of guilt—for he *had* vaulted the horns of his dilemma. *"Stop,"* he bawled, and knew that his voice was hopelessly lost in the general clamor. Everett sprinted between bystanders, knocked a beldame sprawling, caromed into the side of another float. He was still on his feet, still shouting for attention, when the great torso of Yossuf Uri came abreast of the synagogue and disappeared in a blinding flash. A wall of air tossed Everett halfway across the street.

*   *   *

How Jewish can you get? The stable manager fingered the crisp twenty-dollar bill, smiling down at the signature. "I've saddled up a perty spirited mare, Mr. Rabbinowitz," he said, taking in the wistful smile, the olive skin, the dark hypnotic eyes. "Sure that's what you want?"

"Precisely," the little man said, and paced out to the corral. He mounted the mare quickly, gracefully, and cantered her out along the rim of the arroyo. The stableman watched him, puzzled. He was certain he had seen Rabbinowitz before. As the figure dipped below his horizon in the afternoon sun, the stableman laughed. Meticulous silken dress and manner had made the illusion even better, a youthful cosmetic version of a man more character than actor. "George Raft," he murmured, satisfied.

The mare was no filly, but she had Arabian lines. The rider held her at a gallop, imagining

that he was in Iraq and not California. He savored
the earthy scents of this, a small pleasure he
could justify in terms of security. No one, he felt
certain, would bug a bridle trail. Presently he
came in view of San Jose rooftops and at that
moment—precisely—knew that he was being
watched.

He made an elaborate show of patting the
mare's neck, leaning first to one side and then
the other, scanning—without seeming to—every
mass of shrub cover within reasonable pistol
shot. Nothing. His heels pressured the mare. She
was already plunging ahead when he heard the
girl cry out behind him. He had passed her without sensing her? Most disturbing.

He wheeled the mare and returned, erasing his
frownlines for the girl. She was clapping now, a
jet-haired comely thing, slender-boned, with the
lustrous eyes of a drugged fawn. "Ayyy, que
guapo," she laughed aloud, showing a pink
tongue between dazzling teeth. The gold cross at
her throat, the peasant blouse: a latina.

He misjudged her in two ways: "You like the
mare?"

"The combination," she answered, growing
more serious. Her hands were clearly in sight
and he did not see how she could hide a deadly
weapon while showing so much youthful flesh.
But still—Now she stroked the mare's nose,
looking up at him. He liked that. "Like music,"
she said, and waited.

The formula should not have surprised him
so. "Music by Sedaka?"

"Imsh'allah," she said. How convenient that a
popular composer's name should also, in several

related tongues, mean 'gift.' Well, this one would give. Her stealth and cover identity had been, if anything, better than his own. He did not admit to irritation in his response.

He complimented Talith in her deception, dismounting, walking with her to a tree-shaded declivity. The mare tethered, they sat, and now her slight advantage in height disappeared.

"Curious," he began, "how my appetites are whetted by a job well-done." They spoke English and then Arabic, softly, warmly, and when he remounted it was not on the mare. He forced into her immediately, a pain she ignored in her joy to serve. He coupled like a ferret, grinning fiercely, his need unsullied by affection, and Talith knew that she would not be required to simulate orgasm. She extended her tonguetip between her teeth, her own grin lewd in his face, and reached down to find him. She began to contrive for him that redoubled rapture, a Florentine. His restraint was no match for this and, in moments, he was spent.

Presently they drew apart. The girl combed her hair with impatient fingers. "You have seen the media coverage of the Pueblo operation this morning?"

"There was no time for that," he yawned. "I nearly missed my flight to San Jose. But I did hear a bulletin. Did Fat'ah obtain suitable coverage?"

She nodded gravely. "Hakim will be pleased."

"Of that, I am certain." Their great bituminous eyes locked for a moment before, toying with her, he persisted. "But Hakim must have a media center. You are prepared?"

"Prepared? When I hailed you," she riposted, "did you or did you not think I was a local chicana?"

Echoes of repugnance clashed like scimitars behind his quiet words. "You are clever, you are willing. I speak of greater things than—" and paused after using a grossly sexist Bedouin term for his recent use of her. He saw her pupils expand. Pleasure or pain? "I must know whether you have the site, the men, and the equipment Fat'ah requires."

"I cannot say. My instructions are to provide only for the leader himself. He may not arrive, as you know. Or he may." She shrugged.

"You *are* clever. But you are prepared for Hakim Arif?"

"We are Fat'ah."

"And who am I?" He removed his left small finger at the last joint, replaced the prosthetic tip while she regained her composure. "In our telephone arrangements I spoke to you as 'Rabbinowitz'."

"But I thought you would first send—sire, you are Hakim Arif," she murmured, seeming to grow smaller.

"So I am. And angry at continued small talk, and impatient for my media. We have another demonstration to plan, depending on the results we see from this morning's work. You have provided for me, you say? Then show me, Talith."

She quickly explained the route to the site she had prepared, naming each landmark three times. He did not remind her of his old familiarity with travel in the United States, but listened with critical approval. It was best to arrive after

sunset, she said, which also gave her time to alert
the others.

"Chaim and Rashid know you," she added.
The third, Bernal Guerrero, had been recruited
in Damascus, as Talith herself had been, after
Hakim Arif's last sojourn there. Hakim had read
impressive reports on his new followers, and
chose not to say so.

"They will serve," he said, rising to collect the
somnolent mare some distance away. He flung
over his shoulder: "Better perhaps than a woman
who deflects my questions." She could not read
the satisfaction in his face. He wheeled the mare
and trotted her back to the girl. Again he stared
down from a commanding height, stern, refractory: the visage of Fat'ah. "Soon, then," he said,
eyeing the sun.

"Sire," she stammered. Her body was controlled; only her voice betrayed her. "I was led to
expect a lieutenant. Your face is known to few in
Fat'ah."

"Or out of it, as Allah is merciful," he rejoined.
"Perhaps I shall be merciful, too."

"If God wills," she said in Arabic.

"Or perhaps—" he waited until she met his
eyes again, "I shall beat you."

"Perhaps you will," she said, not flinching.

Hakim Arif whipped the mare mercilessly up
the trail with the reins, enjoying the experience,
the control, especially enjoying the memory of
the girl's eyes. They had dilated again at his
threat. Under a westering sun he sped back to the
stable. He was thinking: *spawn of pain. We
Fat'ah are the children of El Aurans after all. . .*

Over an hour later he found the Fat'ah site, temporary as it must be but better situated than he had expected. The bungalow commanded a clear view of the San Jose skyline in the dusk and, on three sides, open pastures beyond carbine range. On the fourth side a swath of scrub oak followed a brook so near the house he could almost leap from its porch into thick cover. He accepted congratulations for his work in Pueblo as though spurning praise, yet Hakim was pleased. He let his distant smiles and nods say so. Let those idiots in the PLO show all the ersatz egalitarianism they liked: Fat'ah, born of Al Fat'h, born of injustice, was effective because he, Hakim Arif, was so. It was essential to strike a balance between fellowship and personal supremacy—yet a little fellowship became a heavy weight.

Only after his site inspection did Hakim conjure a show of warmth, with a ritual embrace for gaunt, silent Rashid and then for Chaim. He traced the new scar tissue across the forehead of Chaim Mardor with a finger. "An honorable wound," he said, thinking otherwise. He caught the gaze of Bernal Guerrero, who stood slightly apart from the others, stalwart in khaki work clothes. "And now, Guerrero: welcome." He offered the handclasp then the embrace.

"My regrets that we could not meet in Damascus," the Panamanian said, his bow formally correct.

Hakim felt the aura of strength, like a physical shield of energy surrounding the strongly-built latino. Independent, ingenious, cold; he would

need firmer leadership than the PLO had provided. "I share your regret," said Hakim.
"Talith, bring us bread."

They sat cross-legged on the living room floor,
Hakim tearing chunks from the uncut loaf. He
placed a piece in each mouth, then chewed a
piece himself. With this ritual he invoked the
ancient Arab law of hospitality; no matter that he
thought it a hollow gesture. Rashid, and perhaps
Guerrero, would luxuriate in the rite that placed
them under Hakim's protection. The site was, for
the time, the home of Fat'ah; and Hakim Arif was
Fat'ah.

Then: "They say you are clever with electronic
devices, Guerrero."

"I can fix a toaster," Guerrero smiled. Then,
sensing that he had been too flippant on such
short acquaintance, he went on. "Or a transceiver, or a squib time-delay. From what I have
seen of the Pueblo blast, perhaps not as well as
you."

Hakim grunted with pleasure. If Guerrero was
hinting for an explanation he was doing it expertly. Besides, a recapitulation of the recent
events might impress them afresh. "Talith, bring
us sweet coffee, and my briefcase. I have some
new devices of French design, manufactured in
Canada. They will be of use." He darted a glance
at Guerrero. "You are prepared to emplace
communication devices tonight?"

"*A sus ordenes*, at your orders," Guerrero
said. "But the roads across the coast range are
few and well-patrolled. In my van is a vehicle
that avoids the highways."

Hakim hesitated. Even an expert cyclist would

have little chance to make good time through
those low precipitous mountains. He said as
much.

"It is not a scrambler bike," Guerrero said easily. "While repairing a small rotary engine last
year I learned that it powered a shrouded impeller. The unit is slung beneath a parafoil, señor.
What I have in the van is my gift to Fat'ah."

He seemed willing to continue, which would
effectively wrest the moment from Hakim.
Worse, it would consume minutes which Hakim
needed to familiarize the Panamanian with the
new microprocessors. "I assume you are profi-
cient," he said curtly, then took the briefcase
from Talith. Moments later he was again the
undivided center of attention. And of control.

Guerrero was quicker than quick, more impressed with the microprocessors than his fel-
lows because he understood their multiple functions without delay. "With the battery packs and
ordinary communication devices patched to
these units," he mused, "Fat'ah can be everywhere at once."

"Indeed," Hakim smirked. "Perhaps I shall
tell you how I used them in Canada. But another
time," he said, seeing Talith check her
wristwatch. "Tonight I shall require remote
voice relays at two telephone locations. Show
me, Guerrero, how you would use my compo-
nents."

Guerrero made mistakes only twice, then correctly assembled the devices three times without
error. At length Hakim was satisfied and called
for a light meal. Talith, in her wisdom, had managed to obtain honey-rich, multilayered *baklava*

as their dessert. Hakim found himself salivating for it and so, perforce, refused it. He had seen the jumble of communication equipment arranged by Talith and Rashid but this, too, he ignored for the moment. Then it was time for Guerrero's departure, and he sent Talith and Rashid out on picket duty.

Guerrero's van combined a short wheelbase with all-terrain tires under a long cargo compartment. At Hakim's acid comment on the garish paint, Guerrero pointed out that, by California standards, it was subdued. The van culture, springing from the recreational vehicles of the seventies, was invading the west coast to such an extent that one could purchase, direct from Detroit, vans covered with tinted plastic bubbles and fantastic painted panoramas. While he enthused over the uses of a van, Guerrero was proving his point.

With Chaim's help, dark green dacron and black-painted aluminum tubing from the van soon became a spidery frame topped by fabric. In places the fabric was taut over the slender tubing; across most of its span it draped limp. The vehicle had no tail surfaces but featured two swept wings, the lower wing staggered behind. Guerrero boasted that the dual wing gave his craft such a low stall speed that, unlike earlier parafoils, it could fly at the pace of a trotting man. Despite the darkness, Hakim could see that Guerrero's perch was a padded bike seat, mounted above the enclosed driveshaft. Ahead of the rider was the little rotary engine; behind him, the shrouded impeller. It started quickly with the rasping whirr of a big lawnmower.

A loaded pack frame leaning against his knee, Hakim cupped one hand to his cheek and leaned forward. "If your landing is not gentle, Guerrero, your cargo will dig your grave."

"I can land in any clearing," Guerrero joked, "with the landing gear I was born with." He flexed his knees and gestured for tho pack.

Guerrero settled the pack straps over his shoulders, adjusting the twenty-kilo mass, testing the freedom of his arms. Hakim realized that, as Guerrero straddled the machine and lifted it clear of the ground, he was momentarily supporting over fifty kilos of dead weight. His takeoff seemed ludicrous for only a moment, a bow-legged trot down the smooth slope of clearing. Then the whirr of the rotary engine was lost in the rush of high-pressure air as Guerrero opened the valve of his air bottle. The great advantage of the air rocket, Hakim saw, lay in the fact that it had no visible exhaust. If it was a relatively low-impulse power unit, it was certainly more than enough for the parafoil.

In twenty meters Guerrero was running in space, then bending forward to lie semiprone as the parafoil wafted upward. A sprinter could have outrun him. The cold-gas rocket abruptly ceased its hiss and Hakim saw the parafoil gently accelerate, now climbing at a shallower angle. Guerrero claimed that the thing could exceed legal highway speeds but only now did Hakim believe him. Guerrero might see by the glow of the city, but his own craft was invisible to Hakim, even its exhaust glow hidden from below.

A whistle from Chaim brought the pickets

back, Chaim taking Talith's carbine with a swift check of its safety. "You will kill one of us yet, Leah," he said as the mechanism clicked. They followed Hakim into the bungalow.

Hakim forced his thoughts away from Guerrero, who was gliding above the starlit ravines somewhere to the west. The parafoil was a technology he deeply mistrusted, but once he had felt the same way about microprocessors. He strode to the living room, determined to hide his delight with the new media center, genuinely concerned that it might not be adequate.

Despite himself: "Ah," he breathed, jubilant as he surveyed the media center Talith had assembled at his orders, with the help of Rashid. Four small TV sets half-encircled a desk which also faced an expanse of window. Four multiband radios were ranged to one side. All sets had earplugs. Three telephones were within reach. Note pads, blank card files, colored pens, typewriter, videotape recorder and two audio tape cassette machines filled much of the working space. The squat table underfoot was almost hidden beneath stacks of directories; Bay Area numbers, Los Angeles numbers, Washington numbers, precisely as he had specified. Hakim knew the dangers of heavy dependence on help supplied by the various telephone companies. There were ways to trace one from his patterns of inquiry. Unless, of course, one mastered the system.

Talith stood near, gnawing a full underlip, watching him assess the media center. "Rashid; Chaim," he rapped suddenly. "Are you prepared to spend the night as pickets?"

Both straightened. "We are Fat'ah," said Chaim. Rashid only nodded.

"Rashid, could you fly that thing?" Hakim was staring out the window toward the mountains again.

"With practice, sire," was the whispery reply. "My experience is all in fixed-wing craft."

"Learn," Hakim ordered, and knew it would be done. He dismissed them both.

Behind him, Leah Talith coughed. He turned, waiting. "Shall I take picket duty?"

"Stay," he said, toying with the HP from his new briefcase. After a moment he continued, "How long have you known Guerrero?"

"Since El-Hamma," naming a Syrian training base. El-Hamma was near enough to Damascus to suit Hakim's purposes—and the purposes of the Syrian army as well. Syrian regular army units, Al-Sa'iqa, the PLO, and the alphabet-soup of irregular terrorist armies all over the world boasted graduates of this ghastly seminary. But Talith seemed to think something more was required and added, "I was with him on a border raid last year. His night vision is supernatural; he always sees things the rest of us miss."

"Or would like us to think so," Hakim countered.

Talith did not speak again for a moment. "He is in awe of you," she said then, sensing a guarded stance in Hakim's attitude. The lie might set the Fat'ah leader at ease. "For one thing, the man is not of our blood. He does not understand all of our customs even yet. For

example, he does not know how to address you."
Her hesitancy suggested that Talith shared
Guerrero's concern.

Hakim had not risen this far by allowing cyni-
cism to show in his voice. "Do we fight for
democracy? Is my name Hakim? Then Hakim it
is!" His face softened, faint lines around his jaw
the only sign that Hakim was entertaining a private amusement. "If you can conceive of a Chris-
tian Trinity, you can hold the dual concept that I
am Fat'ah—but also Hakim."

Talith, deeply ingrained with religious im-
ponderables, accepted this self-assessment by
Hakim as a god, yet an equal of his followers. She
knew how this attitude would be identified by
her psychology professors: mad as a March hare.
It had not occurred to her that Hakim was simply
cynical. Her professors had psychology as their
religion, and Talith had Fat'ah as hers.

Hakim began to play with his new equipment,
not waiting for Guerrero's call, half-expecting to
see a brief new starbloom on the silhouetted
peaks to the west. It was nearly an hour before
the news programs, but the girl flicked a finger
toward the videotape. He fumbled it into operation and saw that she had edited earlier news-
casts into a television festival of the Pueblo horror. Hakim settled back into a chair, note pad
ready, and watched his favorite show.

TUESDAY, 28 OCTOBER, 1980:

Like a dry bearing in his head, a thin pure tone pierced Everett's awareness. "When will I quit hearing that whistle," he demanded.

The white smock shrugged. "It goes with the injury," the physician replied. "With luck, another day or so. No, don't try to sit up, you'll disturb the tubes. Follow orders and you'll be up in a few days, Mr. Everett. You're a big healthy animal; give your system a chance."

Everett glanced out the window of the Denver hospital. The fine cloudless day was lost to him, and he to the Rockies. "Hell of a day to be down."

"But a very good day to be alive," the doctor insisted. "You were blown ten meters, mister. Some others weren't so lucky, including a whole handful of TV people. You have no idea how much outcry the networks are making over those five particular fatalities."

Thanks to the drugs, Everett did not feel his bruised kidney, the hairline fracture, and other modest rearrangements of his middle-aged anatomy. The Denver people had done very well by him. But there were things they could not do.

Curbing impatience, he said, "Let's assume I stay put, don't hassle my nurse, and take lunch in approved fashion," with a glance at the intravenous feeding apparatus.

The surgeon folded his arms. "If," he prompted.

"If I can trade the nurse for a staff member in here to—"

"Contraindicated. We're trying to excite regrowth around that flap torn in your tympanum, Mr. Everett. At your age, a blown eardrum is tough to repair. The nurse stays, the FCC goes."

"My left ear's okay, though. And even a felon gets one telephone call."

After a judicious pause: "You've got it." He spoke to the nurse for a moment, stopped with his hands on the door. "We're starting you on solid foods, provided you make that one call and no more. We can haggle, too. Agreed?"

"Agreed." *More or less,* his tone implied.

"By the way, which note do you hear?"

"I haven't the foggiest," Everett admitted. "Why?"

Deadpan: "If it's 'A' natural, you might take up composing. Robert Schumann heard that note for years; nearly drove him up the chimney."

"Have you ever considered a bedside manner?"

The doctor grinned. "If you needed it, you'd get it. You're on the mend," he said, and walked out.

Maury Everett watched the door swing shut,

thinking of channels. FCC staff to network honchos? Dave Engels? Both too slow, and always loss of fidelity when the message was indirect.

The hell with it. "Nurse, I want you to call NBN Hollywood and get just one man on the line. I want nobody else, I want him with all possible speed, and it might help if you tell him Commissioner Everett is itching to lay the tush of terrorism."

She waited starchily, receiver in hand. "You're to avoid all excitement. Is this an obscene call?"

"Everybody's a comedian," he grunted. "But the only one I want is Charlie George."

* * *

Everett never knew exactly when the whistle died in his cranium. It was gone when he donned street clothes six days later, and that was enough. He was shaky, and he wore an earplug in his right ear, but he was functioning again. A staff member packed his bag because there was no wife to do it, and brought the taxi because he wasn't going home first. The office would simply have to improvise until he had recuperated in Palm Springs—a tender negotiation with militant medics, based on his promise to relax with friends at the California resort city. He did not tell them it would be his first visit, nor that he had met only one of those close friends in casual encounters. He did mail a note to one other Commissioner, outlining his decision. He signed it, 'Zebulon Pike'; Engels would enjoy that.

Everett did not feel the Boeing clear the runway, so deep was he into a sheaf of clippings collated by his staff. A dozen dissident groups had claimed so-called credit for the Pueblo blast, each carefully outlining its reasons, each hopeful that its motive would be touted. As usual, Everett noted with a shake of the massive head, our media system had accommodated them all.

Yet only one group was armed with guilty knowledge: Fat'ah, led by the wraithlike Iraqi, Hakim Arif. Shortly after the blast, a United Press International office took a singular call from Pueblo, Colorado. It spoke in softly accented English of a microwave transmitter hidden in a tennis ball on a synagogue roof. It spoke of galvanized nails embedded in explosives. It correctly stated the exact moment of the blast, to the second.

These details were quickly checked by the UPI. Each detail was chillingly authentic. The caller went on to demand that Fat'ah, the only true believer in Palestinian justice, be given a base of operations for its glorious fight against Jewish tyranny. Ousted by Jordan, then ostensibly from Syria, Fat'ah was simply too militant even for its friends. It had nowhere to go. It chose, therefore, to go to the American people. Its channel of choice was a hideous explosion that left nearly a dozen dead and three dozen injured, half a world away from its avowed enemy.

When the caller began to repeat his spiel, police were already tracing the call. The message was on its fourth re-run when a breathless assault team stormed a Pueblo motel room. Not quite abandoned, the room contained a modified telephone answering device which, upon receiving a coded signal, had made its own prearranged call with a tape cartridge. The device was altogether too cunning: when an officer disgustedly jerked the telephone receiver away, it blew his arm off. The Federal Bureau of Alcohol, Tobacco, and Firearms was still theorizing about the devices used, but was quite positive about the sophistication of the user.

According to a *Newsweek* bio, the leader of Fat'ah was a meticulous planner. When Hakim Arif was twelve years old, U.S. and Israeli agencies were still aiding Iran in the design of its secret police organ, SAVAK. Thus SAVAK was still naive and Hakim already subtle when the boy visited Iran with his father on a routine bribery expedition. During the night, security elements of SAVAK paid a lethal call on the elder Arif. The boy evaporated at the first hint of trouble, taking across rooftops with him most of the emeralds his father had earmarked for Iranian friends. SAVAK knew a good joke when it was played on them, and praised the lad's foresight. They would have preferred their praise to be posthumous; in the Middle East, drollery tends to be obscure.

Hakim took his secondary schooling in English-speaking private schools under the benevolent—and venal—gaze of relatives in Syria, who never did discover where the jewels were. Hakim also came under sporadic crossfires between Arab guerrillas and their Israeli counterparts, and he knew where his sympathies lay. *Newsweek* hinted that young Hakim might have taken additional coursework in an academy of socialist persuasion near Leningrad. How he got into an Ivy-league American school was anybody's guess, but a thumbnail-sized emerald was one of the better suppositions.

Trained in finance, media, and pragmatism, Hakim Arif again disappeared into the east after his American training—but not before leaving indelible memories with a few acquaintances. He quoted the Koran and T.E. Lawrence. He was not exactly averse to carrying large amounts of cash, and protection for it, on his person. He won a ridiculously small wager by chopping off the end of a finger. And he was preternaturally shy of cameras.

Hakim and Fat'ah were mutually magnetized by desire and bitterness, but not even Interpol knew how Hakim Arif came to lead a guerrilla band that rarely saw its leader. One thing seemed clear about his emergence: anyone too devious for Carlos Sanchez developed a certain mystique among the terrorist cadre. Even lunatics have a lunatic fringe; the Fat'ah group developed a positive genius for wearing its welcomes threadbare among groups that were only half crazy.

Thwarted by security forces in Turkey, England, Syria, and Jordan, Fat'ah was evidently fingering the tassels at the end of its tether. Perhaps Hakim had peddled his last emerald; the fact seemed to be that the goals of Fat'ah, reachable by sufficient injections of cash into the proper places, were elusive.

This was not to say that cash could not be raised. According to magazine sources, Libyan

President Muammar Qaddafi had shelled out
two million dollars to Carlos Sanchez for his
Vienna raid on ministers of the Organization of
Petroleum Exporting Countries in December of
1975. Analysts of the Third World eventually
shifted from their initial opinion that Qaddafi
had acted out of personal pique. The final con-
sensus was that Qaddafi and OPEC had simply
sustained a corporate disagreement, just as other
businesses sometimes have disagreements.
Nothing personal; the bullets and the blood had
been morely business. The biggest. As usual.

An even larger investment—some said as
large as five million dollars from Swiss accounts
controlled by Giangiacomo Feltrinelli—had
been made toward the massacre at the Olympic
Village in Munich, in 1972. Hakim Arif had later
contrived a brief and uneasy alliance with the
Black September movement precisely because of
its success; not with the Israelis so much as with
the money they had squeezed from Feltrinelli.

Hakim himself was rumored to have a dark
angel in the person of a sheikh living in and
around an English country estate. The anglo-
phile sheikh could afford a castle, and walled
grounds envied by many a British peer, more
easily than the English could afford the sheikh.
The nabob had been gently dissuaded only in
1977 from driving his special-bodied ten-meter
Rolls across his rolling meadows in search of the
once-tame deer that infested his estate. It was not
the speeding that his neighbors minded; the
Rolls was on very, very private property. The
complaints stemmed from the submachine gun
bullets that sprayed beyond the sheikh's prop-

erty whenever he sought the deer. There may
have been no close connection between the
sheikh's forced moratorium on the deer hunts
and his decision, a month later, to put Hakim
Arif on salary.

No act of terrorism, of course, would be paid
very well by its well-wishers unless it achieved
that crucial phenomenon, media coverage. The
sheikhs, Qaddafis, and Feltrinellis would pay
more for one well-covered disemboweling than
for a thousand committed in secret. Media
coverage, especially on television, gave the
criminal a chance to publicize his motives and
his potency. The news magazines implied that
the emergence of Hakim Arif in the United
States was an omen of spilled guts.

They also gave coverage to Hakim's motives,
and his potency.

Everett paused in his reading to gaze wistfully
out at California's mighty Sierra range that
stretched below the Boeing. Somewhere below,
near Lake Tahoe, was a cabin he knew well;
hoped to visit again. With the dusting of early
snow on sawtooth massifs, the Sierra looked as
cold and hard as the heart of Hakim Arif. What
sort of egoist did it take to shorten his pinkie on
an absurd wager, yet shun photographers? A
very special one, at the least. Everett resumed
reading.

The conservative Los Angeles Times, the previous Monday, had devoted too much space to a
strained parallel between law enforcement
agencies and Keystone Kops. The smash hit of
the new TV season was a Saturday night talk
show in which a battery of clever NBN hosts

deigned to talk, live, only with callers who were already in the news. Soon after midnight after the Pueblo disaster, a caller had identified himself as Hakim Arif. A reigning cinema queen was discussing oral sex at 12:17:26, and found herself staring into a dead phone at 12:17:30. Hakim was speaking.

Incredibly, the Iraqi responded to questions; pre-recording was out of the question. While Hakim launched into the plight of Palestinian Arabs and the need for funding to continue his heroic struggle, network officials feverishly collaborated with police, the FBI, and several telephone companies. Hakim was obviously watching the show, to judge from his critique of one host's silent mugging.

Hakim used no terms objectionable enough to require bleeping. He merely promised to repeat his Pueblo entertainment in larger and more vulnerable gatherings until, in its vast wisdom and power, the United States of America found a haven for Fat'ah. And oh, yes, there was one condition: the country of the haven must adjoin Israel.

While voiceprint experts established the identical patterns of the Pueblo and NBN show voices, a co-host asked if Hakim realized that he was asking for World War Three. Hakim, chuckling, replied that he trusted the superpowers to avoid exaggerated responses to Fat'ah responses to Israeli banditry.

As Hakim chuckled, a Lockheed vehicle lifted vertically from Moffett Field in central California for nearby Santa Cruz. Its hushed rotors carried four case-hardened gentlemen over the coast range in minutes to a parking lot two hundred yards from the Santa Cruz telephone booth which composed one link in Hakim's telephone conversation. Police cordoned the area and awaited the fight.

There was no fight. There was only another clever device in the booth, relaying the conversation by radio. Its sensors noted the approach of the bomb squad to the booth with the 'out of order' sign, and suddenly there was no telephone, no device, and no booth; there was only concussion. The *Times* surmised that Hakim could have been within thirty miles of the booth. No one, including Hakim, knew that the Lockheed assault vertol had passed directly over his bungalow in San Jose. Nor that a sweep-winged parafoil had narrowly missed a redwood tree while banking upward from a school playground near Soquel, California.

Hakim's next call passed through another booth in Capitola, near Soquel and Santa Cruz, to CBS. Hakim was in excellent spirits. Government agencies were in overdrive, steering madly with many corrections. No one was in position to corral even one arm of Fat'ah and when Hakim was good and ready, he closed down his media operation.

By the time his bungalow had been discovered, Hakim had a two-day start. That is, said the private report compiled for Everett by friends of David Engels, if it *had* been Hakim. Fingerprint gambits, falsely planted prints, were common in disinformation games. The Iraqi's M.O. varied, but he always knew how to use available channels, including the illegal importation of some of his materiel from Quebecois sources. There was more, and Everett forced himself to read it. Beyond his old-fashioned reading glasses, his eyes ached. Presently he closed them and tried to ignore the faintly resurgent whistle in his head.

MONDAY, 3 NOVEMBER, 1980:

Two flights and a limousine later, Maurice Everett declined help with his suitcase and carried its reassuring bulk in Palm Springs heat toward a featureless sloping lawn. At least, it seemed to have no features until he strode through a slot in the grassy berm and realized that this comedian knew how to use money.

The berm surrounded a sunken terrace open to the sun. Around the terrace and below ground level lay the translucent walls of Charlie George's hideaway. It reminded Everett of a buried doughnut, its hole a glass-faced atrium yawning into the sky, slanted solar panels more attraction than excrescence. It was thoroughly unlike the monuments erected to Mammon on the nearby acreages: it was logical, insulated, understated. Already, Everett liked Charlie George better for making sense even when he was not compelled to.

Everett was nonplussed for an instant by the

man who met him at the door like a sodbuster's valet. Denims tucked into beflapped, rundown boots; suspenders over an ancient cotton work shirt; a stubble of beard. Yet there was no mistaking the loose-jointed frame or the shock of corntassel hair over bushy brows, familiar to anyone who watched prime time television. Beneath a strong nose was a mouth legendary for its mobility, from slack-jawed idiocy to prudish scorn. Everett realized with a start that it was speaking.

"You wanted it informal," said Charlie George, and ushered Everett to a guest room.

Everett removed his coat. "I thought you'd taken me too literally, Charlie. For a minute I thought you'd set this up in a vacant lot."

"Just doing my bit for the Palm Springs image as the world's most elegant unfenced asylum. Complete with crazy proposals."

"Not in my book," Everett replied. They discussed their strategy while he changed into his scruffies. "I haven't sounded out all the members of the Commission," he admitted, wincing as he adjusted his pullover. "Wills is a reasonable sort, though, and I'll lay it out for him so he'll know how you propose to separate television from terrorism. These panel talks with the AP and UPI sure haven't excited him—or me. I like your scenario much better."

The comedian kept his eyes sociably averted as Everett donned soft leather trousers. "We've been batting out details for an hour," he said.

"Who's 'we'?"

Charlie leaned his head toward the window facing the atrium. "No net veepees, just a couple

of pivotal people I told you about." He led
Everett through a kitchen saturated with fra-
grances of tortilla and taco sauce, into sunlight
toward a buzz of male voices in a hidden corner
of the atrium.

They found two men seated, dividing their
attention between sketch pads and bottles of
Mexican beer. The smaller man made a point of
rising; the taller, a point of not rising. "This is
our friend in the feds," Charlie placed a gentle
hand on Everett's shoulder. "Maury Everett:
Rhone Althouse here, and Dahl D'Este over
there."

Althouse, the compact younger man, wore
faded jeans and Gucci loafers. Only the footgear
and a stunning Hopi necklace belied his undergraduate appearance. He was tanned, well-built,
and his handshake had the solidity of a park
statue. It was hard for Everett to believe that this
pup was a media theorist who deserted
academia for a meteoric rise in gag writing.

"I hope you FCC guys move quicker separately
than you do together," he said to Everett, with
the barest suggestion of a wink.

Everett smiled at the threadbare gibe. FCC decisions never came quickly enough for the industry they regulated. "Don't bet on it," he replied. "I'm still pretty rickety today."

D'Este, doodling furiously on a mammoth
sketch pad, stopped to gaze at Everett with real
interest. "I forgot," he said in a caramel baritone,
"you were the star of the Pueblo thing. Perhaps
you'll tell me about it." His tone implied, *some
other time, just we two.*

Everett accepted a Moctezuma from Charlie

George and eased his broad back into a lawn chair. "All I know, literally, is what I've read since I woke up with tubes running into my arms. I expect to learn a lot more from you three, in hopes it won't happen again."

"Ah," said D'Este, beaming. His elegant slender height was covered by a one-piece mauve velour jumpsuit which, Everett hazarded, might have been tailored expressly for this event. Dahl D'Este affected tight dark curls; his tan was by Max Factor. He hugged the sketch pad to his breast and stood to claim his audience. "Well then, the story thus far—" He paused as though for his host's permission and seemed gratified by some signal. "Charlie has this—*wild* idea that he can ring in a new era of comedy. Instead of avoiding the issue of terrorism in his shtick, and believe me, luv, we all *do*, he wants to create a truly *fabulous* character."

"A whole raft of 'em," the comedian put in. Everett nodded; he knew the general idea but would not rob D'Este of his moment.

"Charlie has seduced the best talents he could find to plan graphics, that's me, and situations, that's Rhone—according to Rhone. Of course it's ironic because Charlie is NBN, Rhone is an ABC captive, and for the nonce I'm doing CBS sets. I don't know how Charlie beguiled his old *enfant terrible*," he smirked at Althouse, "to cross traditional lines in this madness." Everett, who knew it had been the other way around, kept silent. "As for me, I couldn't resist the challenge."

"Or the retainer," Althouse drawled in a murmur designed to carry.

The splendid D'Este ignored him. "While

Charlie and Rhone brainstormed their little skits, I've been inventing Charlie's logo for the new character. A cartoon of the sort of loser who—how did you put it, Rhone?"

"Rates no respect," the younger man supplied. "If he tried dial-a-prayer he'd get three minutes of raucous laughter."

"Well, my logo will peer out at the world from Charlie's backdrop like a malediction. I really ought to sign it. Behold, a very proper Charlie!" With this fanfare, Dahl D'Este spun the sketch pad around and awaited reactions.

Everett was thankful that he did not need to surrogate approval. The sketch was, somehow, the face of Charlie George as an enraged Goya might have seen him. Yet the surface similarity was unimportant. Splashed across the paper in hard sunlight was a stylized symbol of repellence. The head and shoulders of a vicious imbecile faced them as it would glare out at untold millions of viewers. The face was vacuously grinning, and gripped a fuzed stick of dynamite in its teeth. The fuze was short, and it was lit. In redundant arrogance, just exactly enough out of scale as though reaching toward the viewer, was a time-dishonored gesture: the stink-finger salute.

Laughter welled up from the group and geysered. Althouse raised his beer in obeisance.

"Ah,—about the monodigital scorn, Dahl," Charlie wavered, darting a look at Everett.

Althouse held his hands open, cradling an invisible medicine ball. "C'mon, Charlie, it's perfect." He too risked a sidelong glance at the

FCC Commissioner. "And for its public use, our precedent was a recent vice-president."

D'Este: "Of which net?"

"Of the United bloody States," cried Althouse in mock exasperation. "And Rockefellers built Radio City. Yes it's naughty, and yes it's safe!"

"I'm inclined to agree," said Everett, "if it's done by a questionable character for a crucial effect. Chevy Chase, ah, had a finger in that decision."

D'Este leaned the sketch against the solar panels. "A proper Charlie," he repeated, then looked up quickly. "Did you know that British slang for a total loser is a veddy propah Chahlie?"

"Poor Dahl," sighed Althouse. "Did you know that we picked the name 'Charlie George' in 1975 because semantic differential surveys told me they were the outstanding loser names in the English-speaking world? Bertie is good, Ollie is better; but Charlie George is the people's choice."

"Thanks for nothing," Everett chortled. "I always wondered why citizens band jargon for the FCC was 'Uncle Charlie'." Althouse affected surprise, but not chagrin.

Charlie looked back into the middle-distance of his past. "I wasn't too keen to change my name from Byron Krause to Charlie George," he reflected, "until I thought about that poem."

Althouse saw curiosity in Everett's face and broke in. "I tacked up my doggerel on a soundstage bulletin board, and Charlie saw people react, and bingo: Charlie George." He squinted

into the sun as though studying some sky-
written stanza, then recited.

> "Heroes all have lovely names,
> Like Vance, or Mantz, or Lance—or James;
>
> But authors elevate my gorge
> By naming losers Charles—or George.
>
> There's no suspense on the late, late show:
> Big deal—the bad guy's Chas., or Geo.
>
> Goof-offs, goons, schliemiels and schmucks:
> Georgies every one, or Chucks.
>
> Since the days of big Jim Farley,
> Fiction's fiends have been George and Charlie.
>
> No wonder heroes all seem crass
> To any guy named Geo. or Chas.
>
> I think I'll change my name, by golly!
> My last name's George. The nickname's
> Cholly."

Everett grinned around his swig of beer, but:
"Obviously some of your earliest work," D'Este
purred.

"Point is, Dahl, it fitted the image I was after,"
the comedian insisted. "And it's been good to
me. Your logo is great, by the way; it is a proper
charlie." He paused. "I want you to release it to
the public domain."

The ensuing moment held a silence so deep,
Everett's ear hurt. D'Este broke it with a strangled, "Just—give it away? Like some—amateur?

"No—" and there was horror in his hushed, "—residuals?"

"Oh, I'll pay, Dahl; don't I always? But I want the thing available with no restrictions, for any medium anywhere, anytime. PBS. Mad Magazine. The National Enquirer maybe."

"Madness. Madness," D'Este said again, aghast, his normal hyperbole unequal to this task. He reached for a beer.

When Rhone Althouse spoke again it was in almost fatherly tones. "I'm afraid you haven't been listening very closely, Dahl. It's no accident that Charlie and I are planning to spring this idea in different networks. Charlie's the rudder of several steering committees where the power is in some veepee. I have a little leverage in ABC and with any positive audience response we can slowly escalate the trend. IF there's no problem in, uh, certain quarters." He raised an eyebrow toward Everett.

Everett traced a pattern on the label of his beer bottle, thinking aloud. "There shouldn't be any serious objection from us," he began. "It's in the public interest to pit media against terrorism—and if you find yourselves in jeopardy it won't be from the Commission." He could not keep an edge out of his voice. "Personally I think you've waited too goddam long already."

"They nearly bagged an FCC man, you mean," Charlie prodded.

"No. Yes! That too. I can't deny personal feelings; but I was thinking of ENG people from three networks, casually hashed like ants under a heel. That's why network execs care. That's

why your iron is hot. But so far I don't hear
evidence of any broad scope in your plans."

The comedian bit off an angry reply and
Everett realized, too late, that he teetered on the
brink of a lecture that none of them needed.
Charlie and Althouse had broached the idea
months earlier, looking for outside support that
he represented. This group comprised, not problem, but solution.

Althouse rubbed his jaw to hide a twitch in it.
"You came in late," he said softly. "You didn't
hear us planning to expand this thing into news
and commentary. If you've ever tried to apply a
little torque to a network commentator, you
know it's like trying to evict a moray by hand. I
think morning news and editorializing are a
good place to start; more folksy."

"Start what? Boil it down to essentials."

"It boils down to two points: we turn every act
of terrorism into a joke at the terrorist's expense;
and we absolutely must refuse, ever again, to do
a straight report on their motives *in connection
with an act of terrorism.*"

Everett sat rigidly upright at the last phrases,
ignoring the pain in his side. "Good God, Althouse, that really is censorship!"

"*De facto,* yes; I won't duck that one. But
legally it's a case of each network freely choosing to go along with a policy in the public interest. Wartime restrictions beyond what the government demands are a precedent, if we need
one. When countries go to war, their media generally follow that model. Why can't a medium go
to war on its own?

"American television has already seen its

Pearl Harbor in Pueblo, Mr. Everett. It just hasn't declared war yet. And the National Association of Broadcasters could publish guidelines for independent stations. The NAB is an ideal go-between."

The issue lay open between them now like a doubly discovered chess game. Everett saw in Althouse a formidable player who had studied his moves and his opponent. "It's unworkable," Everett said. "What'll you do when some Quebec separatist gang tortures a prime minister? Sit on the news?"

"Of course not, if it's a legitimate story. The medium can give coverage to the event, sympathetic to the victims—but we must deride the gang as a bunch of charlies, and refuse to advertise their motives in connection with an atrocity."

"While you let newspapers scoop you on those details?"

"Probably—until they get an attack of conscience."

Everett's snort implied the extravagance of that notion. "A couple of Southern Cal people did in-depth surveys that suggest there's no 'probably' to it, Althouse. Editors will print assassination attempts as front-page stuff even if they *know* it brings out more assassinations. They admit it."

"Hey; the Allen-Piland study," Althouse breathed, new respect in his face. "You get around."

"I've been known to read hard research," Everett replied.

"And newsmen have been known to modify

their ethics," Charlie George responded. "If this amounts to censorship, Maury, it'll be entirely self-imposed. Nothing very new in that."

"I'm sure this sounds like an odd stance for me to take," Everett smiled sadly, "but I tend to balk at social control. Hell, Rhone, you've studied Schramm and his apostles."

"Funny you should mention that; I remember something you don't, apparently. Most media philosophers claim that, between simple-minded total liberty to slander and hard-nosed total control over the message, there's something we always move toward when we confront a common enemy. It's called Social Responsibility Theory. We used it to advantage in 1917 and 1942. It's time we used it again."

That the issue would arise in the Commission seemed certain. It was equally certain that Everett must select a principle to override others sooner or later. He had a vivid flash of recollection: a willowy girl with gooseflesh and a baton, bravely smiling after an hour of parading, ten seconds before her obliteration. "I don't like it," he said slowly, measuring his words, "but I don't like wars on children either. You make God-damned sure this social responsibility doesn't go beyond the terrorism thing." His promise of support, and of its limitation, were implicit.

"I don't like it either," D'Este spat. "I seem to be part of a media conspiracy I never asked for. Charlie, you didn't ask me here just for graphics. What, then?"

"Commitment," Charlie said evenly.

"I'm working CBS specials! How I'm expected to collar newsmen, writers, producers,

who knows who else, is beyond me; regular
programming is out of my line."

"Nothing in television is out of your line,"
Rhone Althouse began, laying stress on each
word. As he proceeded, Everett noted the upswing in tempo, the appeal to D'Este's vanity,
the loaded phrases, and he was glad Althouse
did not write speeches for politicians. "You're
independent, Dahl; you work for all the nets,
you know everybody in key committees all over
the Industry, and when you lift an idea you pick
a winner.

"Charlie can sweet-talk NBN news into using
your logo when there's a place for it—we
think—while he develops his satire. You know
the old dictum in showbiz; if it succeeds, beat
it to death. I'll start working the same shtick
in ABC comedy—Christ, I'm doing three
shows!—and I can drop the hint that this lovely
logo is public domain. With any luck, the idea
can sweep NBN and ABC both. News, commentary, comedy."

Althouse watched D'Este gnawing a
thumbnail, fixed him with a hard stare. "And
you, Dahl? Will CBS keep out of the fun for some
asinine inscrutable reason? Or will one of its
most active—" he paused, the word *homosexuals* hanging inaudibly in the air like an echo
without an antecedent, "—free spirits, cham-
pion the idea from the inside? That's really the
only question, Dahl. Not whether you can do it,
but whether you *will*."

Intending support, Everett put in, "It'll take
guts, in a milieu that hasn't shown many," and
immediately wished he hadn't.

"No one corporation owns me, Mr. E," D'Este flung the words like ice cubes. "I don't have to stroke your armor."

"That's not what I meant. None of you have considered asking the next question," Everett replied.

Charlie George misunderstood, too. "Ask yourself if it's worth some trouble to keep the Industry from being a flack for maniacs, Dahl. If we don't start soon, ask yourself if you'd like to see the FCC license networks themselves when Congress considers tighter government control."

An even longer silence. "Madness," D'Este said at last, "but in this crazy business—I have misgivings, but I'll go along." He folded his arms in challenge and stared back at Everett. "Licensing? Is that the sword you were brandishing over us, the next question you meant?"

Everett took a long pull at his beer, then set it down. His smile was bleak. "That never crossed my mind, I think Charlie overstated. Here's what I meant: if this idea takes hold, the idea men could be spotlighted, and that means to people like Hakim Arif. I had a brush with their rhetoric, and they weren't even after me. See what it bought me." He peeled his shirt up to reveal the tape that bound the bandage to his right side. Angry stripes, the paths of debris in human flesh, marked his belly and pectorals beyond the tape.

He hauled the fabric down, regarded the sobered media men. "We have a lot of questions to thrash out, but none of you can afford to ignore the next one: if you take them *all* on—Pal-

estinians, IRA, Chileans, Japanese extremists
—what are the chances they'll come after you
personally?"

For once, he noted with satisfaction, Rhone
Althouse sat unprepared, openmouthed. Preparation would not be simple. Everett made a
mental note to talk again with Dave Engels.
Surely Engels could recommend someone as a
bodyguard. Not a woman; certainly not anyone
like Gina Vercours. . .

MONDAY, 10 NOVEMBER, 1980:

Hakim's feet were light on the steps as he hurried from the bank. The sheer weight of bank notes in his briefcase tugged at his left arm but failed to slow his stride. Fourteen minutes to rendezvous; plenty of time unless he were followed. His quick pace was perfectly normal in metropolitan New York City. He checked his timing again before entering the cafeteria. No one followed or seemed to loiter outside the place. He bought a chocolate bar to tempt, but not to entertain, his empty stomach. Slipping the candy into a pocket of his silk shirt away from the newly extended armpit holster, he thought of the pleasures of self-denial. He salivated for the chocolate. Later he would watch Talith eat it. He surveyed the cafeteria's glass front through reflective sunglasses. Twelve minutes; time to burn. He left by a different exit, moving unobtrusively down the street.

It was sheerest luck that the antique store was

placed just so, and boasted a mirror angled just so. Hakim spotted the glance from a stroller to the unmarked green Camaro, both moving behind him and in his direction. The stroller drifted into another shop. A tall sandy-haired man emerged from the Camaro, and in a hurry. Hakim's body braced for action.

He continued his brisk pace. Instead of converging on him they had exchanged tails, which meant he was expected to lead them—whoever they were. They did not move like divinity students. Federals, probably, judging from the cut of their suits. He tested the notion of the Jewish Defense League, a distinct danger in Manhattan, and felt perspiration leap at his scalp. But their methods were usually more direct, and the tail he had picked up must have mooched around the bank for days. And that meant inefficiency, which implied government. He cursed the overcoat that impeded his legs in November cold, then saw the third-rate hotel.

The sandy-haired man entered the lobby as Hakim was leaving the stair onto the filthy mezzanine and wasted seconds on two other passages; seconds that saved him. Hakim found the fire exit, burst the door seal, and slithered past the metal grating to drop into the alley. He sprinted for the street, adjusted his breathing again as he slowed to a walk, then turned another corner and risked a peek over his shoulder. The Camaro was following with its lone driver.

Hakim had nine minutes and needed seven. He wanted that rendezvous, not relishing the alternative risks of public transportation to Long

Island. Nearing the next corner he noted the lack
of pedestrians and made his decision. He broke
into a run, turned sharply, ran a few steps, then
turned back and melted into a doorway. He did
not want the driver to pursue him on foot and
knew this would be the next option.

A small girl sat on the stair in his doorway at
Hakim's eye level, licking fingers sticky with
candy, watching silent and serious as he fumbled in his coat. The silencer slowed his draw.
He flashed the little girl a smile and a wink. The
Camaro squalled around the corner. Hakim
gauged his move to coincide with commitment
to the turn, made five leaping paces, and fired as
many times. The parabellum rounds pierced
glass, cloth, flesh, bone, upholstery, and body
panels in that order, each round making no more
noise than a great book suddenly closed.

The Camaro's inertia carried it into a forlornly
stripped foreign sedan. Hakim held the sidearm
in his coat and retraced his steps, winking again
at the little girl just before he shot her. Then he
reseated the pistol, careful to keep the hot silencer muzzle away from the expensive shirt.

Seven minutes later Hakim hurried up another
alley, squirmed into a delivery van, and nodded
at the sturdy Guerrero who lazed behind the
wheel in coveralls as the engine idled.

The van's engine was mounted between front
seats with an upholstered cover. Bernal Guerrero
had built an extension toward the rear just long
enough to accommodate a small Iraqi; the
makeshift upholstery would pass casual inspection. Kneeling with the extension cover up, reluctant to relinquish control to the latino, Hakim

urged caution. "Drive south first; I was followed." He did not elaborate.

For a time, Guerrero attended strictly to driving as Hakim directed him to the bridge approach. Once over the East River, in heavy traffic, Hakim began to relax but did not stir from his position. Guerrero adjusted an inside rearview. "The funds were on hand, then."

Hakim met his eyes in the mirror. "Was that a question?"

"Deduction, Hakim. The briefcase seems heavy—and you are smiling."

"A wise man smiles in adversity," Hakim quoted, reloading six rounds into the clip.

"I trust Rashid was smiling at the last," Guerrero said obliquely. "We shall miss him."

"Rashid was a fool. You cannot load down an underpowered aircraft and maneuver it, too."

"A fool, then," Guerrero shrugged. "I agree that a satchel charge would have been simpler."

Hakim's irritation was balanced by the utility of the sinewy Guerrero. The Panamanian's suggestions were good, and he did not press them. Yet his conversation always provoked broader answers than Hakim cared to give. "You agree with whom? Have you toured the Statue of Liberty, Guerrero? A satchel charge might disfigure the torch; nothing more. The thing is full of steel girders inside. I planned to destroy it utterly. Think of the coverage," he breathed, and chuckled.

They were past Queens, halfway to the site of Farmingdale on Long Island, before Hakim spoke again. "The new funds," he said as if to himself, "will pour into accounts for Fat'ah exactly as long as our coverage is adequate. But our supporters may not enjoy last night's media sport at Fat'ah expense."

Guerrero nodded, remembering. But to prattle is to reveal, and this time Guerrero said nothing. Amateur films had caught the hapless Rashid, his handmade bomb shackles hopelessly jammed, as he veered away after his first pass over the great green statue, the previous day. The canister weighed nearly three hundred kilos and as it dangled swaying from the little Piper, Rashid must have seen and accepted his imminent death; must have known he could neither land, nor long maintain control. To his credit, he had fought the craft into a shallow turn and straightened again, many kilometers from his target but prepared for another and more suicidal assault. With any luck he might have completed his run, barely off the surface of the harbor, to crash directly into the Statue of Liberty. But the new fireboat hovercraft were very quick, faster under these circumstances than the Piper that careened along at all of ninety kilometers per hour.

Hakim sighed. What ignominy, to be downed by a stream of dirty salt water! Still, "The network commentator made Rashid a martyr," he asserted.

"To what? Idiot liberation, he said. And," Guerrero reminded him, "NBN news did not carry the story well. 'A terrorist quenched with a water pistol,' indeed. It is—*la palabra*, the word? Provocative."

"As you are," Hakim said shortly. "Let me

worry about media, and let the Americans worry about our next demonstration."

"Our next demonstration," Guerrero echoed. It was not quite a question.

"Soon, Guerrero, soon! Be silent." Again Hakim felt moisture at his temples, forcing him to acknowledge a sensation of pressure. Harassment was the guerrilla's tool; when he himself felt harassed, it was better to cancel the operation. Yet he dared not. Something in Guerrero's attitude, indeed in Hakim's own response to the smug mockery of television, said that Hakim must choke that dark laughter under a pall of smoke.

He shifted his cramped legs to sit atop the briefcase as they skirted Mineola. Soon they would roll into the garage at Farmingdale, soon he would bear the briefcase inside with a show of indifference, reviewing the site again to assure its readiness for—for whatever; he did not know what.

Fat'ah must be ready with only four members now, and he could not easily muster more on short notice. The Syrian site would again be secure for a time, now that Hakim could furnish bribes; but Damascus is not Farmingdale, New York and Hakim knew that he was improvising. Fat'ah could not afford always to improvise. Nor could it afford to delay vengeance for the Rashid defeat.

The double-bind was adversity. Hakim forced himself to smile, thinking of smoke. Of black smoke and of media, and of Leah Talith who would be warm against him in the chill Long

Island night. He vowed to deny himself the third, which facilitated the smile, and knew that he could now concentrate on the first two.

* * *

Forty kilometers away in an office of The Tombs, Manhattan, Assistant Chief Inspector Dolby was slavering into his telephone. "Because it doesn't make any goddam sense, that's why," he snarled. "If you were gonna heist a Zee Twenty-Eight Camaro, why pick one that'd just tried to hump a stripped Volkswagen? And when you figure that one out, tell me why you'd take the Volks too. I mean, where's he gonna fence fresh junkers, Damico?"

He listened for long moments, nodding, tapping his teeth with a pencil. "Okay, I'll tell you what I think, I think the officer on duty is also on dago red." Listening again, he began to tap on his cheek. "I don't give a rat's ass how many eyewitnesses he claims, total strangers don't just rush up three minutes after a crash and bodily, BOD-i-ly, pick up two tons of crunched Camaro coupe and cram it into a truck."

Shorter pause. Then a yelp. "Twenty? You can't get twenty men around a Camaro. Well, belay that, maybe you could. But why would you want to?"

He began to experiment, tapping his cheek and moving his lantern jaw. Pause. "Oh, hell, poor little kid. She DOA? Well, at least there's definitely a crime, up 'til now I had serious doubts . . . For one thing, your alleged wreck and your alleged truck and your alleged twenty bad dudes are gone, right? And nobody's reported a theft of any green Camaro today."

Pause. "Look, I can roll when I get a report on the little girl, but you haven't convinced me there was any grand theft auto, much less two. Just some glass in the street, and what else is new? Whaddaya want from me, Damico?"

Listening again, he found the trick and happily tapped his cheek to a simple rhythm. Then sighing: "Okay, right. I will. Hey, my other phone's lit. Yeah—what? Uh, Mary Had A Little Lamb. Talent, huh? S'long."

He punched into the other line in time to take the call. "Dolby here . . . Can you rush it, Canfield? I'm about to go off shift." He started tapping again until his eyes glazed. "Hold it. Let me tell you: it's a green Zee Twenty-Eight, and the Volks ain't got any wheels at all." Pause "I'm psychic is how. Go on."

Dolby started scribbling. Now and then he grunted into the mouthpiece. At last he blew out a mighty breath. "What I think, Canfield, is we don't have enough forms in the Pee Dee. We only got an Unusual Occurrence Report, when we also need a Can You Top This report. Hey, are you sure it ain't some fucking movie crew that staged a wreck in that alley?" His jaw throbbed as he heard the next response. "No, I guess not—for sure they wouldn't leave it with a stiff in it. You sure it's a real live corpse?"

Dolby closed his eyes, pinched the bridge of his nose. "No, Canfield, it's just been a very long Monday for a very short temper. And before you file a report, would you kindly tell me how the Camaro driver could've been dead as long as you say, when he was in another wreck half an hour ago with the same Volkswagen. . . . Never mind, I just know. But you got no lab experience, how come—" He closed his eyes again, very gently. "I see. Not just stiff, you mean cold stiff. How cold? Well shit, take his temperature, I guess . . . For all I care you can shove it up his—wait a minute. You said there was some ID on him?"

Dolby scribbled again. "Ahboudi; courier? Hold it. If the deader had Algerian diplomatic courier status it changes a few things; like, I can dump this in the lap of a Special Services officer, thank God."

Dolby took down more details, then laid down the receiver. After a few minutes he said to Someone beyond his ceiling light fixture: "Let me make You a little bet. I bet You my gold badge if there's a deep-frozen ayrab courier up front, Meyer Cohane's JDL boys are in back of it."

It was a wager even God could not have won.

The New York Police Department found its decision above Dolby, below the Mayor. In return for certain immediate information, the PD elected not to press charges against members of the Jewish Defense League who, all in fun, had removed two vehicles after the collision only to place them elsewhere. The driver of the Camaro, they insisted, had been dead when they arrived at the scene.

This was a luminous understatement inasmuch as Moh'med Ahboudi, an Algerian national with loose consular connections, had been missing from his duties for several weeks. He had been in a freezer for most of that time, after expiring in a brief contest for his freedom. Ahboudi's wounds were frontal skull fracture, broken knuckles, and a ruptured spleen, all of which might possibly be consistent with a very unusual automobile accident. But it also explained why Meyer Cohane, though a full-fledged Rabbi, was persona non grata in Israel. Police records of his enemies tended to be short and untidy.

In the spirit of good fellowship, the JDL fingered the man who had perforated the Camaro—oddly enough, with no bullet holes in the driver— because they had been tailing the gunman. They were virtually certain of his identity: the Iraqi, Hakim Arif.

The JDL was terribly sorry that it could offer no reason why Arif should also be followed by Moh'med Ahboudi, but there it was: Ahboudi was a sloppy tail and had paid the price. Finally, the JDL was sorry they could not lay hands on Arif.

This latter sorrow was genuine enough; after tailing Hakim from the bank in hopes of following him home, JDL men were contrite at their failure. They were even sorrier for young Sammy Greenspan, the original driver of the Camaro. Sammy had died instantly in Arif's ambush. The one bright spot was in the speed with which they managed, in one gruesome practical joke, to get Sammy's body away and to replace it with the cold remains of Moh'med Ahboudi. Now, if the NYPD was willing to take its simplest course, Algerian terrorists and the Iraqi terrorist would find a reason to loathe each other. It was richly

Cohanesque. Sammy Greenspan would have
loved it.

* * *

Chaim and Talith failed to hide their relief at
the sight of the money, stacks of twenties and
fifties, which Hakim revealed in due time. During supper their eyes kept wandering to the cash
until Hakim wordlessly arose and dumped it all
back into the briefcase. "Now we will have sweet
coffee," he sighed, Talith rising to obey, "and
contemplate sweeter revenges. Even today I
struck a small blow; the late news may bear
fruit." He was gratified to see curiosity in their
silent responses.

Hakim did not expect to occupy the ABC lead
story, but grew restive as national, then local
news passed. Had his escape gone unnoticed,
then? It had not, for, "There was an evident
postscript, today, to the blundering attempt on
the Statue of Liberty," said the anchorlady. "If
anyone can make sense of it, perhaps Richard
can. Richard?"

Her co-anchor gazed out at millions, his
backdrop logo a leering idiot that was becoming
familiar on several channels. The newsman
dropped a piece of typescript as if it were defiled
and related little more, factually, than the locale
and the killing of Hakim's pursuer. He went on:
"What places this below the usual level of crime
in the Big Apple, according to one source, is that
the gunman's description matches that of a
Fat'ah charlie; and his victim was an Algerian
Daoudist, from another terrorist group."

Mugging a faint blend of confusion and insouciance into the camera, he continued: "The best current guess is that the victim was trying to make friendly contact, and the gunman mistook him for someone who knew too much." A frosty smile. "Or perhaps that's a charlie's way of hailing a taxi."

Injected by his co-anchor lady: "About the little girl he grazed at point-blank range?"

"Maybe he thought she knew too much, too. And compared to these charlies, maybe she does. She's almost five years old."

Hakim employed vast restraint and continued his televiewing. At his side, Talith said, "But you told us—" until Hakim's hand sliced the air for silence.

The weather news endorsed the frigid gusts that scrabbled at the windows, and Hakim's mood was like the wind. He could not have missed the urchin—and his daring coup was against domestic security forces, he was certain.

Well, *almost* certain. Was it even remotely possible that the coxcomb Daoudists had intended—? On the other hand, government sources could have deliberately lied to the newsmen, with a release designed to confuse Fat'ah.

Talith ghosted to the kitchenette to prepare fresh sweet coffee which Hakim craved, and subsequently ignored, as he lounged before blank television screens. The art of disinformation was but recently borrowed by the Americans from the Middle East, but the west was learning. *But if they know I know that Daoudists could not know where I am*, his thought began, and balked with, *where am I?*

He released a high-pitched giggle and the girl dropped her cup. Hakim angrily erased the rictus from his face and pursued another notion. Daoudists could be behind this, seeking to share the media coverage in its bungling fashion. He, Fat'ah, would need to arrange more talks with his television friends.

Not exactly friends, he amended, so much as co-opportunists who could always be relied upon to give accurate and detailed coverage if it were available. *Except in wartime,* whispered a wisp from a forgotten text. It was unthinkable that American television networks could perceive themselves to be at war with Fat'ah.

Unthinkable, therefore Hakim thought about it.

The same grinning salacious fool was becoming the prominent image behind every news item on terrorism. On competing networks! He thought about it some more. While Fat'ah planned the attack that was to cost Rashid his life, Ukranian dissenters had made news by murdering three enemies in the Soviet Secretariat. A scrap of dialogoue haunted Hakim from a subsequent skit on the Charlie George Show.

INT. SQUALID BASEMENT NIGHT

CHARLIE wears a Rasputin cloak and
villainous mustache, leaning over a
rickety table lit by a bent candle.
He scowls at CRETINOV, who cleans a
blunderbuss with a sagging barrel.

TWO-SHOT CHARLIE AND CRETINOV

CHARLIE
Comrade leader, I say we must
kidnap everyone who calls us fools!

CRETINOV
(bored)
Nyet; where would we keep
five billion people?

This established the general tenor of a five-minute lampoon, redolent of fools and of impotence, on terrorism against the Kremlin. The Ukrainians had enjoyed the sympathy of the United States Government. Perhaps they still did, but obviously American television moguls thought along different lines.

When had Hakim last heard a sympathetic rendering of the justice, the demands, the motivations, of a terrorist group? For that matter, he persisted, any factual rendering at all? A harrowing suspicion fostered a pattern that coalesced in Hakim's mind as he absently reached for his coffee. Every datum he applied seemed to fit the undeclared war that he should have expected from this medium, sooner or later. A medium upon which Fat'ah was all too dependent: newspapers brought details, but TV brought showers of cash from Fat'ah well-wishers. Had the Americans at last conspired to rob him of his forum, his voice, his cash?

Hakim retrieved his mental images of smoke and media, this time imagining a greasy black roil erupting from a picture tube. It should be simple enough to test this suspicion. If the suspicion proved to be accurate, Hakim vowed, he would bring war to this monster medium.

He sipped the tepid coffee, then realized that he had forbidden it to himself. Rage flung the cup for him, shattering it against a television set that squatted unharmed. The girl's gasp paced Guerrero's reaction, a sidelong roll from his chair from which the latino emerged crouching, his Browning sidearm drawn. Guerrero was not particularly quick, but his hand was steady. In the soundless staring match with the latino, Hakim told himself, he dropped his own eyes first to atone for his rashness.

Hakim stood erect and exhaled deeply from his nose. "We need rest," he said.

"Yes, you do," Guerrero agreed, tucking the automatic away.

Hakim did not pause in his march to the far bedroom. Talith knew that he would not ask her to follow, knew with equal certainty that he expected her to do so within minutes. She collected the debris that lay before the television set, unaware of its symbolic content, then stood before Guerrero, who was slicing excerpts from newspapers.

He glanced up. "I will take sentry duty until four A.M.," he said.

"That is not my topic," she replied quietly, too quietly to be heard down the hallway. "You came very near disrespect, a moment ago."

"I meant no disrespect." Guerrero seemed to think the matter was closed.

She chose her words carefully: "You left room

for an inference that Hakim's stamina is less than
your own."

Guerrero frowned; it was something she rarely
saw. "He had a brush with disaster; anyone
would be exhausted," he explained, watching
carefully to assess her response. "Under the
circumstances—"

"Under *any* circumstances, Hakim is your
superior. In every way. Believe what you like,
Bernal, but pay service to that idea in his presence. *Always.*"

From a camp chair near the window, Chaim:
"More than with your training instructors in
El-Hamma, Guerrero. I know him: before he
would accept your insolence, he would accept
your resignation." Chaim Mardor flicked the
safety back and forth on the weapon across his
knees. Guerrero heard, not taking his gaze from
Talith. He nodded. It was unnecessary to state
that no one resigned from Fat'ah while he was
still breathing.

"I must go. I want to go," she corrected herself
quickly, and disappeared into the gloom. Guerrero stared after her, then began to detach
another clipping for Hakim. He was smiling.

Hakim lay in his bed awaiting the girl. He had
read the latino's implied criticism, but would
absorb it for now. He could not afford to waste
Guerrero. Yet.

MONDAY, 10 NOVEMBER, 1980:

As Hakim awaited the girl, Maurice Everett's evening had hardly begun in Colorado Springs. He selected a fresh log from the bin and thrust it into his fireplace, holding it with two fingers like a rolled newspaper.

"It'll catch," David Engels grinned from his chair, waving the mug lazily. "Sit down, Maury, you're nervous as a bridegroom. Forget she's coming."

"I'd like to," Everett said, dusting his hands. He reached for a poker, then realized it was more makework, more fuel for Engels whose amusement was beginning to grate on the nerves. "Some more rum in your toddy?"

"I'm fine." Engels placed a hand over the beverage. At times of stress, he knew, Everett drank sparingly but wanted everybody else drunk as lords. "It's Vercours you should be plying with booze. I'd rather you did it tonight, out of your own pocket, than later with contingency funds."

"That raises a nice question, Dave. I'm grate-ful, and I won't ask what contingency funds those are—"

"Wouldn't tell you anyhow."

"— But who decides when I need Vercours? Let's assume my intuition's screwed up, and it works out so well I use her for every public appearance. That's twenty times a year."

"Fifty thou? Pretty steep," Engels replied. "I'd probably palm you off on a bureau man; maybe switch 'em around."

"So you do decide." He saw the Engels fea-tures become opaque and knew that he was right. "Well then, why didn't you suggest that to begin with?"

"I told you on the phone, and I told you today, and for the last time I'm telling you: if a female can handle this work, she's better. She raises fewer suspicions. The Secret Service used to make bodyguards obvious on the theory that it'd put a case of the shakes on the assassin. But for some of these fanatics it just shows 'em in which direction to start the spray of lead."

"Or at least that's the current theory."

"All God's chillun got theories," said Engels, and sipped. "If you don't like ours, pick another one."

"And fund it myself."

Engels winked: "You got it. Look, Maury, I can't locate any bureau women who'd be as available. Besides," he went on, ticking off de-tails on his fingers, "Vercours takes it seriously. She's been taking lessons in defensive driving at Riverside. And Wally Conklin likes the ENG coverage she does on him. She even tapes his speeches. What more could you ask? I'll tell you one thing sure, Wally Conklin isn't going to be singing any hosannas over your hiring her away."

"Your hiring her away!"

One eye closed in an outre horsewink: "If you won't tell, I won't tell."

Everett's laugh rattled crockery in the next room. "Okay, you bastard: so you foot the bills and I take the heat. And what'd you say about Vercours and defensive driving? What doesn't she do?"

"She doesn't do-wacka-doo, if that's what you mean," Engels said archly. "Not with our likes, at least. Think of Gina Vercours as one of the boys."

"But she might run off with my secretary?"

"Doubtful. Wouldn't be good business, and Vercours sounds like all business on the phone. She picked the time tonight—"

The door chime echoed. Everett stood up too quickly, then forced himself to move toward the door as though relaxed. He told himself that it was not lack of self-confidence. It was simply that he did not know how to behave with most women, never had, which was why his early marriage had failed early. He was ill at ease because—all right, then, it was lack of self-confidence with women. While traversing his carpet, Maurice Everett had made a valuable discovery.

He made another as he swung the door open. Gina Vercours, in heels, was taller than most men. Her "Hi," the smile on the wide mouth, and the handshake were greetings to an equal. He ushered her in, saw her drape the suede coat and a bag that was half purse, half equipment satchel, on his closet doorknob. Everett's crockery rattled again.

David Engels hurried toward them. "What'd I miss?"

"That's what I do," Everett said, pointing to the coat and bag. "But I put my coat in the closet tonight to—to—you know," he said feebly.

Gina nodded, then studied the closet door. "If you'd put a dozen doorknobs on that wall, you wouldn't need a closet. I'll bill you later," she said, shaking hands with Engels. "Or you can buy me off now with whatever I smell in the air."

In five minutes, Everett had forgot his fidgets over Gina Vercours. She sipped the steaming toddy and asked for more rum, then knelt to warm her hands at the fire. She meddled with the antique kettle that swung on its bracket over the hearth. "God, this iron kettle must weigh ten pounds."

"Five kilos," Everett corrected.

"I'm old-fashioned," she said, grinning.

"Sure you are. I don't think it's polite to fly false colors."

Still grinning, she said, "Then I don't think you should ever do it," and he laughed again. It was his own stance, *here I am, take it or leave it;* but she wore it more gracefully.

Engels, an expert interviewer, drew Gina out with ease, dropping asides on Everett now and then. A service brat, Gina had attended schools in Texas, Virginia, Texas, California, Mas-

sachusetts, and Texas before parlaying a tennis
scholarship into a business degree at Arizona
State.

"Funny," Engels frowned in faked concern,
"you don't look like a jock."

"The hell I don't," she countered, pinching
her browned forearm. "I'll have skin like an al-
ligator when I'm forty."

"Which will be—?"

"In four years, Mr. Engels, don't be coy. I'm
not." Everett inwardly seconded her observation. She had no reluctance to list her strengths
or her weaknesses. Health, lack of attachments,
and media training were her perceived
strengths. "But I'm not really a people person, if
you follow me," she admitted. "I like to live
well, and I'm pretty selfish."

"That's laying it on the line," said Everett.
"Why are you interested in this escort, bodyguard, iffy kind of work? It isn't exactly steady
employment, Gina. As you must know, I may not
need you at all."

For the first time, the smile she turned on him
was wily, secretive, somehow very female, the
wide-set hazel eyes steady on his. "You'll need
me," she insisted softly. "Maybe not tomorrow
or next month, but if you have heavy clout in
media, sooner or later you're going to need
somebody." She smiled to herself. "I still keep
ENG contacts in Phoenix, and of course I mix
around when I'm on duty with Conklin. If you
never before saw reporters looking over their
shoulders, you can see it now. It's a feeling you
can reach out and touch," she finished.

Everett persisted. "So why do you like it?"

"I don't like it, Mr. Everett. I like the money. Let's say you use me twice a year and Wally does the same. Added to my fees in tennis, that's a new 'vette every year." She arched an eyebrow. "You could use some work on the courts, Commissioner. Work off some of that, ah, good living."

Engels laughed at Everett's discomfort. "He thinks he's a bear, Gina. Fattens up every autumn, snores all winter, runs up mountains every spring. Catch him early in the morning and you'll think he's a sure-nough grizzly."

"I don't expect to be chasing him early in the morning," she replied smoothly, and patted Everett's knee as he flushed the hue of berry juice. "Nothing personal, Mr. Everett—but it seemed worth clarifying."

Everett cleared his throat, wondering how he had triggered this conversational trap. "Understood. But you can be personal enough to call me Maury. I don't know what to call a Corvette freak, but I'll think of something suitable."

David Engels sat back, watching the automobile buffs unload on each other. Everett's dislike for 'big iron' was easily supported by every datum an ecologist might cite. At one point he threatened to show photographs of Mini-Coopers beating factory Corvettes at Laguna Seca. Gina claimed to be wary of any car that could be stolen by a tumble-bug. "Not that I blame the tumble-bug," she cracked; "one little ball of crap looks pretty much like another."

Eventually, after a pizza had been delivered and demolished, Gina Vercours stretched the strong svelte legs and yawned. Everett noticed the highly developed calf muscles swelling above slender ankles, and remembered something else as she arose. "You used to have different hair, didn't you?"

"Still do," she said, tugging at a brunette curl. "It's under here. You can pile a lot of hair under a wig." A throaty laugh: "I even have a gray one. One of my mannnny dis-guis-es," she said, without elaboration.

Everett snorted good-naturedly. "You wouldn't fool a leg man at two hundred paces."

It seemed that Gina had two laughs; this one was a whoop, unabashed and piercing. She promised to wear knickers with the gray wig and readied herself to leave.

Engels strolled companionably with them toward the closet. "One thing more, Gina: what sort of martial arts training have you had?"

She broke off a sentence to say, lightly, "Nothing, really, until the past few weeks. I'm going twice a week now—"

"Horseshit. I mean before you met Wallace Conklin."

Something came into the yellow-green eyes that did not affect the voice or smile. "I told you. Oh, I picked up a few tricks from a friend in Tempe, back in college."

Engels was not smiling. "Horseshit," he repeated.

She shrugged, expressionless, and reached for her coat.

"We've both seen videotapes of you taking that kid with the Schmeisser, Gina," Engels said to break the silence. "Those were killing techniques; black belt stuff."

She continued with the coat, calm with her buttons and collar. She reached for her bag, then turned. Her face was still noncommittal, the voice calm and pleasant. "Wallace Conklin thinks of me as a brilliant opportunist, Mr. Commissioner David Engels. He would not like to think of me as a deadly weapon. Help me keep it that way." She came to some decision as her shoulders dropped. "All right. You won't be satisfied until I give you a motive. So.

"When I was fourteen, I was raped. He was a friend of my father's, an old army buddy on a visit. Bob was very macho, very old-shoe. I guess he was what he was all the way through. I knew it would destroy an important friendship with my dad if I said anything. So I didn't say anything. Six months later, Bob came to visit again." The voice was edged with obsidian now. "And raped me again."

"Oh, Christ," Everett whispered. "Hey, forget it, I understand why you'd want to gloss over it."

"You don't understand shit," said Gina Vercours. "The next morning I started looking for an academy. It made me scrimp and lie about going to the library, but it was worth it. Good ol' Bob paid us another visit a year later."

Engels was smiling now, expectant. "Took him fair and square?"

"I bushwhacked the sonofabitch," she said, "after I kissed him, the first time we were alone. He could've taken me or made it a standoff, I know that now. But he had it coming. And he got it, collapsed cheekbone and all. My dad never understood how Bob could've taken such a beating on a little flight of stairs."

She reached for the outer door, opened it, still speaking to Engels. "To my knowledge, Bob never came around again. But you can't appreciate—and I didn't want to tell you—how much I enjoyed going through it in my mind twice a week at the academy for the next two years. I still enjoy it. I don't like you very much, you know. I mean you, collectively. Actually you two are okay, and that has affected my judgment. I'm still willing to be your escort if you ever need it, Maury."

"You mustn't ever lie to me again," Engels said, making it avuncular.

"And if I ever do, you mustn't pick me up on it because it'll be something I figure is none of your Goddamned business. I've done research on you, too. Sorry for the outburst," she said, raised her free hand in a wave, then pulled the door shut behind her.

For perhaps twenty seconds the two men stood motionless, listening to the long stride as it faded. Then an exchange of sheepish grins. "So much for the ineffable power of our federal government," Engels grumbled, and swigged his toddy.

"She's her own man, by God," Everett said. He nodded absently as if testing his phrase and finding it apt. They shuffled back to the conversation pit to be near the fire, Engels beginning to chuckle, Everett taking it up. When they had finished, the Engels rasp and the Everett boom still hanging in the air, they made fresh drinks.

"I don't know why that was so funny," Everett admitted. "Charlie George's friend Althouse could probably tell me, the little fart is as sharp as a broken bottle."

Engels gestured toward the blank TV set in one corner. "All this stuff I'm seeing on terrorists and charlies is his idea, you said?"

A nod. "But will it have any effect?"

"Oh, it'll have one. Dear God only knows what it'll be in the end, Maury. And old Lasswell might have a guess. What'd he call it when you get some media effect you didn't expect?"

"Latent function," Everett grunted. "And when your media brainstorm turns around and chews your ass off, that's dysfunction." He leaned back on his couch, rubbing his temples. "Lord, don't I know it! Dave, you think I should get a permit for a gun?"

Shrugging: "Depends on how much time you'd put in with it. You can't walk around casually holding a blunderbuss; might cause talk. And if you're not reasonably good with it, a concealed piece is murder. Yours. You take Gina Vercours, now—"

"A perfectly appalling idea," Everett staged a shudder.

"But she goes heeled with Conklin, according to my source. A Beretta in a videotape cassette, which she uses once a week. Like I said: she takes it seriously."

Everett whistled. "That lady has more balls than a bowling alley," he rumbled. "I like her."

"That could be a problem."

"No, I mean I like the idea, because I don't like her. Wait, I'll get it right in a minute. Yeah, Dave, sure I like her, butch or no butch. But better still,

I like knowing there's no chance of a personal attachment. Like parts in a machine: we link up, do our jobs, and disengage again. I can dig it."

Engels studied his mug, his thoughts surveying engagements of another day. He had seen some unlikely relationships develop between agents working closely together under pressure. Unrelenting pressure was the lens that gathered and focused emotions to white heat. It could leave permanent scars. So could a Schmeisser. "Well, you're a big boy, Zebulon Pike," he said, and drained his mug. "Are you going to use Vercours for the NAB convention in Reno?"

Everett yawned and banked the fire for the night, talking as he worked. "I thought about it. No, I guess not. Things haven't come to that point and I really don't think they will. You want to share a room at the Mapes or somewhere?"

"I won't be there," Engels smiled. "I'd rather see pornography than hear you drone on about it. And speaking of pornography, how would you rate Vercours's legs on a scale of one to ten?"

"Cut it out, Dave, I need to sleep, not sweat. But how does ten-point-five strike you?"

"That's what I thought," Engels chuckled, walking toward the guest bedroom. He turned at the doorway. "Parts in a machine, hm? Sure, you can dig it." Then David Engels turned in. He knew Everett too well to push it.

WEDNESDAY, 26 NOVEMBER, 1980:

As long as the National Association of Broadcasters wanted to hold a convention during Thanksgiving holidays, Everett admitted, it was nice that Reno was its choice. He wandered among the manufacturer's exhibits in the hotel foyer, grudgingly accepting some responsibility for the presence of so many new security devices. The Oracle Microelectronics display drew his attention briefly before he moved on. You could say what you liked about media men, their self-interest was intelligent. Cassette systems shared display space with microwave alarms. One import drew his admiration: an outgrowth of the English medical Thermovision system, it could display so small a mass of metal as coins in a pocket—unless they were at body heat, no more, no less.

A voice behind him said, "Neat. Any charlie who sneaks his forty-five past that rig will have

to carry it as a suppository," and Everett wheeled
to face Rhone Althouse.

Everett's delight was real, though brief. "It's
nice to see somebody I can ask questions of,
instead of just answering 'em," he said.

"I heard your speech on porn," was the reply,
"and I can't believe you have any answers. Seriously, I did want to—well, uh, actually Charlie
George, ah—oh, shit." He cocked his head to one
side. "The fact is, our little Palm Springs conspiracy has become the worst-kept secret since
the Bay of Pigs. Dahl D'Este couldn't sit on such a
juicy tidbit for long. To begin with, his lady-love
is a gossip columnist."

"It's a little late, but thanks for the warning.
Lady? D'Este makes both scenes?"

A one-beat pause. "Yeah, ob and epi; and
thanks for the straight line. Charlie and I thought
you should know that the word will be leaking. It
should have a positive effect in the Industry,"
Althouse added quickly. It had the sound of an
excuse.

Everett nodded, hands thrust into pockets of
his stylishly discomfiting jacket. "Well, you're
answering my questions before I ask. I'll have to
deny my part in it for the record; but just between
us, Rhone, I'm willing to let it live as a rumor.
The Commission is interested in this ethical
epidemic, naturally. I've been asked how long
you can keep it up." Raised eyebrows invited an
answer.

"Hell, it's popular," the writer beamed. "With
CBS taking it up, it's a trendy thing—oh," he
said quickly. "You mean the reprisals?"

Everett's nod was quick. "Those Fat'ah pismires cost NBN a bundle when the net refused to air that videotape Arif sent them last week."

"Fortunes of war," Althouse grimaced. "Don't think our own Charlie isn't hurting, even if he doesn't flinch. He's got a piece of several stations, and those transmission towers Fat'ah destroyed didn't do the dividends any good. Insurance tripled."

"Arif didn't flush out any friendly envoys from the nets to pay him off, I suppose."

Althouse squinted in the subdued light. "I think I would've heard if that were in the offing. If that's the crux of your concern—officially, I mean—I can't answer for the whole industry.

"Maury, it's become a grass-roots movement, just as I hoped. Doesn't have a single spokesman, and that's where its strength lies. But it looks to me like a full-scale media war brewing." He hesitated, glanced around, bit his lip. For the first time, Everett saw something in the writer that was not young, something of the mature hunted animal. "We haven't forgotten those scenarios you laid on us. Do you have—no, cancel that, I don't want to know. Do you think we should have around-the-clock protection when our names hit the newspapers?"

"Let me put it this way: you and I both know D'Este can put us all on the list of endangered species. You think our names are due to hit the newsstands?"

"I know they are," said Althouse, with a sickly smile that told Everett why the writer had flown to Reno: face-to-face admission that Everett

could expect the worst. There could be little
pleasure in a print-media hero label that doubled
as death warrant.

No point in asking how Rhone Althouse knew.
His pallor said he knew. "Tell Charlie George we
are about to learn what it's like to be a popular
politico," Everett remarked, fashioning a cross-
hair 'X' with his forefingers. As an effort at levi-
ty, the gesture fell sprawling. "How long before
our oh-so-responsible press fingers us?"

"Tomorrow."

Everett drew a long breath. "Goddam the
world's D'Estes, we ought to put out a contract
on that guy ourselves. Well, I can't say I didn't
expect this sooner or later."

"My fault. I knew Dahl was a gamble."

"Uh-huh—with odds they'd be ashamed to
quote in this town. I don't like the stakes, either."

"What're you going to do?"

"Find pressing business somewhere else. One
thing I won't do is stick around in Reno. Thanks
again; and luck, Rhone." Everett turned and
moved off.

Althouse stood and watched the big man,
wondering if Everett would hide, wondering if
he too should disappear as D'Este had already
done. He took some comfort in Everett's refusal
to blame him for the original idea. But the Commissioner had known the danger, even while he
lent tacit bureaucratic support. D'Este gone to
ground, Everett forewarned: better than nothing,
yet a poor defense against the fury of terrorism
which his own scripts had turned against them
all.

An unfamiliar itch between his shoulders

made Rhone Althouse aware that he was standing absolutely inert, alone and unarmed in a hotel, a perfect target. Althouse walked away quickly. He did not care who noticed that his path was a zigzag.

THURSDAY, 4 DECEMBER, 1980:

The news magazines spread across Hakim's bed made up in depth what they lacked in immediacy. The article before him was satisfyingly thorough under its head, "TV: No More Strange Bedfellows?" It began:

For weeks, every pundit in the sprawling television medium had matched his favorite terrorism rumor against the rumors in the next studio. The scathing satire on terrorism, newly unleashed and widespread in TV, was said to originate in an oval office. Or, less likely, that it was a propaganda ploy jointly financed by Israel and England. One pollster claimed that the new scripts merely reflect what the American viewer wanted to see.

The truth, as it filtered from CBS last week, was both likelier and stranger than whodunits. There had been no tugs at domestic political strings, and no foreign influence. But in the persons of four highly regarded media men, there was definitely a plot. The top banana, to no one's great surprise, turned out to be NBN's answer to Jacques Tati, the protean Charlie George. Of considerably more interest to media analysts was the reputed anchorman, anomalous FCC sachem Maurice D. Everett (*see box*). . . .

"All bedfellows are strange," muttered Hakim, patting the rump of the girl who slept as he scanned the stack of clippings. He read the four-page article carefully, marking some passages with a flow pen, then concentrated on the verbal sketch of Everett:

The Commission will not provide some trendy new definition of pornography every two years, or even every election year. True, our job is as the traffic cops of broadcasting. Well, we'd like to enter into a sort of public collusion with the National Association of Broadcasters: we won't give you speeding tickets, if you won't be too racy on public information channels. Fair enough?"

These were the closing words last Wednesday in an NAB address by Maurice Everett, the FCC's strapping executive-turned-Commissioner. The only son of a Des Moines merchant, his mother a 1936 emigre from Haifa, the eclectic Everett brings a lively open mind and informal clarity to media problems.

Everett, 42, has always marched to the music of a contrapuntal drum. His unpredictability was well-known as early as his undergraduate days in California Polytechnic where Everett switched majors four times while holding his position as second-string fullback. He emerged with a double major in American History and Engineering, and has not been second-string at anything since.

The Vietnam conflict drew Everett for a tour of combat duty where the towering young lieutenant won a Silver Star and, not incidentally, picked up fresh ideas on electronic information-gathering systems. His subsequent marriage was brief, ending in divorce in 1964.

Everett's career with a Colorado microelectronics firm seemed to orient the salty-tongued young executive toward narrow technical areas but, in a clean break with other industrialists in 1970, he thrust his hulking shoulders in with Denver ecologists. Between frequent solo jaunts into western wild areas, Everett championed several hobby and special-interest groups in what, at first, appeared to be playboy enthusiasm. But Everett, long regarded as one of Colorado's most eligible rebounds, rarely followed the playboy mold. He supported the Equal Rights Amendment, small sedan racing, cross-country skiing, and bicyclists in a pattern that developed squarely in opposition to the philosophy of conspicuous consumption.

For the past two years a member of the Federal Communications Commission, Maurice Everett had seemed to be settling into a liberal position, confining his aggressiveness to the handball courts, even after a chance encounter with the Pueblo bombing that hospitalized him for a time. But late last week, acquaintance and set designer Dahl D'Este revealed an apparent about-face by Everett. Previously a staunch friend of press freedoms, the Commissioner was reportedly a key figure in the sub rosa group that planned a broad media counterattack on terrorism (see Media). Central to the group's strategy was a new treatment of the act of terrorism per se; and to some pundits this treatment was a dangerous

excursion into media control. For free-swinging
libertarians, the choice lies between the Scylla of
manipulated media and the Charybdis of ram-
pant terrorism. Whichever course the Commissioner charts, he will create new enemies. Judging by his demeanor last week in Reno, Maurice
Everett is losing little sleep over it.

Hakim made special note of the Commissioner's
unpredictability, his stress on physical fitness,
his military background, his direct methods of
dealing with the world. Hakim did not find these
details pleasant; the man could be a formidable
challenge. Yet the element of surprise still re-
sided with Fat'ah. Presently Hakim riffled
through other clippings, finding—as he had
expected—invaluable data on his enemies. His
sullen longing found focus in names which he
listed in alphabetical order: Althouse, D'Este,
Everett, George.

Print media made one thing pellucid: no matter how brilliantly successful his coup, the terrorist was still to be treated as a charlie, a fool, on
television. Hakim saw this dictum as a simple
clash of wills. These strategists might give up
their brave posturings if one of their number
paid the price. Fat'ah might even subcontract the
job.

If the *fait accompli* carried no leverage, Fat'ah
could relocate again and try the threat. No hollow promise, but one steeped in potency. The
sort of threat one could employ when the enemy
is reduced to a softened target; isolated, im-
mobile, helpless. Hakim wondered which of the
four he would concentrate on first. Perhaps he

could find some means to make object lessons of
all four, he thought, and felt a lambent surge of
rekindled strength. He turned off the light and
nudged Leah Talith. It had not once occurred to
Hakim that others, less cautious than he, might
react with a blinder savagery.

SATURDAY, 6 DECEMBER, 1980:

Young Donny Flynn drenched himself in misgivings before he had driven the provos an hour out of South Boston, Massachusetts. It had been all very well to parade these two micks on the streets of Old Southie as his mysterious and powerful friends— even though the elder Flynn himself had never set eyes on them before they showed up, the previous Sunday, bearing the nearest thing to an illiterate letter of introduction anybody could ask for. It didn't matter if they'd written the letter themselves, thought Donny; when you were nineteen and a recent flunkout from Boston College you could use the street status these old soddy friends conferred. Donny had made sure everybody knew he would be disappearing with them for a time, for Something Very Important. But cooped up in the goddam BMW with these jabbering drunks all the way to Colorado? Donny would go out of his gourd.

He remembered his father's confusion when Flaherty, the tall slender one with the voice like a fiddle string, and McTaggart, the nervous red-head, walked into their house in Old Southie. Da kept up with soccer and he read the *Irish News*, but he wasn't much for writing letters since Ma died and Donny couldn't recall when he had last seen a postmark from Ireland.

Donny had never seen Ireland and couldn't care less. Da spoke less about the Irish question than most of their friends, and was definitely not interested in visiting the country of his youth even though as a machinist in nearby Chelsea, he made enough to buy a nice place and little things like a twenty-thousand dollar BMW 733i. Other people went back to visit. Why not Da?

McTaggart, talking for the both of them, dumped a flood of lilting patter the minute he walked in. He wasn't much older than Donny but any dumb shit could see he'd been around. And if he couldn't see it he could hear it from McTaggart. Donny had heard it, dropping his *Playboy* on his bed and putting his ear to the wall that separated him from his father's hobby room. McTaggart's musical brogue was a tune to make Donny smile, but the lyrics did not please his father much.

It was weird: the sound was muffled to begin with, but in addition to the opaque Irish slang of McTaggart it seemed that Da's own speech had curiously peeled its American frosting away so that Donny was listening to a father he had never heard before. Da had laughed a lot at first. And then Flaherty, the older one, had talked a little in that squeaky voice, not much, and after that Da

wasn't laughing much and when he did, it had
an undertone Donny did not recognize at first.
But when he recognized it, he liked it. It was fear.
Donny could use some pointers from anybody
who could walk into his father's house and immediately make his father seem less like a fuckin' knowitall and more like a man who could
listen to reason. Who had to listen.

It was all mixed up with some old friend, a
provo, who felt that it was time Da earned his
keep. It was the Irish Republican Army, and
again it wasn't. Donny might be lost in a classroom but he was bright enough to assemble the
fact that provos, of the Provisional Wing of the
IRA, had abiding disagreements with the IRA's
main body. Jeez, it sounded like two entirely
separate armies.

It also sounded like a lot of shit about Da earn-
ing his keep and Da had made that point himself.
But to the provos it seemed that you assumed a
debt, boyo, by leaving the ould sod, especially if
your machinist's skills were needed for weapons
repair, and most particularly especially if you
had planted a tin of jelly, whatever that was, in a
London railway depot.

Sure, said McTaggart, an' it *was* a wee time
back, but the sojers hadn't forgot and the fookin'
protestants hadn't forgot but, as luck wud have
it, ould Flynn had the chance to make the provos
forget. And that wud break the chain of
memories. All square, all debts repaid.

So Da had decided to think about it. The two
micks had seemed to notice Donny for the first
time after the talk in the hobby room, Flaherty
succinct, McTaggart effusive. By bedtime,

Donny was trying to get the hang of their
melodious jargon, quick to realize that when Da
was working during the day, Donny would be
their guide and if he could manage it, their confidante. They went to the snooker hall on Monday with Donny, and found new friends with old
brogues who helped them become chummily,
gloriously drunk while Donny worked to confirm the image of Donny Flynn as a man with
connections. But no matter how he hinted and
pried, no matter how many stories he began
about the swath he cut among the little broads
from Brookline to Newton, somehow Donny
Flynn was the outsider. He learned, as McTaggart might say, fuck-all about the provo
mission—which was to say, nothing whatever.

But Donny found them happy enough to talk
about the United States. They found Boston ac-
ceptable, though there was much to be said for
Quebec, where they had visited before coming
down, legal as the Pope, to see the States. The
people in Quebec had a villainous language but
they understood repression and martyrdom better, and their connections with rich men in Libya
and Syria were excellent. Still, the Irish here in
the States knew how to give for a good cause. At
least they did until thon bunch of blirts on the
telly started blatherin' like eejits, makin' sport of
the provo cause.

Then Flaherty made an observation, eloquent
for him, that thanks to the newspapers he knew
how they could be accountin' w'it.

McTaggart had then suggested that Flaherty
shut his gub. It was hard for Donny to tell
whether McTaggart was the superior or merely

the more loquacious. Certainly McTaggart was
the talker. Donny wondered what might be Flaherty's special talent.

The next nights had been a pleasure since Da
had supplied Donny with money and, Jasus,
even the car, so he could enjoy himself in Boston. Donny would have loved to know what the
men talked about at home while he cruised in the
metallic blue BMW, looking for—he tried the
phrase—some wee hoore. Actually he took in a
movie each night, and remembered subplots so
he could inject himself into them to describe his
conquest of the evening, in case McTaggart
might ask, or might be willing to listen. McTaggart never asked, and hardly listened at all. It
was hard to tell whether Flaherty was listening,
the way those yellow-gray eyes roamed from
deep in the narrow head. In fact, Donny was
beginning to think he had made no impression
on the visitors until Thursday, night before last.
On that night, McTaggart had brewed up a real
Irish stew, all by himself.

Halfway through the meal, articulated at the
tail of a monologue extolling the luxuries of Old
Southie folk, McTaggart singsonged, "An' ye've
been a gracious host, Mr. Flynn sur, none better
seein' the bloody great wad ye donated to buy us
some proper togs in this cold weather. Mind, the
Flaherty and meself, we cud hardly want fer
more. But there'll be one more wee askin' fer the
cause, and that'll be all."

The harried machinist laid down his spoon
with a grizzled hand, wearing an expression of
disgust. "An' that'll be what?"

"A car, sur; as the wee lad says, some wheels,"

McTaggart said, with a laughing wink, bestowing on Donny a camaraderie he had previously withheld. "A car an' a driver, d'ye mind, it's the papers to drive that we're needin' and between the Flaherty and meself there's nobbut—"

"Be damned t'ye," Flynn said, coloring. "Rent one. I'll buy ye airline tickets, if that's it, and then ye both can—"

"The BMW," Flaherty said then, his thin voice scything through Flynn's anger, scattering it like dead leaves. "Rental won't do, d'ye see? Ye trust the lad to drive. Aye, all he has t'do. On my honor an' then we'll be away on. Ye'll niver see us more."

There was a long silence, the two provos watching critically as old Flynn, now older than sin itself, picked up his spoon and nodded. "After that, we're quits," said Flynn. "We won't want to know ye."

McTaggart seemed about to take up the monologue again but he caught the look from Flaherty. Donny caught it too, there was enough of it to go around. It said *stuff yer gub an' don't tinker wi' yer victory*. Donny felt victorious as well. No one had asked him, but wherever they needed to go he was willing, especially cupped in the leather seat behind the wheel of the BMW. He'd take them clear to New Haven, if that was what they wanted. But they wanted Denver.

Denver, for Christ's sake! That was just one stop short of Mars, to Donny Flynn. And his father was willing! Perhaps 'willing' was too strong a word, but he was going to permit it, Donny sought one of his new phrases—sure as flies on dog dirt.

Last night then, Friday, Donny's father had drilled him on ice conditions, tire pressures, uses of a credit card, and—repeatedly—on various cautions when riding with strangers. Donny reflected that Da spent more time talking with him that evening, while the micks were out buying clothes with Flynn money, than he had spent in any previous month Donny could recall. It almost gave Donny a feeling of being dear, valued, even loved. For a wild moment he considered saying the hell with it, he'd stay home and maybe talk with the old man sometimes in the evenings, but Donny Flynn sensed that it would not, could not turn out that way. The flesh had its patterns; he knew they would not talk like this many times.

Donny had not helped load the car that night, but packed food and cans of juice into a cardboard box as McTaggart swaggered back and forth to the car, wearing his new trenchcoat even though the weather was mild. Donny packed a single bag for himself, swiped Da's driving gloves and both pairs of sunglasses.

Finally, this morning, well before light, Donny had hurried to warm up the car. Presently Flaherty padded out, followed by McTaggart. Da waved for Donny, who left the car idling and ran up the steps. McTaggart was arranging packages in the back seat. Flaherty was staring toward the house. Donny was about to enter the house but found that Da wanted him to stay there in full view.

In the predawn he could see, on Da's face, a look he had not seen since the funeral in '71. The father put his hands on the son's shoulders,

gripped them, seemed about to embrace Donny.
He said, quietly, "I can't counsel ye further than
this, boy, but if ye ever listen to advice, listen
now." There was little of the pure Irish in his
voice; it was his Da, but burdened with some
new yet old and unspeakable dread. "Break no
laws, even speed laws. Don't argue with those
two. Think of them as grown children. Your job
is to drive, nothing more. Nothing more, d'ye
understand?"

Donny nodded, wincing under the steely grip.
After a moment his father continued. "Maybe
I'm lending ye to them for your own sake, maybe
just for mine. I don't know. But the bargain is just
for driving. Whatever ye do, do not let either of
them put a weapon into your hands."

Donny nodded again.

"Swear it." The grip was excruciating.

"I swear to God I won't, Da," said Donny
Flynn, wondering why his father's face made
him want to cry.

"Ye've sworn it, Donegal Flynn," his father
said, and then released him. A gentle fist tapped
his bicep. "Ye know our telephone number, if it
comes to that. Keep the credit card in your
pocket. An' now, get yer arse out to Route
Ninety-five afore the weekend rush."

At first Donny was too busy driving to pay
attention to his passengers. Once on the interstate route, he began to listen. McTaggart,
nursing a bottle of booze, luxuriated in leather
cushions and entertained himself with an endless curse on American luxury. Bunch of girnin'
soft cunts they were, aye, who'd risk nobbut
filthy fookin' money fer the cause.

Occasionally Flaherty responded, snoozing, his legs stretched out as he slumped in the rear seat gloom. Once Donny tried to join in by agreeing. They ignored him. Boozing and snoozing, they ignored Donny's route past Pawtucket and Providence, ignored his brief panic on the stretch of ice outside Warwick. It was not until he suggested a stop at New London, trying to invent some clever phrase from the bits and pieces he had collected, that they stopped ignoring him. He made the mistake of referring to them as oul sods.

The open-handed slap across the back of his head made Donny swerve, sent bright gobbets of light dancing across his vision. "What the fuck kind of answer is that," he yelled, half turning.

"The kind ye earn, ye wee bastid," Flaherty piped, "callin' yer betters sods." Flaherty would have made a good soprano, Donny thought, but a lousy debater.

McTaggart started to cackle, understanding the problem, explaining at great length between swigs that the oul sod was holy, but a couple of oul sods were sodomites. He did not blame Donny for his mistake. He did not blame Flaherty, either. Flaherty had made no mistake. Flaherty had simply made his point in a way that even a wee lad could not fail to remember. Donny Flynn shook his head to clear it, and remembered.

In Newark they bought the biggest, most grossly oleaginous giantburgers the micks had ever seen, and Donny located two fresh bottles of John Jameson. Donny perceived something ritualized in their insistence on that particular

whiskey from that particular part of Ireland, did
not understand, and knew better than to ask. For
one thing, McTaggart was so smashed he could
not have interceded if Flaherty had fancied some
fresh offense by Donny.

Donny wondered if the leather seats would
ever be the same after McTaggart dropped his
giantburger on his fly and, in a rage, ground the
mess into the seat before hurling the debris from
his window. It was shaping up to be a great little
trip, thought Donny.

The following day, Sunday, Donny found it
necessary to tell McTaggart about antilitter laws
as they sped across Virginia. McTaggart cared
fuck-all about that until Donny explained about
the highway patrol cruisers that blossomed in
thousands across the land like winter wildflow-
ers, sitting in hidden spots to surprise the jaded
traveler. Flaherty said nothing, only patting the
Christmas package, nearly as long as his arm,
that Donny had seen carried from his father's
hobby room.

McTaggart saw the gesture. "None o' that, ye
eejit," he cautioned, laughing; "ye'll have a
chance in Colorado, by Jasus, an' not afore."

Monday, the whiskey consumed, Donny tried
to find more John J. in St. Louis, feeling more
like a nursemaid to grown men at every futile
stop. Bushmill's was heretical, any Scotch just as
bad. Donny bought two gray stoneware jugs of
local Platte Valley straight corn and smiled at the
sight of the two provos, slouching in new but
outdated trenchcoats, cradling their booze and
swilling it even as they reviled it. They looked

wholly harmless, old-faced children in Sam
Spade suits, playing at some unfathomable international game. Donny wondered if their mission was to pick up money from some Denver
Hibernian Relief fund. He was a little vague on
that; couldn't they do it by mail? Or maybe they
were carrying money to Denver, hundreds and
thousands of dollars or pounds or whatever, in
those packages. Couriers of the night, Donny
thought, teasing himself with it. Maybe he was a
key piece in some enormous intrigue. Maybe,
while the BMW purred across central Missouri,
cornfields a ragtag stubble in the hard snow-
blown earth around him, Donny Flynn was a
romantic figure.

He felt a chill blast of air on his scalp and
sighed, expecting McTaggart to dump another
load of trash along the deserted stretch. Then he
heard a giggle. The next instant he was dodging
hot brass casings amid a hail of small explosions
inside the car. "Steady on, boyo," McTaggart
slurred happily as the BMW lurched across the
shoulder of the road, Donny slapping at the
spent casing that sizzled between his collar and
his neck.

It was a very close miss as Donny turned the
wheel into the slide, waited for the Michelins to
grip—or for the blue missile to plummet down
into the cold dead cornfields below them.

At length, Donny could speak again, so
shaken he did not care whether Flaherty liked it
or not. "You gotta warn me, goddammit," he
pleaded, trying to see what was happening behind him. "I thought I'd been shot."

"Had ta check out the oul persuader, lad,"
McTaggart crooned, fiddling with a small automatic weapon. "Yer da keeps nice toys an' he
knows his wurruk, but I had ta check on it, d'ye
see? Away on, Donegal Flynn, an' it's a foine
thing ye're doin' fer the cause, me lovin' lad."

Donny knew what one of the packages contained, now. And knew why his father had
called him 'Donegal', a name reserved for use
under only the most serious possible circumstances. At every kilometer sign, Donny wished
more devoutly that he was back home and away
from these knotheaded assholes. It would make a
great story, holy Mary it would make him a legend on the streets, only nobody would believe a
fourth of it. But in the meantime, he must endure
close company with men he wouldn't introduce
to a wino. He tried to make himself smaller in the
driver's seat, experiencing an unfamiliar emo-
tion, neither fear nor anger. It was embarrass-
ment.

How could you reconcile their professional
standing in a holy cause with the swaggering
boozing carelessness of this pair? Maybe you
couldn't. Maybe this arrogant self-destructive
romantic stupidity was the rule, not the excep-
tion, which could've been a hell of a good reason
why Da had left Ireland to begin with. One sure
thing, McTaggart and Flaherty were the kind of
friends your enemies would gladly donate. Why
shit, they were worse than those skits he'd seen
on TV; a proper couple of charlies.

Well, they'd be in Denver in another day and
then, according to McTaggart, they'd do some
surveillance. And after that maybe they would

go away, or he could drive them back to Old Southie. Donny would do it, would go anywhere they told him, as long as he only had to drive. He would obey his Da. Surely, surely just driving couldn't get him in much trouble.

FRIDAY, 12 DECEMBER, 1980:

Maurice Everett urged his Mini-Cooper up the ice-slick highway out of Golden, Colorado, the rallye tires biting hard through the gentle curves. He needed a weekend of solitude. Briefly and with a touch of cupidity he had thought of hiring Gina Vercours to go along. She was a skier, after all. But he had refused that notion, and the snub-nosed piece in a shoulder holster, on the same grounds: they would both cramp his style and they might call attention to him. He had already caught somebody's attention through the postal service but, during his new celebrity, the Denver office had intercepted only the lone ceramic letter bomb. Perhaps he was exaggerating his importance, but he would feel safer spending his weekend at one of the little rental cabins outside the little town of Empire. Even do a little winter stalking, who could say?

The three who could say, kept well to the rear.

For a time the driver sweated to keep in sight of the Mini, settling for occasional glimpses of the tiny vehicle as the terrain permitted. There were few turnouts available after the new snow, and the further Everett isolated himself, the better two of them liked it.

Everett chose the roadhouse on impulse, backing the Mini in to assure easy return. The flakes were dusting down again, powdery dry on his face. He ordered coffee and began shucking his furlined coat before he realized that he was alone with the counterman. He slapped snow from the front of his winter hat, then saw the dark blue BMW ease off the highway. Everett took his coffee with hands that shook, watching through fogged windows as the sleek sedan began to emulate his parking maneuver. No, not quite; the BMW blocked his Mini, and only one of the car's three occupants emerged. Three coffees to go, or one Commissioner?

Everett saw the tall trenchcoated man cradle his long, gaily-wrapped package, speak briefly to the young driver; Everett noted the Massachusetts license plate and used his time wisely. He walked to one end of the roadhouse, far from the windows and counterman, and piled his coat high in the last booth, placing his hat atop it. The coffee steamed in the center of the table, untasted bait.

Everett stepped directly across the aisle from his end booth into the men's room, hoping that his circumstantial case was nothing more than that, hoping that the lean trenchcoated man would get his coffee and go on to Empire, or

Georgetown, or hell. He did not close the door or try the light switch.

There was nothing he could see in the semidarkness that would serve as a weapon and as he settled on the toilet, fully clothed and staring at his coffee three meters away, he felt the toilet seat move. One of its two attachment wingnuts was gone. Gently, silently, Everett set about removing the other, unconcerned by the stench of urine below his nose. Early or late, he reasoned, the audacious bird gets the worm.

He heard the front door of the roadhouse sigh shut, heard a mumbled exchange—one voice had a high lilt to it—at the counter ten meters from him, heard the counterman open a refrigerator. So Mr. Trenchcoat wanted more than coffee. Cheeseburgers, or diversion?

Under the clank and scrape of short order cookery, Everett heard soft footfalls. He stood, breathing quickly and lightly through his mouth, gripping the toilet lid with no earthly thought of what he would do with it. He felt like a fool: *oh, hello, I was just leaving, sorry about the lid, it didn't fit me anyhow* . . . And then Mr. Trenchcoat stepped to Everett's booth as if offering his package, one hand thrust into the false end of the package and he must have seen that he was confronting an uninhabited hat and coat just as Everett swung the lid, edge on, against the base of his skull from behind and to one side.

Everett was appalled at himself for an instant. He had drygulched a harmless holiday drunk, he thought, as the man toppled soundlessly onto Everett's coat. The contents of the package slid

backward onto the floor then, and Everett reflected that harmless drunks do not usually carry
sawed-off automatic shotguns, in Christmas
packages with false ends.

Everett's snowshoes were in the Mini and
without them he would be stupid to run out the
back way. The counterman, incredibly, was busy
incinerating three steaks and had noticed nothing. Everett wrote the BMW license number on
his table with catsup, though he could have used
blood, and wrestled the trenchcoat from the unconscious man.

The only way out was past the BMW. He
hoped it would flee at his first warning shot,
then realized that the occupants were waiting to
hear that shot. How would Mr. Trenchcoat exit?
Backward, no doubt, holding the shotgun on the
counterman. Everett's trousers were the wrong
shade of gray but he could not afford to dwell on
that. The trenchcoat was of a cut he had not seen
in years; perhaps they would not think beyond it
for a few seconds. Then too, the blowing snow
might help mask him for a moment. Or it might
not.

He slid into the trenchcoat, which pinched at
the armpits, turned its collar up, retrieved the
shotgun and checked its safety. Gripped in a
glacial calm that he knew would not last, he
reminded himself of Pueblo and quashed his fear
with one thought: *my turn!* Everett had time to
pity the counterman, but not to question his own
sanity, as he moved past windows near the door
and turned his back on the door.

Everett's shotgun blast tore a fist-sized hole in

the floor and sent a lance of pain through
Everett's bad ear. The counterman ran without
hesitation out the rear door into a snowdrift,
screaming, and Everett backed out the front door
fast. The driver of the blue car seemed to be
screaming as well. The BMW engine blipped
lustily and a voice called, "In, in, Flaherty, ye
fookin' twit," and Everett spun to see a red-
haired man holding a rear door open with one
hand, a machine pistol forgotten in the other.
Everett did not forget the weapon and aimed for
it. His first shot blew the weapon and a hand out
the BMW's front window from the inside.

Donegal Flynn accelerated to the highway, the
left rear door of the car flapping open, and Everett fired twice more. The next shot sent pellets
caroming through the inside of the sedan and his
last was a clean miss. Everett flopped hard into
the snow and only heard, but could not see, the
shiny BMW slide off the highway. It was a long
vertical roll to the river and by the time they
reached it neither of the occupants minded the
cold water, being dead at the time.

Everett burst into the roadhouse to find that
his first victim was still unconscious, a stroke of
luck since Everett had neglected to check him for
concealed weapons. There were things to set
right. The counterman must be tamed, the telephone must be used; but first things first. He
needed that toilet lid for a mundane purpose,
and right now.

*   *   *

By the time the FBI mobile lab was en route

from Denver, Highway Patrol units had things
well in hand, had taken a sullen silent Irishman
away in handcuffs, had even located the ruined
sedan some distance down the river in three
meters of water. Everett apologized for a dozen
things including his prints, muddying those already on the shotgun; the instantaneous defec-
tion of Smiley Bohlen, the counterman; and all
the trouble he had caused in trying to defend
himself. Despite his unquestioned identity,
Maury Everett knew he was under informal ar-
rest until the unmarked brown van pulled up
outside the roadhouse. The atmosphere warmed
quickly after that. Two of the FBI men in parkas
mapped out the area while the third, an immacu-
late cigar-chewing gentleman named Will Fulton, sat with Everett over coffee and a tape recorder.

As soon as a tape ended, Fulton would take it
to the mobile lab for a fast-track transmission to
Denver. Someone located the weapon Everett
had blown from the BMW, which tickled Fulton
no end even before its analysis in the van. Finally grown hoarse, Everett asked, "How much
longer do we go on, Fulton? I needed a rest
before any of this happened, and right now all I
want is to get in the Mini and disappear."

"Hard to say," said Fulton, glancing at his
watch. "I got a bulletin from the van telling us to
wait for a reinforcement. Somebody's flying into
Denver, apparently, if the weather'll permit it.
Besides, Commissioner, you thought you'd disappeared this morning. Care to think again?"

As Everett shook his head, a little fellow in a
parka came in with a friendly nod to them both,

then dropped a clipboard at Fulton's elbow before returning to the van.

Fulton, shifting the cigar no-hands, scanned the pages at length. "It was a hit, all right," he said finally as if to himself. "A Mr. Flynn owned that four-door BMW in a Boston suburb. Flynn's a naturalized citizen from Belfast, and he's already made a statement. Anxious to cooperate; even more anxious about his son. Would you recognize a facsimile photo when it comes in?"

"Not likely," Everett admitted. "I feel rotten about those two guys in the car."

"Because they didn't get a shot at you?"

"Sounds crazy when you put it that way. There was no doubt about that charlie with the shotgun, though. Was there?"

"None. Just got factual verification of your story; a print tally from him on the weapon. Yours too, of course." Fulton pursed his lips obscenely around the unlit cigar, running a forefinger along the lined paper. "Who's Sean McTaggart?"

"Never heard of him. Or Flynn, that I recall."

"Eoin Flaherty?"

Pause. Headshake. "Nope. Wait; the guy with the automatic pistol? I think he called me 'flirty'; maybe 'Flaherty'. But why is some Boston Irishman I never heard of financing a hit on me? Doesn't make sense."

"Flynn claims he'd just met the two Irishers, mutual friends back in the old country and so on. Loaned 'em the car with his teen-aged son to drive it, out of a sense of loyalty. Claims he had no idea what they intended to do here beyond sightseeing."

"Should we believe in that?"

"Sure; that and the Easter bunny." Fulton lifted a page to read another. "We have Flynn's prints too, and they're also on the magazine we took from the Vzor."

"Come again?"

"Vzor seven point six-five millimetre," Fulton said with satisfaction. "A Czech automatic with magazine, takes a silencer. Little thirty caliber slugs, more or less; it sprays 'em out the barrel like shit through a tin horn. The shotgun barrel was shortened very recently by an expert. And Flynn is a machinist. I'm betting we find metal from that shotgun barrel around his shop somewhere."

Everett put his hands over his face, sighed into his palms. "Why would American citizens be helping these people?"

"Lee Oswald was American. Charlie Manson, too," Fulton said. "But there's more to this attempt than your garden-variety political lunatic, Commissioner."

"How do you know? No, tell me later, Fulton. I've got a case of nerves that won't quit. What if I just drive out a ways, find a motel, and come back later if you need me? I'd call here and tell you where I am."

The FBI agent inspected the tattered wet end of his cigar, discarded it, and drew another from his vest pocket before answering. "Go out back here and yell your head off for a minute. Cry, if it'll help. I would, and no apologies," he said, smiling candidly into Everett's face. "But someone you know has made you my responsibility until I'm relieved, since I'm senior in the office.

Shouldn't be long."

Everett squinted, then smiled back. "Dave Engels," he said flatly.

A shrug. "A minute ago you were curious about something that I *can* tell you. Yesterday we got some information from a gent we can deport at any time. Jersey City fella; as long as he gets in touch now and then, he doesn't have to chase goats up hillsides in Sicily, or whatever the hell they do there.

"There are a hell of a lot of thorny types in the FLQ—that's the Front de Libération du Quebec—who funnel arms to the Irish Provisionals. Some of the stuff is American, and some like the little Vzor comes from Eastern Europe through Libya and Syria to Canada. Long way around, but some countries are very sloppy about checking imports. Those are the same ones where the Customs people live on tips, like waiters.

"So the FLQ is well-placed to be middleman for terrorists. And that's where you came in; or rather, didn't come in."

"You've lost me," said Everett. "Can I borrow a cigar?"

"Long as you don't light it," Fulton grinned, fishing out another stogie. "They stink. Well, early this week the FLQ offered three hit contracts, a matched set, to—ah—certain undesirable elements, all with names ending in vowels, in the Big Apple area. That territory includes Philly and Jersey City. Ordinarily I suppose the contracts would've been fulfilled and we'd have three more unsolved snuffs on our hands, probably from twenty-two pistols they're using these days and don't ask me why.

"But when the local banditti learned the names of the marks—people they were to hit— they turned the FLQ down flat." Fulton cocked his head; one side of his mouth twitched. "I like that; even the Mafia has scruples. You'll be interested in the marks," Fulton continued, holding up three fingers. "A script writer named Althouse," he turned down his ring finger; "an artsy-fartsy swish named D'Este, and—" he turned down his forefinger, leaving the middle finger thrusting up in emulation of a familiar TV logo.

"And Charlie George," Everett supplied.

"You got it. Our informant says it was ol' Charlie who queered the whole job. It was suddenly obvious that this was a political thing, and believe it or not Charlie G. is a favorite of the Mafia boys. Who knows, they may own a piece of him."

"Nobody owns much of Charlie," Everett replied, wondering how accurate he was. "But I'm beginning to get your drift."

"Well, even your corrupt, stodgy old small-minded FBI can add the fourth name that belongs there."

"Mine."

"Only it wasn't. Why not? Then we got the call from the Colorado Highway Patrol about lunchtime, and somebody was awake in Washington, and now we think we know why not. The FLQ knew there was already a group setting you up. They must've taken that contract from another bunch, and had the money, and why waste dough they could use to buy more plastique? You were already spoken for."

Everett stared out the window, squinting as headlights swept the roadhouse in the evening murk. "What does the FLQ do now? What do I do? I mean, do they just give up, or is there an underworld all-points bulletin out for the four of us?"

Fulton almost laughed. "Nicely put. We don't know who the FLQ finally set it up with, but there must've been somebody. Which brings me to some very unpleasant news. But first, I think what you should do is take a new ID. That's unofficial, man-to-man, Mr. Everett. But I think you should let us tell the media you did a long yoo-hoo-hoo over the cliff in the BMW. Flaherty won't tell on you; we can put him on more ice than Admiral Byrd."

Headlights swung toward them as a Pontiac Firebird slithered into the parking lot. Everett slapped the table. "That'll be Dave Engels."

"I doubt it," said Fulton, studying his cigar, "unless he's had a recent sex change."

The dark hair that emerged from the Firebird was unfamiliar, but the shoulder bag and the stride could not be forgotten. Everett began to smile as Gina Vercours hurried through the snow.

Her greeting was offhand, unhurried, anodyne for Everett's twanging nerves. Fulton stood up, a thumb tucked under the ornate buckle beneath his vest. "Good thing I remembered about the weather," she said, stamping her feet as she tossed her wrap over a booth. "It was eighty-seven degrees in Phoenix today. And don't tell me what that is in celsius, Maury," she grinned.

"Gina; still old-fashioned," he said, taking her hand in his.

"And you still don't believe me," she countered, then turned to the other man. "Are you agent Fulton?"

Fulton nodded as she said, "I'm Gina Vercours, which Maury will verify, and in lieu of a pass phrase they said to give you this." She offered him the tiny tape machine, which he took after lowering his hand from his midriff. "Better than working with Wally Conklin," she added; "I don't have to rent cars, and at the air terminal they hand you a synopsis on tape with a ve-ry sex-y voice."

"Can I hear her?" Everett asked.

"Her? Him, fella." She tossed him a mock-suspicious frown. "So what's the drill, gentlemen?"

"Bury him somewhere," Fulton aimed his cigar at Everett, then clamped down on it again.

"What if I hadn't been me," Gina asked innocently.

"I'd have been disappointed." Fulton tapped his buckle. "Gas projector. You'd be in barf city," he explained. He took his coat and snap-brim hat, adjusting them with care. "And let us know where you bury him, Ms. Vercours, which means stay near a telephone. We may pick up more information for you. They gave you a phone scrambler?"

She nodded, patting the shoulder bag. As Fulton was leaving, Everett recalled their unfinished business. "One more thing, Fulton, if you don't mind. How do you know the Canadians found somebody to take their contracts after the Mafia refused?"

Fulton stopped, glanced toward Gina, then took Everett by the arm. Outside, his breath frosty, Fulton said, "Somebody bagged Dahl D'Este about one ayem this morning in San Francisco."

Everett sagged against the railing. "How?"

"That's what I didn't want to say in front of the lady. D'Este seemed to think he could lose himself among all the other homosexuals in the Gay city—Bay City, that is. He must've been cruising the gay strip near the downtown hotels where they make a lot of pickups off the streets. Pathetic little guys carrying overnight kits, feet hardly touching the pavement, waiting for a score like any other hooker; makes you sad to see it, Mr. Everett," he muttered, smug and sententious.

He picked up his cadence. "Well, we don't know how the contact was made but somebody got into D'Este's Cadillac with him. After shooing the others off the street, maybe, I don't know how. We're checking. Anyway: A little later the Caddie piled into a building on O'Farrell Street. Must've been moving at a crawl. They found D'Este behind the wheel and an overnight kit on the floor.

"And it smelled like he'd been having an orgy with almond extract. Somebody had snuffed him with a dildo. You know, those rubber dicks they fill with who-knows-what? This one was full of hydrocyanic acid, prussic acid, same thing. He'd taken a full shot of it in the face, and they found the dildo in his mouth. Enough cyanide to snuff an elephant, I kid you not. No prints, just rubber goods."

Everett hugged himself and shivered. "Jesus. Oh, Jesus, what a way to go."

"Show me a nice way; I might take it," Fulton grumbled. He started down the steps. "But pass the word, Mr. Everett: beware of almond dildoes."

Everett, his thoughts racing forward, called out: "Fulton!"

The agent stopped at the van, unconsciously coming to attention. "Sir."

"Have you told Althouse and Charlie George about this?"

"Was Edgar Hoover a fed? Of course, Mr. Everett, we're not amateurs. At least Mr. George knows. Nobody's raised the Althouse guy yet but they'll get to him."

"Or somebody will."

"Is that a fact," Fulton said drily, and slammed the door.

Two minutes later, Gina and Everett were arguing. "Anybody could bully us off the road in that crackerbox of yours," she spat.

"*If* they could catch us in this ice, which they couldn't without a Porsche turbo and front-wheel drive," he returned.

"And besides, how many more crazy Irishmen know you drive that Mini."

"Good God, Vercours, who's the boss here?"

She dropped her shoulders and her voice. "You are, of course. I'll get my things out of the Firebird."

"You will like hell," Everett grunted. "I have the better car, but you have the better argument." He grinned. "Anyhow, the Mini's heater isn't worth a damn. The 'bird it is, ma'am."

They were laughing before his weekend gear was repacked in the Firebird. He drove back down the highway toward Golden, explaining that they needed more food. As they neared the town, she was glancing backward. "When you stop, pull out of sight and face the highway," she suggested.

He pulled in near a market, turning the car end-for-end in a rum-runner's switch on the icy ground. They waited. After several minutes a big tandem rig came steaming past, chains singing on the pavement. Then nothing. "I'll go in," she said; "I know what kind of junk food I like. And you can keep warm with this," she added, laying a compact automatic on the seat.

She was back very soon with a single brown sack, celery poking from its top. Everett eased the Firebird onto the highway, soon passed the roadhouse and his forlorn Mini without a glance. Near Empire they slowed at a neat row of cabins with overhead telephone lines stretching away to the office.

Quickly, then: "None of this two-adjoining rooms crap, Maury. We're together. That's my job."

He nodded and punched the car's nose through crusty snow into the drive. The owner was pleased to rent his best and most secluded cabin to Mr. and Mrs. Marks.

"Soda pop and cigarettes here, Mr. Marks," he

said, "but I'll be locking up shortly."

"We'd appreciate it if you'd patch the phone in so I can make calls directly."

"Can't do that." He found that he could indeed, with a fifty-dollar nonrefundable deposit.

"One more thing," Gina said. "We were supposed to meet some folks tomorrow who love to surprise us—and I detest surprises. If anyone asks for us —" A moment's thought "—tell them we're an old couple. And as soon as they leave, please give us a ring."

A collusive smirk spread across the leathery features. "I got it," he said archly, not getting it at all.

Inside the chill cabin, Everett turned up the heat and found a bonus in the dry wood piled beside the fireplace. Gina, blowing on her hands, checked the windows before taking a portable door lock from her bag. She emplaced the heavy steel assembly at breastbone height, wedged into the facing by a heavy setscrew. Then she made a call, using her scrambler over the mouthpiece, which reduced her conversation to gibberish for any monitoring device. Maury Everett imagined himself as a push-pin relocated on some FBI map, and knew he had no real alternative.

As the tiny blaze began to lick upward into the kindling, Maury turned to study the place. Well-furnished, plenty of blankets, electric range and a decent shower. Behind the cabins, he knew, lay an unbroken white expanse leading into the soaring trees beyond. Too bad he had only one set of snowshoes for his morning trek, but— "What on earth are you doing, Gina?"

"Setting our detectors," she said absently, adjusting a dial on the device she had taken from her bag. "I can sleep with this little rig, and I don't want to be roused by every passing field mouse."

"That's new Oracle hardware," he laughed, and stood up to see. He explained his history with the firm that marketed her detectors, oddly warmed to find that the little wireless motion sensors were as useful as his sales people had claimed they would be. With one inside the Firebird, a second dropped into the snow outside the bathroom window, and another placed adhesively under the eaves away from steady winds, they would be forewarned of approach by anything larger than a rabbit. Gina emplaced the sensors while Everett rummaged in their groceries. When she returned he had spread the stuff on the table. He saw her turn quickly to sit on the bed, her head down.

"Problems?"

"I don't know," she said groggily, her breathing deep and rapid. "It's not time for my period. I just feel like a wet rag." She looked up, hearing him chuckle. "I'm glad it meets with your approval" she growled.

"The altitude," he said gently, and turned his chair to sit facing her. "Hey, lady, you're two kilometers high, here. Takes a few days before you can scurry around, jock or no jock, without getting spots before your eyes."

He placed a tentative hand on her shoulder, felt her stiffen, patted her once, withdrew the hand. "Prescription is simple: just keep breathin'," he said, and moved back to the table. "Prognosis is simpler still: you'll be hungry as a hoot-owl in another five minutes."

Presently, as he sliced a second hunk of the petrified salami to go with his corn chips, he heard bedsprings creak. A moment later she was sitting across from him, the brunette wig discarded, her hair gleaming beryllium bronze in the firelight. "Don't mind me," she said, her buoyancy gradually returning. "When I'm not fully fit I feel vulnerable. And when I feel vulnerable, I am not the easiest person to approach. You know?" Her frown was questioning, serious.

He nodded. "Like being fresh out of videotape when the bridge collapses," he offered.

"At least," she smiled, then sniffed. "What's this stuff?"

He watched her finger the soft disc of cheese he had taken from its airtight tin. "Camembert. Give it an hour to soften, and it makes the worst beer in Colorado taste like dark Lowenbrau."

"Can't just be dead, huh? It has to putrify."

She saw something shatter behind his eyes before he squeezed them shut. He shook off the outward display, turning to stare into the fire. "I'm sorry," she whispered. "That was stupid of me."

Everett told her, inflections low and halting, of the youth who almost certainly lay under swirling rapids in his expensive metal coffin several kilometers away. "I keep hearing him yelling. He was scared out of his sphincter, Gina. I don't think he knew what was happening."

"My synopsis said he had an automatic weapon. He knew."

"That was the third guy, the one in the back seat; the one I—I aimed at."

"Then you didn't actually pull the plug on the kid driving?"

"Not intentionally." He swallowed with an effort. "I'm not like you, Gina. I don't have the killer instinct very well honed." He saw her start to protest and held up a restraining hand. "I've seen you move in when you didn't have to, lady. And I'm grateful, I admire you for it. Wouldn't want you any other way. Okay?" She gnawed her lip and gave silent assent. "But I think, I honestly *think* I wouldn't've pulled that trigger if I hadn't found myself within spitting distance of that Czech automatic. I was going to round the bastards up. I think."

She began to tear small shreds of celery leaf, placing them atop corn chips like hors d'oeuvres. "And I think we simply have different views of what constitutes self-defense," she mused, voice low and calm. "You defend only against immediate threat to your life. I have another view: when something has demonstrated that it is ready and willing to screw me good—and I'm wearing my Freudian half-slip there—I'm likely to defend against the possibility; one demonstration is all I need."

"Screw me twice, shame on me," Everett quoted.

"Absolutely. I got screwed twice, 'way back when, and it left me with a sense of shame I don't want to feel again. *Ever*," the last word intense.

A thin piercing tone stuttered from the Oracle detector. Gina flashed to it, flicked off the audio alarm and checked the tiny lamp glowing on the detector face. "In back," she whispered. "Leave the lights alone but get *down*." He followed instructions, watched her check the Beretta before she closed the bathroom door. A musical laugh, barely audible from the bathroom: "Come here a minute, Maury. This, you have to see."

He found her peering through the back window, the scene outside a dazzling blue-white against black. Twenty meters away, a sleek four-point buck stood quartering toward them, the long neck arched up, antlers stark against the sky. "Testing our scent," Everett breathed, lips brushing her hair. They watched in silence for a long moment. "He doesn't want to get screwed, either."

"Is he in season?"

"Not for me. Always, for a camera. Maybe we can track him tomorrow."

"You're out of your mind," she chuckled. The buck, startled perhaps by some faint transmission of her voice, swung gracefully around, sprang away into the trees with vast heart-stopping leaps.

"Nijinsky," Everett said. "They used to say his leaps were magic. Maybe he was just part deer."

Moving back toward their catastrophic array of foods on the table, Gina paused to reset the detector audio. Everett found his wine, wrenched the cork out, found two coffee cups and poured, yawning as she sat down again.

"Did I understand you right?" She was smiling quizzically. "You only hunt with a camera?"

"Don't let it get around. Some of my friends wouldn't understand."

"Or maybe they would, which'd be worse."

He swigged the wine, crooning happily. "Much worse," he agreed. "Don't get me wrong: I shot an elk once, to get his hide for a pair of trousers. Could've just bought the goddam hide but if I really needed a set of elkhides I figured it was only right to get 'em the hard way."

"How did you feel afterward?"

"Pretty good, to tell the truth. I packed a hindquarter down with the green hide. God, I was a bloody mess. The trousers turned out to be heavy as guilt, but I still have 'em. And if I ever need another pair, I'll go after another elk. It's all the shit we go after that we don't need; that's what puts my hackles up."

She tasted the wine. "Sherry? Wow."

"Harvey's Bristol Cream," he nodded. "The dirty old men with their Madeira just haven't discovered this stuff."

She slouched in her chair, feeling for the rungs beneath his own, and he moved his legs companionably aside. "You don't need a whole lot, do you," she asked shrewdly. "I mean, you don't chase after much. Women, trophies over your mantel, man-of-the-year nominations—"

"Mark of the year, maybe," he snorted.

"Mr. and Mrs. Marks," she said; "I noticed that. But you're avoiding my interview, Commissioner."

"Ah, yes." Pompous clearing of his throat. "I chase what I need, Gina. Well, hell, sometimes I don't even do that. When my wife left me a lo-o-ong time back, I needed her. It wasn't pride that kept me from chasing her. It was knowing she'd just leave again. I didn't have what she needed, you see. Someone who'd stay down off the timberline and build furniture, mix drinks, mow lawns, lust after a silk tie or a smoking jacket."

That throaty laugh again. "David Engels was right, then. You're solitary as a bear. No wasted effort, no chasing all the lady bears out of raunch season. And definitely, no learning to ride a bicycle just to be a circus bear."

He sipped, took a bit of cheese. "Yeah, Dave's probably right. I'd like to think of me as being like Nijinsky out there," he nodded toward the back of the cabin, yawned. "But deer are gregarious critters, full of grace and helium. And they don't hibernate, and I do." He stretched until his joints cracked. "You must've figured out some sensible sleeping arrangement."

"The best. You under a sheet, me above 'em. Best-kept secret of the New England bundlers, or so Conklin tells me. But you go ahead. I'll stoke the fire later and set the detector up close."

He undressed, wondering that he felt no particular unease in her presence. Once she glanced toward him and smiled, raising her cup in a silent toast, then faced the fire again. He doused the lights and, scissoring his legs briskly between the sheets to warm them, heard her low chuckle. "Now what," he asked.

"That's what I do," she said. "Go to sleep."

He rolled onto his side, faced the wall. Just

parts in a machine, he insisted to the image of Dave Engels. *You don't know everything, buddy.* Yet the last image he recalled that night was the halo of yellow made by lambent firelight on the mane of Gina Vercours.

SATURDAY, 13 DECEMBER, 1980:

He awoke to the odors of omelet and coffee, sat up quickly, noting that Gina evidently slept in a loose culotte arrangement. "Whoo," he rubbed hands briskly over his face as she turned; "for a second there, I forgot all this. Mind-bending."

"Your friends in Denver wouldn't let me forget," Gina replied. "You had a call a few minutes ago. Agent Fulton; I promised to have you coherent when he calls again. Did I lie?"

"Nope, unless you promised I'd be decisive, too." She gestured with a plate and he nodded, waving it to him with both hands. He took the steaming plate and settled it into his lap.

"Don't expect this kind of service every morning," Gina teased, going back for the coffee. "I'm feeling sorry for you today, is all."

Between mouthfuls of omelet: "Why?"

" 'Cause you're indecisive."

"Did I talk in my sleep?" He had stopped chewing, the cup poised halfway to his mouth.

"No-oo," she said, a full-octave drop within that one word managing to convey mild irritation, bewilderment, and desire to drop what had begun as banter. "Or if you did, I didn't listen. What's got into you—or should I ask?"

He destroyed the rest of the omelet before replying; and when he did, it was with reluctance. "I know what Fulton wants. And it isn't an easy decision. When I didn't respond to his hints yesterday, he finally laid it on the line. The FBI thinks I should drop out of sight, with a faked media release about my going into the river with those two men in the BMW."

"You mean take a new identity? Pretty drastic," she said, the hazel eyes unblinking over her cup.

"You have a real gift for understatement. But I've been thinking it out, and there may be an alternative," he said, as the telephone rang.

The scrambler was not perfect, requiring him to speak slowly for clarity. "Thanks, Fulton, I'm fine," he said, grateful that Gina had chosen to take her shower during the call. "Yeah, I've thought about it. God knows how you'd get total silence from that little cook, uh, Bohlen? And I couldn't very well continue to perform my Commission duties from the grave, so to speak."

He listened, nodding as if into a videophone. "I'll take your word for that, but look: what if I were listed as seriously injured?" Pause. "I don't know; Walter Reade, San Diego Naval Hospital, Brook General maybe; whatever sounds convincing. You could say I'd been shot or whacked, and collapsed later. Internal hemorrhage, even a relapse from the licking I took at Pueblo. Hell, call a doctor and work it out; I'm open to suggestion, so long as it'd let me continue my work through a mail drop."

He sipped the coffee through a longer pause, one corner of his mind occupied with the liquid slither of a nude blonde soaping herself a few paces away. *A nude blonde butch,* he reminded his libido; *forget it.*

Then he heard Will Fulton's last suggestion, which made it easy to forget women. "Oh no, fella; that's out." Brief pause. "I can't tell you why, exactly, but the idea lacks appeal. I've been Maury Everett too long. And who'd foot the bills?"

He barely noticed Gina's return, immersed in a debate he felt that he was losing. "Okay," he said at last. "I'll think about it, and you set up a scenario. I'll be around here somewhere until you can convince me this'll work. Remember, Fulton, in some ways I'm like any other working stiff." He watched Gina as she sat on the bed to slip from culottes to slacks, then forced himself to look away. "Sure; and I appreciate it, Will. 'Bye."

Everett would not discuss his problem with Gina until he had thought it out in a more pleasant setting. Over her objections, they canvassed Empire, then Golden, for an extra set of snowshoes. She objected again at the price, observing that they made the ugliest, most expensive pair of hand-chewed tennis racquets in her experience. It was past noon on Saturday before they were properly shod for the trek, Gina quickly learning the widestance shuffle, carrying her shoulder bag easily for the first hundred meters.

Maury Everett stopped frequently to let her rest, and laughed as she stumbled down a slope. "Lean back until you have the hang of it," he advised. "You're not on skis."

Grumbling pleasantly, wiping snow from her goggles, she moved with him across the mounded blue-white wilderness, pausing now and then to inspect animal tracks. They had covered more than a kilometer before Everett found a sunny overhang sheltered from the wind and, with his clasp knife, cut boughs for insulation. They took off the snowshoes and sat on them, leaning against the green boughs, silently sharing cheddar and crackers.

The sunlight was warm on her face, distant peaks sharply visible in the thin clear air. It was no longer so difficult to see how a man of solitary habits might prefer winter in the Rockies, alone, to any other time, any other place. She said as much.

"Only we're not alone; and neither is Nijinsky," he replied, and indicated a copse of trees in a ravine far below. Gradually she traced the patterns that revealed several deer among the mass of conifers, as Everett launched into a discourse on the fleet animals.

"My fanny's like a waffle from sitting on these snowshoes," she said, shifting, and provoked a lecture on the differences between her bobtailed 'bearclaw' snowshoes and the long-tailed types used for less rugged country. Gina suddenly realized that the big man was temporizing, focusing on familiar topics, using her as a stimulus to deflect his thoughts. From what?

"My face is frozen in a permanent squint," she said then, to change the subject. "Could we get moving again?"

Single file, they followed the mountain's contours, Everett taking the lead. Eventually Gina admitted that her stamina was waning again in the high altitude and, after another quiet breather, they retraced their path. In another hour they stood in a grove of trees above the cabin.

"Let me go first," she insisted. "I'll wave you in if it's okay."

He hesitated, then shrugged. "I'll never get used to this," he said, motioning for her to go ahead.

He watched her circle the cabin, aware that there were ways to locate and deactivate the Oracle sensors, ways to counter the most sophisticated passive system. Gina Vercours herself was the active system that must probe the site. She disappeared into the cabin then, finally emerging to scan the heights where he stood.

At Gina's wave, Everett lurched forward in a shambling lope, traversing the steep declivity in a series of shallow zigzags. Exhalations condensed in his wake, wafting upward in the still air, and as he trotted in, she was grinning. "You leave a contrail like a 747," she marveled.

"Just out of condition," he puffed, hyperventilating. "Can't afford to inhale fast, it'd shrivel all those poor little alveoli."

"I'll take your word for it," she said quickly. "No more lectures, please; whatever's bothering you, suffer in silence!"

He unstrapped the snowshoes, amused, then

followed her into the cabin. "Am I all that transparent? Well, humor me, babe; I just need time to get used to new ideas."

She was heating water for instant coffee. "Such as?"

"Such as undergoing cosmetic surgery," he said, and was grimly pleased to see that the notion disturbed her. By tacit agreement they eased onto separate sides of the bed, sitting side-by-side, sipping coffee as they argued the problem out.

At one point, Gina reached over to take the roll of fat at his waist between her thumb and forefinger. If he lost thirty pounds of suet, she joked, nobody would recognize him.

"That's the crux of it," he objected. "I hate being forced to extremes because a half-dozen gangs of charlies want my hide on their walls."

"Then repudiate your stand. You'd have all the media coverage you could want."

He was damned if he would. The very fact of his being hunted, he said, implied that young Rhone Althouse had found an Achilles tendon in terrorism. But between repudiation and a new identity there was an alternative. He could continue as always, but with tight security around him.

That, Gina said flatly, was suicide. "And I won't be a party to it," she warned. "Get yourself another boy, fifteen of 'em. It might delay the inevitable but sooner or later—" she broke off, laid a hand on his arm, not looking at him. "You're not seriously considering that, are you?"

Everett laid his big paw over her hand, turned

to face her. "I considered it, yes. But General Patton was right: don't die for your country; make some other sonofabitch die for *his*. I'm no martyr, Gina." He withdrew his hand, powerfully conscious that she had made no move to retreat from this small evidence of a growing rapport.

Gina levered herself up to sit cross-legged, facing him. The act somehow lent her a gamin charm; in other circumstances he would have worn a wide grin. "So you're damned if you'll repudiate, and you won't paint a bull's eye on your butt," she urged. "That leaves us with a new you. Any other alternatives?"

"Only the choice between stories that I'm comatose, and stories that I'm dead. I like the coma; *that*, you can come back from. Only I'd have to come back with a different face."

"Just thinking about it must be a downer, huh?"

It was not so much a fear of surgery, he said; Fulton had hinted at temporary cosmetic techniques. The weight loss was a good idea in any event. He sighed, "I guess I'm just worried about the effects on the few people I care about."

"Ah," she breathed; "relationships." They were silent for a time before she added, "You have a solid self-image, Maury. No matter who you see in the mirror, you'll still be you."

He stared hard at her. "Tell me that when I have a new face."

"I will—assuming you'll still need me." It was a clear request for clarification; even a bit wistful, he thought, his gaze softening as he sought the frank hazel eyes.

To avoid making a fool of himself he swung from the bed. "That's your safest assumption of the day," he said. "I have a phone call to make."

Will Fulton did not have every detail worked out, but Everett accepted the story they had concocted for the press. Severe head injury during a kidnap attempt, condition improved but still critical, under heavy guard at an undisclosed location. "We can take you to Beverly Hills, Tucson, or San Antonio for the plas—uh, cosmetic surgery," Fulton said.

Everett glanced across the bed. "Tucson it is," he said, and exchanged slow smiles with Gina. "But why don't I just drive your Firebird down to Las Cruces and across?"

He frowned at the answer. "Okay, then the lady can do the driving and I'll hide my wallet. That's the way I want to do it, Fulton . . . I'm not *asking* you to take the responsibility."

There was more along this vein, the FBI loath to take chances on some accidental unmasking of Everett, and Everett determined to have his way. Everett finally terminated the call, met Gina's glance.

"What now?" she asked. There was something in her query that was calculated, yet far from cold.

"We head for Tucson tomorrow; and I start losing weight today. Get into your snowshoes," he smiled; "I'll tell you about it on the mountain."

She lay back on the bed, flexing the long bare legs in languid sensuality. "Tell me here," she purred. "I can think of better ways to lose weight." Her invitation left no room for misunderstanding.

Returning her smile: "I do believe your sense of duty is boundless." He took the hand that reached up for him, eased down beside her.

"Never think that," she whispered, graceful fingers sliding along the muscles corded at his neck. "I told you I was selfish." She felt his hands on her, tremblingly tentative, gentle in their vitality. "I won't break," she laughed, and thrust her breasts against his cupped hands. Murmuring with pleasure, she kissed his throat and then, her eyes wide and unfocused on his own, traced the surface of his lips with her tongue.

Maurice Everett, maltrained by a lifetime of cinema caresses, roamed weightless in the depths of the artless green-flecked eyes. It was a token of commitment, of sharing, that ravished him in its directness.

"When did you decide this was what you wanted," he asked, his hand moving down the voluptuous swell of her hip.

"When you called me 'babe'." she murmured, lips fluttering against his, "and I didn't mind. Shut up and give me."

That lesbian contralto had fooled him badly. The moon was well up before he thought of snowshoes again.

Mr. and Mrs. Marks left their cabin on Monday, after defacing many kilometers of snow with their prints and breaking two slats in the bed. They found a motel in Socorro, New Mexico that night but were abashed into more quiescent

love-making at two A.M. by the insomniac
pounding on their wall. Tucson boasted a wealth
of motels, at least one with a vibrating mattress
and naughty movies on television. When Everett
showed up Wednesday at the Tucson office of
the FBI he was four kilos thinner, randy as a goat,
and full of ideas for further weight reduction.
Gina Vercours drove the Firebird on to Phoenix.
En route, she saw the contrail of a commercial
airliner at it lanced toward Los Angeles from El
Paso. Gina stroked her thigh and smiled, thinking of the contrails Maury Everett made when
loping over snowdrifts. She did not consider the
passengers of the aircraft, who included Hakim
Arif and, several seats ahead, Leah Talith.

Neither Bernal Guerrero nor Chaim Mardor
were on the flight, having driven the little van
earlier with its fresh Quebecois supplies. There
was just no way to get surface-to-air missiles
through a baggage inspection, not even the little
shoulder-fired SAMs Hakim had earmarked for
his war on media. . .

SATURDAY, 27 DECEMBER, 1980:

Charlie George's solution to the security problem was outlandish. He had paid a slather of money to NBN's best sound stage architect and three slathers to several independent special effects crews. The moving van that had backed up to his earth berm in Palm Springs contained twelve blue-tinted, shallow reinforced fiberglass trays, each nearly three meters across; enough structural aluminum to erect a small dirigible; and panel after panel of clear two-centimeter polycarbonate lying atop ultramodern furnishings.

It had taken twelve days and over two hundred thousand dollars to put the materials in Palm Springs in holiday season. After another five days of furious labor by picked men, Charlie's atrium had disappeared. Now, in its place, was a pond formed by the interconnected trays, holding eleven thousand kilos of water, complete with fountain and a ridiculous naked cherub for

lagniappe. In the geometric center of the pond
was a gorgeous rectangular dwelling, mostly
clear polycarbonate and white aluminum, conforming to Charlie's idea of a three-holer by Mies
van der Rohe. Anyone who climbed the new
stairs over the berm could see, though not learn
much from, the pair of armed churls who kept
house there. He could not see into the fake
fieldstone bathroom, which hid the stairs leading down to Charlie's original lair.

The pond and the bulletproof plastic house
rested on tubular aluminum columns that rose
here and there from the atrium floor. Since the
house and pond also had translucent floors,
Charlie still had some daylight in the place. The
sight of the aluminum maze in his atrium only
made him madder, more determined to press his
peculiar attack on the shadowy bastards who
made it all necessary.

At least Charlie could feel secure behind
rammed-earth walls, below the liquid armor,
and beyond his stolid guards. He churned
through his pre-opened mail alone on a warm
Saturday afternoon in late December, fighting
post-Christmas anomie, wishing there were
some way he could tempt Rhone Althouse from
his hideaway at Lake Arrowhead. The highly
publicized fates of Maurice Everett and especially of Dahl D'Este had reduced Althouse to
something that approached paranoia. Surely,
thought Charlie, I can jolly Rhone out of this
mood. So far, he had been unsuccessful; even
Charlie could not cheer a melancholy gagman.

But Charlie found a way, beginning with the
package from the office of Commissioner David

Engels. It contained an individualized telephone scrambler, and a number with a six-oh-
two area code. He called the number. Two minutes later he was struggling with tears of re-
pressed joy, partly because he no longer felt guilt
over the Everett affair. The voice on the other end
had the right scrambler, and he asked if Charlie
still lived in a vacant lot.

"Maury, God *damn*, you sound terrific," Charlie stammered into the scrambler. He carried the
wireless phone extension into his kitchen for a
beer, knowing he sounded like a manic-
depressive caught on the upswing, caring not a
whit. "You weren't? It was all hype, the coma,
the kidnapping, all of it?" He listened to the
explanation, his expressions a barometer of his
moods as he followed Everett's tale.

After twenty minutes, a sobering thought
began to nag him. "As much as I like knowing
you're skinny and tan and full of garbanzos,
why'd you tell me? I mean, how d'you know I'm
not another jabbering D'Este, God rest him?" He
took a swallow of beer and nearly choked on it.
"A JOB? You mean a real, union-dues-paying,
NBN-salaried *job*?" Long pause before, "Nobody
has to know your function but me, Maury; hell,
even I don't know what some of my retinue do.
And if you really want to work for nothing, yeh, I
see your point; it'd be legal. But don't blame me
if you get zapped for conflict of interest, one
day."

The woman was another matter, but: "So long
as NBN doesn't realize she's an armed guard. If I
pass you off as a situations consultant, she can be
your aide; carry a clipboard, gopher coffee, all

that crap." He listened for another moment.
Then, "I'll have to tell Althouse, you know. He'll
see you on the sets anyhow and you won't fool
him for long."

Charlie listened again, starting to laugh. "I
know what he'll say; having the FCC doing un-
paid liaison is like having God cry at your wed-
ding . . . All right, then, private consulting; don't
go bureaucratic on me now, for Christ's sake."

When Charlie broke the connection, his
cheeks ached from smiling. He immediately
made a call to Lake Arrowhead, a two-hour drive
away, and enticed Rhone Althouse to risk the
trip. It was news, said Charlie, too heavy and too
light to carry over telephone lines.

There was heavier news to be shared by the
time Althouse drove up in his cover identity,
carrying a five-gallon bottle of distilled water
into the van der Rohe miniature. As Charlie had
spoken with Maurice Everett, a traffic watch
helicopter had exploded in midair over South
Pasadena while airing its live remote broadcast
on a Los Angeles station.

The debris had fallen on a freeway cloverleaf
to tangle in the clotted weekend traffic, with
eight known fatalities and over thirty injuries,
including the chain-reaction wrecks that re-
sulted. Eyewitnesses had seen the faint scrawl of
smoke that led from the ground to terminate in
the aerial firebloom of metal, fuel, and flesh.
Again, the group calling itself Fat'ah clamored
for recognition of a direct hit with its SAM. But
this time the news services reported no competing claims. On the contrary, both the Palestine
Liberation Organization and the more recent

Chicano 'Raza' group called to make specific denials.

It was hideous news, Althouse agreed, dropping into his favorite chair in Charlie's living room. "But there's a meta-message under it," he said. "It says maybe there's hope now. Three months ago, every unshelled nut in California would've been jostling the others to claim responsibility. At least today they're making a show of clean hands for a pure civilian atrocity." He glanced sharply at Charlie. "Now for the good news I risked my ass for."

Charlie told him.

The Althouse reaction was mixed and thoughtful: "I'll be glad to see Maury when I wander onto the set, but—I dunno, Charlie, all of us eggs in one basket?" He lifted one hand, made it waver in the air.

"If you're going to lay Cervantes on me, try Twain: he said put all your eggs in one basket, and *watch that basket,*" Charlie retorted, pleased to recall his classics.

"Twain was a lousy administrator," Althouse grunted. "It's getting pretty late in the game for aphorisms, Charlie. You and I and Maury Everett shouldn't even occupy the same hemisphere!"

"Aw, Rhone, don't be skittish," Charlie said gently. "We've started a war, right?" He got an answering nod. "So think of this as a nonstop, floating summit meeting."

"All right," Althouse flashed, jerking a thumb toward the sky, "and you can think of that SAM as a commando raid. We're all crowding into L.A. together, Charlie, and God protect us if this leaks to the wrong people." He donned a

horrendous prissy smile, spoke in a nasal sac-
charine falsetto, "What great big handsome
nose-bobbed FCC Commissioner, initials M. E.,
is hiding out on the set with what terrorist-
baiting NBN star? Are they just good friends, or
is it one-on-one, fellas?" He dropped the sham
and glowered, "That's all you need, bubbe."

"If that should happen, we'd split," Charlie
shrugged.

Althouse drew an imaginary line with his
forefinger from throat to groin. "You might get
split, Charlie. That Fat'ah bunch is getting too
close." He stared into the gloom at nothing in
particular. "Too damn close," he muttered.

Silently, Charlie scared up a pack of cards. He
could think of no better answer.

THURSDAY, 8 JANUARY, 1981:

In the heyday of Paramount Studios it had been easier to locate watering troughs of the grips, gaffers, construction men and engineers who form an utterly indispensable lower echelon of the visual arts industry. Yet every shift of media brought shifting locations, and many a gaudy gin mill has passed through its own eminence to become musty and forgotten as technicians found work, and cheap bar whiskey, in other sections of Los Angeles.

It was Chaim Mardor, moving quietly among the devotees of arts and crafts, who first learned the site of one after-hours bar in current vogue with Industry people. There are many industries north of Wilshire Boulevard, but only one capital-I Industry.

Hakim's instructions to Leah Talith were explicit. "Call me from each location before you make inquiries, Talith. I must know your sequence. These people may have their own security elements and you could arouse interest."

She applied a fresh layer of scarlet to her mouth, cinched her belt to pull the blouse more tightly over her breasts. "How well you put it, Hakim," she said, studying the image in her compact mirror.

He swept his eyes over her body, impassive. "How readily you pose as a prostitute," he remarked.

"A New York prostitute, Hakim. Here I will pass as a secretary. You will see."

He would not argue. "Fat'ah is not interested in failure, Talith," he said. "Make certain your contact has access to the comedian's work."

"It may take several evenings of my time."

"Then you shall spend it," he said softly. "Spill no blood, but bring Fat'ah what you can, however you can."

She put away the compact, adjusted her feet to the new high-heeled sandals. Then, subdued: "Pray that I do not have to charm another woman."

"Fat'ah does not pray," he said, still more softly. "You will do what you must."

"And repeat the details to you later?"

"If you would arouse me," he answered obliquely, "learn where the comedian can be reached."

She averted her face, nodding. Leah Talith sought the emotional tripwires of her leader in vain. She had no motive beyond the desire to cement Fat'ah together, which meant that she must please Hakim. Yet she knew his hostility against any prying into his own motives. Many of his actions seemed consistent with simple masochism, and she knew him to be jealous of her flesh. Yet he was able to cloister his desires with a dreadful efficiency. Classroom psychology, she reflected as she drove away from their Glendale site, was unequal to Hakim Arif.

The bar on Ventura Boulevard was nearly a waste of time. She invented an acquaintance with NBN to cloak her questions in innocence, and heard of a spa on San Fernando Road. Cursing the endless urban protraction of Los Angeles, she drove to the suburb of Pacoima, and resumed her inquiry. At last, just north of Burbank, she found in a quintet of listless drinkers two men whose varicolored badges had the NBN imprimatur. They were quiet, middle-aged folk who found less charm in the girl than in their highball glasses, and Talith fought against frustration. But the bartender, defending the honor of his turf, claimed the young lady was much too late for interesting conversation. Most weekdays during happy hours, he said morosely, the place was acrawl with NBN hardhats.

The young lady thanked him, nursed her ouzo while she listened to the quintet that steadily plastered itself into the booth. A carpenter from a cinema crew did his best to impress her. She was demure, cool, disinterested; he had nothing she needed.

She returned to Glendale long after midnight to find Hakim a sentry in the kitchenette. Somehow she knew that what she had overheard would trigger arousal in Hakim. "The network

has a backlot, a great fenced area, north of Burbank," she told him. "I believe the men were
connected with the Charlie George show."

An hour later she slid from their bed to take
sentry duty, using her compact mirror as she
daubed antiseptic on the marks left by Hakim's
teeth on her shoulders and breasts. Perhaps, she
told herself, psychology was a useless tool after
all. She could intuit the onset of Hakim's savage
needs, but despaired of discovering the main-
spring that drove him. She wondered what
Hakim would do if he learned that her nimble
fingers gentled Chaim during the nights, as one
might gentle a long-abused stallion. He would
do nothing, perhaps. Anything, perhaps. It mattered little, so long as Chaim Mardor continued
to function in the interests of Fat'ah. A less patient man than Guerrero, modifying their vehicles in their garage, might have found Chaim's
help unacceptable.

Smiling to herself, she slipped to the bedside
of Chaim, listening to the measured breathing.
Presently, at her manual urging, his respiration
quickened. She spoke to him then in their ancient tongue, gently leading him as he slept. It
never occurred to Talith that, in her role as suc-
cubus, she had performed a displacement. To
Chaim, Fat'ah was embodied, not in Hakim, but
in Leah Talith herself.

The next morning, a few kilometers to the
northwest, Gina Vercours introduced herself to
Charlie George on the NBN backlot and indicated her strapping—and foolishly smirking—
blond companion. "And you know Simon Kenton here," she said.

"Holy gawd," Charlie gaped, staring hard. In his costume as Idi Amin's twitchy analyst, Charlie was a study in contrasts. He glanced from the big man's stylish sandals to the yellow hair two meters above. "You're new!"

Everett hugged the comedian. "Refinished," he corrected. "We were glad to see tight security at the backlot gate, by the way. Hey, I think they're ready for you."

Charlie moved away toward the waiting crew; glanced back with an admiring headshake. He then proceeded to blow his lines so badly that his director suggested a break. "My mind is well and truly blown," Charlie admitted, taking his visitors by the arms. He guided them to a bench, out of the paths of technicians, and studied the face of Everett carefully. "Even the eyes," he said, bewildered. "I've seen a few good nose jobs in my time but Jee-zus, I'm even wondering if you're really you."

"Panoramic contact lenses," Everett said. "Would you believe they're as good as bifocals? The hard part, they told me, was dickering with my vocal chords. I'm supposed to fool a voice-printer, too."

"In-damn-credible. Excuse my staring. You look thinner, too; what'd they do to your cheeks?"

Gina began to laugh. "Mostly kept food out of 'em," she said, as Everett strained to look aloof. "That was tougher than surgery, Mr. George. It still is."

Charlie darted a keen glance at Everett. "Something I keep trying to recall," he said, "about the meeting at my place. Somebody was sketching something." He seemed expectant, uneasy.

Everett sucked at a tooth. "No—except for D'Este, of course."

"Go on."

Everett spread his hands, nonplussed, then suddenly burst into laughter. "Charlie, you're testing me! You really aren't sure," he accused. "I feel more secure every minute," the comedian replied. But the concern did not leave Charlie's face until Everett passed his exam. The comedian apologized for his suspicions, to Everett's genuine delight. At the end of the ten-minute break they had banished their reserve and Gina was saying 'Charlie' instead of 'Mr. George'.

The comedian's reaction underlined for Everett the success of the cosmeticians in Tucson. Incisions at jaw and scalp had brought other subtle changes in the planes of the rugged features, and Gina's companionship accounted for much of the startling weight loss. Dental work, bleach, and a new hair style completed the process, though nothing had been done to alter Everett's fingerprints.

The name was a conceit, one he had demanded over the objections of David Engels. He had chosen the name of an obscure early Kentucky woodsman, from whom he could claim descent. He claimed it gave him a built-in background, but with his obligatory change in clothing style, knew it was a substitute approach to his mountain-man fantasy. Gina, he found, had been wrong: no self-image could stay wholly unchanged under such an implosive assault.

Lunch was a set of informal choices between the NBN mobile lunch truck and a caterer's van, both parked outside the mammoth sound stage. Charlie insisted on buying. "Don't worry about fitting in today," he said around his mouthful of ham and cheese; "just get the feel of the place. We're doing all my stuff on the backlot these days. Find the head, the script girl, and the union steward, and then you'll know where all the power is." He turned to Gina. "That place you rented: does it suit you?"

"Three exits, one from the patio," she nodded, "and a video monitor to check visitors. Besides," as though auditioning for *Little Women*, "who could possibly be interested in us?"

"Autograph hunters," Charlie said. "You two make an imposing pair. I might get you both some walk-ons if you like, Maury."

"Sy," Everett said quickly.

"Shit," Charlie hissed. "Sy it is. Keep harping on it." He became his imbecile bumpkin: "I ain't the quickest study on the set."

"As for going in front of cameras, we'll decline with thanks," Everett said, explaining Gina's need to maintain a low profile. "Face it, Charlie, union scale for bit players is a poor trade for the salary she rakes in now."

Charlie studied the auburn-wigged Gina with new interest. "Somehow I thought you had, uh, personal motives."

Gina bit into an apple, chewed a moment before: "Mr. Kenton is, as they say, my main man; no reservations on that, Charlie. But let me save you a lot of unasked questions: my client happens to be a very, very dear friend, and that's a

bonus. Still, I am not independently wealthy."
She aimed a forefinger toward him to punctuate
her next phrase: "And I intend to be. That means
I must think about other clients next year, and
the next."

Charlie blinked. "You're very direct, Gina. In
this business I tend to forget there are people like
you."

"There isn't anybody like her," Everett chortled. "She'll con you with a candid serve, but
look out for her backhand."

This reminded Charlie of the nearby tennis
courts. Before returning to the set, he advised
them to get familiar with the self-contained
world of the backlot. NBN officials had assured
Charlie George that the vast fenced area was
secure, far better than a leased location and near
corporate offices as well. They had not added
that their own security chief disagreed and
avoided mentioning the obvious: the backlot
was relatively cheap. The new passes gave an
added measure of security with their integral
electronic ID. It was a measure that diminished
geometrically with the issuance of every new
pass.

Larry Farquar toyed with his drink after work
on Friday evening and assessed the dark
roman-nosed beauty through the bar mirror. He
had spotted her the previous evening, her huge
serious eyes studying a carpenter from Warner's
as he tried for a one-nighter that simply was not
in the cards. For one thing, the wood-butcher's
line was a string of Industry names, dropped like
pennies in a trail to his sack. None of those
names had done much for the girl, who seemed

more interested in the baggy-eyed old NBN guys in the back booth.

But then, the carpenter didn't have the confidence of a Farquar, the best damn' electrician on NBN's backlot with a profile just a trifle too three-dimensional to make it through a screen test. Well, Farquar was a star at what he did, and knew that a steady job was as good an aphrodisiac as most girls needed.

Farquar decided the slender, high-breasted girl was not the sort to reveal what turned her on, and this turned Farquar on like a quartz-iodine key light. Genuine or faked, impassivity in exotic women was a challenge to be overcome. Internally as Larry Farquar moved in, he was buzzing like a housefly. Leah Talith saw him from the edge of her vision, and waited in the web of her secret smile.

Sunday, Farquar learned from an honest bartender in Burbank that his wallet had turned up minus cash, but with papers intact. He would never know whether he had simply passed out on the bed Friday night, or if the girl had spiked his drink; but whatthehell, she hadn't trashed his apartment or taken his stereo. He retrieved the wallet, saw that his licenses and the new NBN security pass were accounted for, and had a drink to bank the fires of his confidence. He vowed to forget the girl with the dark eyes and the Gioconda smile. If he reported the temporary loss to NBN it would only make trouble. Besides, he had the security pass. How could you copy its electronic ID?

Fat'ah could have told him.

TUESDAY, 20 JANUARY, 1981:

It was midmorning, a week after Guerrero first drove into the backlot to test his forged pass, before Charlie George and his writers were mollified with the script. It was a tepid takeoff on an attempted prison break by Raza terrorists the previous week.

The skit had two things going for it: Charlie's Chicano accent was uproarious, and he could do pantomimic wonders as a terrorist sapper trying to wire a bomb and chew gum at the same time. They threw out the line identifying the leader as Irish. It was faithful to the new connections between terrorist gangs, but it was also confusingly unfunny. Charlie fumed inside, wishing Rhone were around to bandage the wounded script. But Rhone Althouse was now ABC. He was also scared shitless.

The caterer's van left Glendale on time as usual, on its normal route. The driver noticed nothing unusual until a few minutes after some idiot girl swerved into the space ahead of him on Glenoaks Boulevard. He heard several metallic impacts as he started away from the stoplight but was not worried until his engine started to overheat.

He managed to coast safely to a stop when the engine seized, the girl in the little sedan now all but forgotten as she extended her lead and disappeared into Burbank traffic. He did not see the sedan pass him again, this time with a scarfaced youth at the wheel; he was wondering how his radiator had suffered so many punctures. Neither he nor anyone else had seen Chaim Mardor, prone and peering from a slot in the trunk of the little sedan, empty the clip of his small silenced target pistol into the radiator of the van.

By low-static FM citizen's band radio, Talith informed Hakim that the baby was sleeping soundly and without complication. She dropped Chaim where his rig was parked in the north end of Burbank, radioed again when they were in sight of the access road that lay between the NBN acreage and a freeway.

Bernal Guerrero replied from the inside of the backlot. All was well at home; the front door had not stuck and the side door would open.

Talith signaled to Chaim with her arm, and both moved over to the shoulder of the road. They took a small calculated risk in stopping, but far greater chances were being taken across the heavy chain-link fence.

The Charlie George crew managed a halfdozen takes before noon and, as lunch vans began their setups at unobtrusive locations away from the exterior set, Charlie's nose directed his

eyes toward the new van which advertised hot
Mexican food. Charlie's mania for Mexican food
had been duly noted by news magazines.

"Okay, it's a wrap," the unit director called.
"Eat it!" Charlie threw off his prop raincoat,
ignoring the free spread by NBN. He drifted instead, with Everett and Gina Vercours, toward
the menudo and its vendor, Bernal Guerrero.

Only one side panel of the van was raised, for
the excellent reason that one side was rigged for
lunch, the other for Charlie and one of his crew.

The comedian awaited his turn. The latino
appeared to recognize his patron only at second
glance, bestowed a grave smile on Charlie and
said, "For you, Señor Carlito, something special.
Bring a friend; there is enough for only two."

Charlie motioned with his head to his tall
blond companion. "Rank hath its privileges,"
Everett muttered to Gina. "If you're nice, I'll
share with you." She made a face and turned
back to study the unfamiliar food. Somewhere in
the far recesses of her mind, an alarm chittered
for attention. But it was only something about
the food, which did not tally with the Mexican
dishes she knew. They were, in fact, Panamanian. Prepared by Guerrero, mercury-poisoned
by Hakim. Not that mercury was so lethal; it was
really a matter of tradition.

Had Charlie not followed Guerrero to the hidden side of the van, Hakim could have shot him
with the veterinarian's tranquilizer gun from inside the van, through one of the thin silvered
mylar panels. Guerrero would then have been
obliged to take their second hostage, preferably
one known to the comedian, with the hypoder-

mic. The second hostage was to be, in Hakim's
wry parlance, the 'demonstrator model'. But the
tranquilizer was a recent fast-acting drug, and its
dosage was determined by guesswork. Sometimes the target animal died within minutes.
Hakim, peering closely through the mylar,
poised himself to choose whichever target Guerrero left him.

Gina turned, started to follow the men, then
was rediverted by one of Hakim's deft touches as
entire racks of warm lunch items began to spill
from the display racks onto the macadam. She
rushed instinctively to help minimize the spill-
age.

On the other side of the van, Guerrero heard
the commotion Hakim had initiated. Charlie's
smile was tentative until he felt Guerrero's needle enter his side like a cold lightning bolt. He
cried only, "Hey, that hurts," not convincingly,
before Guerrero's gristly fingers numbed his
diaphragm. Everett spun, had time to wrench
Guerrero around as Charlie began to slump before a fletched dart caught the big man high on
the left pectoral muscle, Hakim's round a muffled slam as he fired pointblank from inside the
van.

Guerrero ducked under Charlie George to
catch him by the thighs, then lifted, hurling the
limp NBN star against the featureless side panel.
Guerrero had delayed the operation for days,
tinkering with pivots and countersprings until
those panels worked to perfection. The panel
swung inward, dumped Charlie at the feet of
Hakim, and swung shut again. Hakim snatched
up his stockless submachine gun and swung it

toward the laughing group whose own minor
panic had masked the sounds from Charlie's side
of the van. Hakim would squeeze the trigger, a
spray of forty rounds into their faces, the instant
Guerrero dumped the second hostage inert at his
feet.

But Everett, knocked too breathless by the dart
to cry aloud, was a bigger specimen than Fat'ah
had expected and was slow to succumb. He
found the dart, gasping, tore it from his flesh,
and took a step toward Guerrero whose foot
caught him squarely in the crotch. The Panamanian whirled him by his collar, slammed him
against the panel, finally managed to thrust him
inside, though mauled by the long legs that
kicked as Everett began to lose consciousness.
Hakim spat the single code word, "kuwa,
power," and dropped over the struggling blond
giant to smother his hoarse cry.

Guerrero rounded the rear of his van to find
Gina Vercours stacking food on the lip of the
narrow counter. "Charlie, Sy," she was laughing, "come see what we've got."

Guerrero made a gesture of helplessness, said,
"Keep it," and dropped the side panel which
sideswiped Gina's head as it fell. She dropped
to her knees as Guerrero reached the driver's seat
and a technician, aghast, leaped to Gina's aid.

Guerrero was hard-pressed to keep from draw-
ing his Browning parabellum sidearm because
he could hear, two hundred meters away,
screams from the script girl who had seen it all.

The van squealed away as Gina, swaying to
her feet, realized who was missing and where
they must be. She fumbled in her shoulder bag

for a heartbeat too long and Hakim, locked against his second victim, heard two rounds from the Beretta ricochet from the chassis beneath him. She had missed the tires, and knew better than to fire blindly into the van's rear panel.

Gina, staring helplessly after the careening van, replaced the Beretta before she retrieved the tranquilizer dart, holding it by its needle tip with a tissue. "Warn the gate and get me to a telephone," she slurred, dizzied by the blow against her temple. All the way to the sound stage, two thoughts vied for primacy in her head. They were, *I've lost Maury,* and *I've lost my job.* She could not decide which thought had occurred first.

As the van howled between two of the hangarlike sound stages, Guerrero bore far to the right to begin his left turn. He had thirty seconds on his pursuers but Hakim had made it clear that they must expect communication between the exterior sets and the guarded backlot gate. Guerrero smiled, hearing Hakim's curses as he struggled with dead weights greater than his own, and sped toward the perimeter cyclone fencing. Outside the fence was the access road, deserted except for a small foreign sedan and a larger car towing an old mobile home. These vehicles were motionless.

Guerrero slapped the button in plenty of time but was not gratified. He slapped it again, then pressed it with a rocking motion as he tapped the brakes hard. Five meters of cyclone fencing peeled back as the bangalore torpedo at last accepted its microwave signal, and Guerrero felt

the pressure wave cuff the van. He angled
through the hole, negotiating the shallow ditch
with elan, and exulted in his choice of a vehicle
with high ground clearance. As he made a gear
change, accelerating toward escape, he could
see Chaim in his outside rearview, dutifully towing the decrepit mobile home into position to
block immediate pursuit along the access road.
For once, Chaim Mardor performed above ex-
pectation, the mobile home teetering for a moment before it rolled onto its side, a barricade
stretching from the ditch to the opposite side of
the road.

Talith waited for Chaim in her small car, the
only vehicle of their regular fleet that was not a
van. Guerrero waited for nothing, but tossed
quick glances to check the possibility of air surveillance. Van Nuys airport was soon sliding
past on his right, and they would be vulnerable
until he reached the state university campus
where their other vans waited.

Minutes later, Guerrero eased the van into a
campus parking lot. Hakim was ready with the
crate and together they wrestled their burden,
the bulk of a refrigerator, from their vehicle into
the rear of a somewhat smaller van. As Hakim
urged the smaller vehicle away, encouraging its
cold engine with curses, Guerrero wheeled the
kidnap van across the lot and abandoned it along
with his vendor's uniform. It might be many
hours before the abandoned van was noticed,
among the hundreds of recreational vehicles on
the campus. Guerrero knew what every undergraduate knew: a recreational vehicle was lim-
ited only by what one defined as recreation.

He moved then to his last vehicle change, flexing his hands in the thin gloves as he waited for the engine to warm, for the flow of adrenaline to subside, for the next item on his private agenda. He had carefully planted Hakim's fingerprints on the abandoned kidnap vehicle after wiping away his own. On the other hand, Hakim had given him only a public rendezvous some kilometers to the west in Moorpark and not the location of the new Fat'ah site which, Guerrero knew, might be in any direction. Hakim's monolithic insistence on sole control was a continuing problem, but Guerrero had to admit the little *palo blanco* was thorough. He checked the time and grinned to himself; it wouldn't do to be late picking up Chaim and Leah. Guerrero's masters were thorough, too.

By six PM, Hakim was so far out of patience that he fairly leaped from his seat in the Moorpark bus station at his first sight of Guerrero. The Panamanian bought a newspaper, saw Hakim stand, then ambled out into the street. It was too dark to read the fine print but, waiting for Hakim to catch up, Guerrero saw that they had once again made the front page above the fold. Fat'ah still had friends in print media—whether they knew it or not.

Though Guerrero walked slowly, Hakim sounded breathless. "I told the *girl* to make rendezvous," he said, as they paused for a stoplight. "And you are four hours late!"

"The Americans had other ideas," Guerrero growled convincingly. "Talith and Chaim tried to run a blockade."

"Escape?"

"I was lucky to escape, myself. They were cut down, Hakim."

Hakim's voice was exceedingly soft. "This you saw?"

"I saw. It may be here," he lied again, brandishing the folded newspaper, ready to grapple with the Iraqi if he saw his cover blown. Hakim Arif only looked straight ahead, and fashioned for himself a terrible smile.

They walked another block, forcing themselves to study the window displays, checking for surveillance as they went. "The hostages will be conscious again soon," Hakim said as if to himself. "They will be noisy, no doubt. Your delay forced me to inject them again." Then, as a new possibility struck him: "Was your van compromised?"

Guerrero gave a negative headshake, very much desiring to keep his own vehicle. "It is just ahead there," he indicated. "Do I abandon it now?" Always, he knew, Hakim was perversely biased against an underling's suggestion. He had seen it work many times for Leah Talith; but Talith would use it no longer.

"We have expended twelve thousand dollars in vehicles, and two Fat'ah lives this day," Hakim snarled. "No more waste. Stay here, wait for my van, then follow."

Guerrero nodded and sauntered to his parked van as Hakim hurried away. He knew that distant friendly eyes were on him, but made no signal. One cigarette later, the latino saw Hakim's vehicle pass. He followed closely in traffic, then dropped back during Hakim's double-back maneuvers. When Hakim was satisfied that only Guerrero was following, he turned north onto Highway Twenty-three toward the mountains.

Well beyond the town of Fillmore the lead van slowed abruptly, loitered along the highway until it was devoid of other traffic. Then Hakim swung onto a gravel road. Guerrero sensed that they were very near the new Fat'ah site and philosophically accepted his inability to share that suspicion with the men he reported to.

After two kilometers they turned again, and Guerrero saw that the new site was a renovated farmhouse in a small orchard. He hurried to help Hakim unload the crate at the porch, ignoring the awful sounds from inside it. Only when the crate was opened in the house did Guerrero learn why the massive blond hostage, gagged and tightly bound, was such a noisy passenger.

On both hostages, the legs had been taped flexed, so that muscle cramps would almost certainly result. More tape looped from necks to thighs, assuring that tall men would make smaller packages. Heavy adhesive bands strapped arms across their chests, the left hand of the second hostage heavily retaped over a crimson-and-rust bandage. Guerrero did a brief double-take, rolling the captive over to see the maimed left hand. Both hostages were conscious. Despite his gag, the injured hostage moaned at the rough movement. From Guerrero, a sigh: "Will you rid the world of fingers, Hakim?"

The Fat'ah leader knelt to examine the bandage while Charlie, eyes wide in horror as he saw the hand of Maurice Everett, tried to speak through the gag. "An ancient and honored cus-

tom, my friend," said Hakim, smiling, and back-
handed Charlie viciously to quell the interrup-
tion. "I mailed his left small finger by special
delivery to the National Broadcasting Network
people. I added a promise to forward more
pieces—some of them yours—until my demands
are aired," he continued, staring into Charlie's
face as he spoke. He wheeled to regard Guerrero.
"I might have delivered it myself while waiting
for you!"

"Your demands, not Fat'ah's," Guerrero
mused aloud.

"I am Fat'ah," almost inaudible.

"It is reducing itself to that," Guerrero agreed
ambiguously, then blunted the goad. "What may
I do now?"

Hakim retained a precarious control. "Familiarize yourself with the house, cook a meal,
mend your tongue if you would keep it. I shall
arrange for our guests to—entertain us."

As the dusk became darkness, Guerrero found
that the nearest lights were over a kilometer
away, too far to carry the sounds of Charlie
George's interrogation. The Panamanian took
his time, kept away from the torture room, and
waited for Hakim to kill their captives in outlet
for his frustration. It sounded as though Hakim
was devoting all his attention to the comedian.
When the screams subsided, Guerrero began to
heat their stew.

Charlie George had more stamina than either
of them had thought. He managed to walk, a
tape-wrapped garrotte wire looped as leash
about his throat, to the table, but fell trying to sit
in the folding chair.

Hakim's smile was a beatitude, so well did his captive behave. Charlie's nose was a ruin, his right ear torn—"It will come off anyway," Hakim chuckled—but his mouth had been left equipped for conversation. He was not disposed to eat and his hands shook so badly that Hakim laughed; but Hakim needed say only once, "Eat it all," softly. Charlie George ate it all. The second captive, trussed with tape and wire, moaned unheeded in the torture room, a supply of parts which might be maintained or dispensed at Fat'ah convenience. He was, Hakim felt, of only secondary importance.

Hakim produced a huge chocolate bar for dessert and helped eat it. He felt no desire or need to deny himself the stuff, while the garrotte wire was in his hand. After the chocolate: "An hour ago, you maintained that this satire is too widespread to halt," he prodded the exhausted Charlie, "and I say you will halt it, piece by piece."

"You underestimate their greed," Charlie replied, scarcely above a whisper. From time to time he clenched his teeth hard. "Every nightclub schlepper in the Catskills is inventing stealable material—and the public loves it." he managed something that could have been a smile. "You're a smash, Charlie."

"You will call me 'Hakim'." The Iraqi flicked the garrotte wire, then looked at the wall a moment. "And the new series you mentioned? What is the investment?"

"One on ABC, one on CBS," Charlie said. "Buy 'em off if you can. Start with ten million apiece; they'll laugh at you." With this unfortunate phrase he trailed off; exhaustion tugged at

his eyelids. Hakim reached out with delicate
precision and thumped the bloody ear.
"Ahhhh—I don't see what you gain by torture,"
Charlie grunted. "I have no secrets." It was not a
lie. Nor was it accurate.

Guerrero, taking notes, gestured at the captive
with the butt of his pen. "Perhaps you do not
know what you know."

"And perhaps you are being punished,"
Hakim murmured.

"What else is new," Charlie said, and was
rewarded by a sudden tug on the wire. "Sorry,"
he managed to croak.

"Repeat after me: 'I beg forgiveness, Effendi',"
Hakim smiled, and tugged again. Charlie did it.
"Now, the amputee in the next room," Hakim
continued. "What is he to you?"

The uncomprehending gaze became wonder
as Charlie grappled with a new surmise. "Sy?
Simon Kenton?" Charlie steeled himself for the
garrotte.

"If that is his name. He is a close friend?"

Charlie swallowed. "We get along; I don't
hunger for his bod. He's a consultant; why is he
here?"

"You will not question Fat'ah," Hakim
thumped the ear again, almost gaily. Charlie,
through his agony, caught something subtly in-
quisitive as his gaze swept past the face of Guerrero. The Panamanian said nothing. Hakim
pressed on with, "But the network will know
him by the fingerprint." It was a question.

"They have his prints but he's my consultant—like twenty other people from time to
time."

"Now tell me again how NBN amassed those tapes to be aired in the event one of their people was taken." With the change of topic, Charlie felt surer that the disguise of Maurice Everett had not been penetrated, that Fat'ah had kidnapped a major enemy by a fluke and still did not know it.

But how long before newspapers, in their zeal for all the news, made these murderous fanatics a present of the crucial datum? Perhaps Charlie could temporize, could claim he did not recognize Everett in his new guise, could hope for clemency. In his heart, Charlie knew it was all a crock of shit. They would tear him to pieces when they found out. Unless Everett's contacts could do a nose-job on the news, too. It was possible. Not likely, but. . .

Charlie, glad to change the subject, repeated the truth about NBN's contingency tapes. The networks had all considered the possibility that their stars might be ransomed, or worse, by terrorists. They would feel no pain.

The hostages would absorb all of that.

Hakim probed for some weak point in network thinking, asked questions that sometimes led nowhere. Eventually he saw that the answers were becoming more disjointed, less useful, and led the unprotesting Charlie to the torture room.

Guerrero saw the captive trussed flat on a tabletop, feet toward the door, before Hakim was satisfied. Guerrero kept the butt of his ballpoint pen aimed at the doorway, putting away his gear as Hakim returned. Slumped in a corner, radiating silent hatred, the second captive gripped his wrist and stared at nothing.

"I will set up the media center," Hakim said

mildly. "You will feed the big one, Kenton, then install this lock on their door." He handed Guerrero a heavy push-bolt affair.

Guerrero ascertained that 'Kenton' could feed himself with one hand temporarily freed, saw in the steady motions a reservoir of strength. He offered the big man a glass of water which was emptied in one draught, and reclaimed the glass by spreading his fingers inside the rim. Hakim had not seen the exchange. Guerrero caught the captive's eyes with his. "You are wondering how you can surprise me while securely lashed with wire, Señor Kenton," he said evenly. "Of course, you cannot. Even if you could, you cannot surprise us both. You would be dead in seconds if you tried. It would be small loss. Suit yourself," he added.

"I hear you," was the growled response. No promises, no pleas, no hollow threats.

Guerrero had seen the same stolid calm in *corridas*, as a wounded Miura waited for the matador to make one little mistake. But Bernal Guerrero had graduated from Panama by making very few mistakes. "Just remember that I know, and Hakim knows, what you are wondering," he said.

Guerrero was wrong. Everett was wondering why they called him 'Kenton' even after capturing him; why the Iraqi had grilled Charlie George about so many things without once mentioning Maurice Everett; whether it was all part of the torturer's art to wear him down by forcing him to stay in the room, to hear the guttural screams of a friend in agony without being able to cover his ears.

It simply had not yet occurred to Everett that he was a target of purest opportunity, a means to distribute more tokens of Fat'ah power and Fat'ah horror without killing the comedian too quickly. Everett considered the care with which Guerrero had handled his water glass. Not with aversion, but with delicacy, as though his own use of the glass had made it special. Yet all he had given it were smudges. Fingerprints. And why study those when they already had him?

Unless they didn't know they had him.

A filament of hope began to glow in the core of Everett's being. He did not think Fat'ah had access to print files. In this he was correct, but at certain levels of international quid pro quo, a more potent organization than Fat'ah did have access.

Guerrero set about clearing the bowls away, taking care with the water glass, as Hakim brought his HP unit and media monitors in. "I saw lights of a village from the porch," Guerrero reported. "With only two of us left, you might brief me to that extent."

"I might—when you need to know. Information is at a premium now, is it not? We have not even a telephone here. But no matter," he said, setting his small portable TV sets up. "We can do what we must."

Guerrero paused, framed another guarded question, then thought better of it and went after tools for the door lock. From his van, he saw that the windows of the torture room were boarded. Returning with the tools, he installed the simple lock, pausing to watch the monitors with Hakim. There was no mention of a shootout between

Chaim and police—naturally—but there was also absolute silence on the daring daylight abduction of Charlie George and the consultant. Guerrero saw Hakim's subliminal headshakes and was emboldened; the Iraqi might have doubted Guerrero's story if the kidnapping, but no capture of Fat'ah elements, had received major coverage. As it was, Hakim focused only on television as his primary source of dis-, mis-, and non-information.

When the last newscast was done, Hakim read and made notes on alternative courses of action, now and then consulting the HP unit which lay among his media equipment. The HP told Hakim what he already knew: Fat'ah was nearing bankruptcy now.

At last Hakim put away his tools of strategy, ascertained that Charlie George was breathing heavily, and sought his own bedroll. Then, for the first time, he missed Leah Talith until he thrust the image of her youthful body from him. "We shall see, tomorrow," he said to the sentry, Guerrero. Then he fell into a sleep of confidence.

The next morning, there was still no news of the abduction on television. Hakim made a quick trip into town for newspapers and chocolate, vaguely aware that his supremacy over the hostages permitted him to relinquish some control over his simpler desires.

The Panamanian checked the lashings of his captives as soon as Hakim was gone, loosening the wire that looped from behind Everett's knees to his neck. He withdrew the Browning automatic from his waistband, held it up, then replaced it. "A unique weapon," he said. "A bit heavy, but it carries seven rounds for each of you. See that you do not move closer together. I shall be back immediately."

They heard the bolt grind into its socket, heard the floor creak and the door slam. Charlie, taped supine to the table, moved his head to see his friend staring back at him. Neither spoke until they heard the engine of Guerrero's van start, a peculiar whine piercing its throb.

"He's leaving," Charlie wheezed.

"No he's not. Probably bugging us from outside."

Charlie considered the possibility. The engine note was unchanging, a fast idle. "Sorry I got you into this," he said, choosing his words carefully. "It's not as if you were responsible for it."

"I'm beginning to think you're right," was the reply. "But they're gonna snuff me anyhow."

"Maybe not. You have a better chance than I do, sure as your name is Simon Kenton."

A nod to Charlie. "Maybe if I stir around a bit I can get circulation going." With heels and rump, he began inching toward Charlie.

Charlie knew the words had covered another intent, but: "You can't chew wire, Simon. And there's dust on the floor." Fear in the voice. It was a thinly disguised plea. "I'm sorry, Simon."

After a long hesitation: "It was just an idea."

"Not one of your better ones." Charlie flexed his left hand, twisting the wrist within the tape. "How's your *hand*," he continued, straining to see if his motion was visible from the corner.

"Hurts like a bastard," Everett replied. "Not as healthy as yours."

Charlie continued to strain against the tape,

perspiration aiding him as he gradually worked
his wrist free of the adhesive which still bound
him, like a manacle, to the table. A few moments
later, Charlie heard the engine die outside. "I
don't think we can play out this hand, Simon."

"They'll deal us another one."

But it was several minutes before Guerrero
returned, sliding the bolt loose and waiting a full
minute before he flung the door open. He eased
to a vantage point that let him view the recum-
bent Charlie, risked a quick look toward the
corner, then walked in, the Browning drawn.

From the corner, "You don't take just a whole
lot of chances."

"More than you know," Guerrero laughed, his
spirits strangely buoyant. He strode to the corner
and replaced the wire around the big man's
throat with one hand, the muzzle of the automatic against the stubbled jaw. When he had tested
the bonds of Charlie George, he added more tape.
He chuckled ruefully to see Charlie's wrist raw
from its struggle. "I would do the same as you,
Carlito," he said, retaping, "but I would expect
punishment for it."

"You   don't   think   I'm   being   punished
enough?"

"I think this conversation is pointless." From
outside came the sound of an approaching vehicle. Quickly, Guerrero stepped to the next room,
leaving the door open as he moved to a window.
"Hakim is prompt," he said.

"You know what I think," Charlie said softly.
"I think that sonofabitch is afraid to talk to us."

Charlie was partly right. But Guerrero did not

need to talk to them so long as the equipment in his van functioned properly.

Hakim's morning newspapers carried headlines on a reported kidnapping, although television sources still refused comment. Hakim released the comedian, his wrists taped, ankles hobbled, and forced him to eat a mighty breakfast—which was also lunch. He smiled fondly as Charlie complied. Charlie had bled a little during the night and morning but, Guerrero judged, not nearly enough. Hakim seemed content to sit in their orchard site until their food ran out.

Only once did Charlie attempt to reason with his captor. "Look, you've made your point with that poor devil in there," he jerked his head toward Everett in the torture room. "We don't even know where the hell we are. Maybe if you took him blindfolded and released him somewhere. It'd be a sign of good faith to—"

Instantly Hakim was on his feet, eyes glaring in a bright vacancy. He drew his knife from a pocket, rushed into the other room. Charlie heard a cry subside into a long groan before the Iraqi returned, flinging something onto Charlie's plate. "Shall I force you to eat that?"

It was a small piece of scalp, pinkish gray on the underside, the blond hair flecked with blood. Charlie George closed his eyes and swallowed convulsively. He shook his head.

"Good faith? That is the sign of my faith," Hakim said, his breathing very deep. "At your next suggestion you will dine on your friend Kenton." He then described the meal in detail.

Charlie saw that he was in the hands of a rabid animal and kept shaking his head long after Hakim moved away.

It was some time before Hakim thought to have Guerrero tend the new wound, and by that time the captive was faint from loss of blood. It was not a killing wound, Guerrero decided; but like all scalp wounds it had bled excessively. As usual, he said nothing.

The early evening news was innocent of Fat'ah, but Hakim was ebullient, hinting at his motive for optimism. "Your new show time is at eight tonight," he reminded Charlie. "If your people place any value on you, we shall have what we demand."

"The show was taped in pieces weeks ago, you know," Charlie replied, constant pain from his broken nose diluting his voice. "Before they moved us to Wednesdays, even. They don't have to worry about dead air."

"I shouldn't talk so casually about pieces or death if I were you," Hakim rejoined. "I shall bet you one ear that we get coverage."

Charlie made no reply, but tried to read a paperback which Guerrero had discarded. Shortly after his own show began, the captive showed signs of distress. Hakim handed the leash wire to Guerrero who waited in the bathroom while Charlie lost his supper. The audio was up, the door nearly closed. Guerrero took a calculated risk.

"You will not leave here alive, *Carlito*. If you hope, throw that up, too."

Charlie knelt, face in his hands as the ear began to bleed afresh, rocking fore and aft. Muffled by his hands: "Why d'you think I'm so puking scared? NBN won't cave in; we agreed on that tactic. I wish I could retract it now but I can't. And if I could, they still wouldn't." He looked up through streaming silent tears, his hands bloodily beseeching. "And if they would?"

"You would still die," Guerrero said, wondering if it were true. "It is an ancient custom among the bedouin to dismember their captives. Hakim is a bedouin in his heart."

"What can I do?" It was an agonized whisper.

"Die. Slowly, appeasing him, in a week; or quickly, avoiding pain, if you anger him enough." Their eyes met in a long moment of communion. Charlie retched again briefly, and the moment passed.

The Charlie George Show passed as well as Charlie sat near Hakim, the garrotte wire in place. There was no reference to the kidnapping until the end of the show. Charlie normally traded jokes with his audience for a few moments but, instead of the sequence Charlie had taped, his rotund second-banana comic appeared. Standing before a familiar logo, a fiercely satirical sketch for which Dahl D'Este had paid with his life, the chubby comic mimicked a gossip columnist with barbed one-liners. Finally, he said, there was no rumor in the truth—his tongue pointedly explored his cheek—that Charlie and a friend were in a plummet conference with stagestruck terrorists. They wanted a big hand, but Charlie's boy only gave them the finger.

Hakim watched the credits roll, snapped off

the set, and treated Charlie George to a malevo-
lent smile. "You win," he said, "and you lose."

"You got coverage," Charlie husked, "and
anyhow, you're going to do whatever you want
to. NBN got your message, and you got theirs."

"I have other messages," Hakim said, and spat
in Charlie's face.

Charlie saw cold rage in the zealot eyes and
accepted, at last, that the network would not
save him from consequences of events he had
shaped. He spoke to Hakim, but looked at Guerrero. "Have it your way, you pile of pigshit. We
did a skit on that: used your profile on a sow's
merkin, it's the only coverage you rate—"

The garrotte cut off the sudden tirade. Without
Hakim's tape over the wire, Charlie would never
have drawn another breath, as Hakim used the
leash to throw Charlie to the floor. Hakim held
the wire taut, kicking expertly at elbows and
knees until his victim lay silent and gray on the
red-smeared floor. Hakim squatted to loosen the
wire and nodded with satisfaction as the unconscious man's breathing resumed in ragged
spasms, the larynx bruised but not crushed.
Guerrero kept his face blank as he helped drag
their burden into the torture room, then laid his
ballpoint pen on a shelf while Hakim trussed
Charlie to the table. In the corner, surrounded by
the odors of close captivity, Everett breathed un-
evenly as he slept.

"Keep them alive for awhile," Guerrero urged.
To his dismay, he heard Hakim grumble assent.

"The comedian must not cheat me of his
awareness," the Fat'ah leader explained, "when
I take more souvenirs." He paused, studying the

inert hostage, then jerked his gaze to Guerrero. "What was he really saying, Guerrero? *Damn you*, or *kill me*?"

"Does it matter what the tree says to the axe?"

"If only your questions were all so cogent," Hakim laughed. "That was worthy of El Aurans himself—he who understood pain so well. No, it does not matter. Feed Kenton when he wakes. Let him eliminate his waste elsewhere. Tomorrow the comedian will be replenished, and wrung empty again." Hakim turned in immediately. He did not hear the engine of Guerrero's van cough to life an hour later, its exhaust further muffled by a cardboard box.

THURSDAY, 22 JANUARY, 1981:

The man they knew as Kenton woke crying a name. It sounded like 'Jeana', thought Guerrero, forcing himself alert after only four hours of sleep. He handed a cup of cold soup to the bloody wreck of a man and returned to the kitchen, grumbling like a servant. He had taken an enormous risk in contacting his superiors but, he reflected, he was amply repaid in information.

Charlie was half-dragged to their morning meal; one arm useless, the other barely functional. He moaned softly as Guerrero and Hakim attacked their cereal. Then Hakim, using his own traditionally unclean left hand in private amusement, gravely took Charlie's spoon and began to feed him. Charlie knew better than to refuse, saying only, "You are one strange man."

"You must continue to function—and it is easy to be polite to an inferior. Another thing," watching Charlie's difficulty in swallowing, "your schoolboy taunts will not compel me to kill you. Fat'ah is not compelled. Fat'ah compels. And Fat'ah punishes."

"The monitors," Guerrero said, indicating his wristwatch.

"You will watch them when we have taken the comedian to his room, and after you see to the consultant." Hakim had tired of his game with the spoon and, with the implacable Guerrero, conveyed Charlie George to the room he dreaded.

Hakim trussed Charlie to the table again as Guerrero helped his charge to the bathroom some distance away. Then Hakim tugged Charlie's torso to the table's edge. The captive lay face up, hanging half off the table, his head a foot from the spattered floor. He saw Hakim produce the knife, elastic bands, clear plastic tube and gossamer bag, and tried not to guess their uses. Hakim taped him firmly in place as blood gradually pounded louder in the ears of Charlie George.

Hakim brought the knife to Charlie's throat, smiling, and Charlie closed his eyes. Hakim tugged at the torn ear until Charlie opened his eyes again and then, in two quick sweeps, he severed the ear.

The big man in the bathroom stiffened as he heard the scream. With the Browning nuzzling his jaw, he had no option but self-control. At the moment he found the cool water in the basin far more important than anything else on earth. The raw flesh at his temple had clotted heavily, a black patch intruding into the yellow hair. As he inspected it in the mirror, he saw the Panamanian's reflection. It revealed faint sardonic amusement and something else, fainter still. It might have been pity.

"Look closely, Señor Kenton," the reflection said, in tones that would not carry far. "Not at the wound, but at the scalp around it." Everett did so, always conscious of the gun muzzle at his throat. "Is it possible that your hair is growing dark instead of gray?" Their eyes locked for an instant. "Very odd, no?"

Again the cold water over his face, to buy time. "I dye it," he said at last. In a few days, if he lived that long, they would know that much anyway.

"I am sure you do." Guerrero moved aside to let the other man drop his trousers.

"It makes me look younger." Everett strained against constipation, the necessary outcome of his forced inactivity.

"And those faint scars at your hairline; what do they do? What other little secrets do you have in store for me?"

This ape-raping little wetback was toying with him, Everett decided. Either the guy knew everything, or nothing. "It's very common—in the Industry," he grunted.

"Of course it is," Guerrero said in tones that implied denial. He waited until the gore-smeared trousers were in place again, his amusement more pronounced as he backed from the cubicle. With the Browning he waved toward the room where Charlie George lay.

Charlie fought his own screams through clenched teeth, sobbing, straining against his bonds. His face a study in dispassionate interest,

Hakim stanched the flow of blood and, holding
Charlie by his hair, sprinkled a clotting agent
over the grisly mess before he applied a rough
bandage. Guerrero again trussed his own captive, this time in a different corner. He did not
look toward Hakim but he no longer showed
amusement. Guerrero placed his ballpoint pen
on the shelf and laid the adhesive tape near it.

It took Charlie George four tries to say, between gasps "Why?"

"Questions, questions," Hakim sighed. "Your
ear will go to the Los Angeles Times, and its
coverage may provoke your television people.
This may even start a modest war between
media. And this is because I choose," he continued, quickly pulling the flimsy polyethylene
bag over Charlie's head. At this point Guerrero
glanced quickly toward Hakim and then stalked
from the room, the spool of wire lying unused on
the floor.

Hakim snapped the elastic bands around
Charlie's neck and stood back, watching the red
stain spread past his bandage inside the bag.
Charlie's eyes became huge with horror as his
first breath sucked the bag against his nose
and mouth. After twenty seconds, as Charlie
thrashed hopelessly against his bondage, Hakim
thrust the plastic tube under the elastic and into
Charlie's mouth before tugging the bag back into
place. The tube was short and not entirely flaccid, and Hakim pulled his chair near to hold the
free end of the tube away from loose ends of the
bag.

Hakim waited until the breathing steadied.
Charlie's eyes were closed. "Open your eyes,"

Hakim said gently. No response. "Open them,"
he said, placing a fingertip lightly over the tube's
end. Charlie's eyes flew open and Hakim's finger
moved back.

"Have you heard of the dry submarine, my
friend? You are wearing one. The wet submarine
is favored in Chile; it features a variety of nasty
liquids in the bag. Yours may soon qualify as
wet," he added, seeing the runnel of crimson
that painted the bag's interior in Charlie's feeble
struggles.

Hakim did not glance toward his second captive. Had he done so, he would have seen the big
man tearing with his teeth at the fresh tape, gums
bleeding, heedless of the pain.

"Why, you ask, and ask, and ask," Hakim continued, crooning near as though speaking to a
valued confidante, a beloved. "Because you will
perhaps return to your sumptuous life, if it
pleases me. You will be my message to your
medium, a man who knows he has been totally
broken. El Aurans, the Lawrence of Arabia, broke
after long torture and found ambition gone. Few
were his equal but," the dark eyes held a soft
luminosity of madness as he quoted, "'My will
had gone and I feared to be alone, lest the winds
of circumstance ... blow my empty soul away.'
I do not think you can avoid carrying that message," Hakim added. "This is true eastern martial art: corner the enemy, and leave him nothing.
Your Machiavelli understood."

From the other room came Guerrero's call:
"Coverage, Hakim!"

The little man turned in his chair, picked up
the severed ear, and released the tube which lay

nearly invisible against the bag. In three strides he was through the door, to loom at Guerrero's side.

The item was insignificant, merely an admission that an NBN star was a possible kidnap victim. Television was carrying the news, but obviously was not going to dwell on the event. "So, I must contact another medium," Hakim said, and held up his ghastly trophy.

Guerrero blinked. "You do what you do only too well, Hakim."

"Praise, or criticism?"

"It is my mission to help you do all you possibly can." Guerrero smiled at the sharp glance from Hakim; he had spoken the truth, yet not all of it. Nor could he boldly state what he knew about their second captive. It must seem a brilliant suspicion. "I have been studying Kenton very closely, Hakim," he went on. "I believe that his face is a masquerade. Either he or the comedian might be persuaded to discuss the point."

"The comedian?" Hakim barked a laugh. "Not he; not now."

Guerrero was very, very still. "It *has* been quiet in there."

"He no longer complains," Hakim answered, deliberately vague.

"You are finished, then," Guerrero persisted.

It was Hakim's pleasure to joke, thinking of the abject terror in the eyes of Charlie George. "Say, rather, *he* is finished," he rejoined, and turned back toward the torture room.

Guerrero followed unbidden, his excitement mounting, with only a glance toward Everett, whose hands were hidden in his lap. He saw

Charlie George hanging inert like some butchered animal, his head half-obscured in glisten-
ing red polymer. He could not know that Charlie
had spent the past moments desperately inhal-
ing, exhaling, trying with an animal's simplicity
to bathe his lungs in precious oxygen. Charlie's
mind was not clear but it held tenaciously to the
fact that Guerrero was anxious for his death.
Mouth and eyes open wide, Charlie George
ceased to breathe as Guerrero came into view.

Guerrero's mistake was his haste to believe
what he wanted to believe. He saw the plastic
sucked against nostrils, the obscenely gaping
mouth and staring eyes. He did not seek the thud
of Charlie's heart under his twisted clothing and
failed to notice the slender tube emergent from
the plastic bag. "The poor *pendejo* is dead,
then?" He rapped the question out carelessly.

Hakim's mistake was the indirect lie, his automatic response to questions asked in the tone
Guerrero used now. "Truly, as you see," Hakim
said, gesturing toward Charlie George, amused
at Charlie's ploy.

Hakim's merriment was fleeting. From the tail
of his eye he saw Guerrero's hand slide toward
the Browning and, in that instant, Hakim re-
solved many small inconsistencies. Still, he
flung the knife too hastily. Guerrero dodged,
rolling as he aimed, but could not avoid the chair
that struck him as he fired. The Iraqi sprang past
the doorway, slammed the door and flicked the
bolt in place as chunks of wallboard peppered
his face. He had counted five shots from the
Browning against the door lock, but knew the
damned thing held many more. Half blinded by

debris from Guerrero's fire, Hakim elected to run rather than retrieve his own sidearm. It lay at his media display in the path of Guerrero's continued fire against the door. One slug hurled scattered fragments of his beloved Hewlett-Packard unit into the face of a video monitor.

Hakim reached his van quickly, almost forgetting to snap the toggle he had hidden beneath the dash, and lurched toward the road with a dead-cold engine racing and spitting. He dropped low over the wheel, unable to see if Guerrero followed. Hakim had cash and the Uzi, an exquisite Israeli submachine gun, as Fat'ah emergency rations behind him in the van.

Hakim considered stopping to make a stand on the gravel road but checked his rearviews in time to reconsider. Guerrero was there, twenty seconds behind. Hakim would need ten to stop, ten more to reach and feed the weapon. He would fare better if he could increase his lead, and guessed that Guerrero would withhold fire as they passed through the village of Piru. It was worth a try.

Slowing at the edge of the little town, Hakim saw his rearviews fill with Guerrero's van. Whatever his motive, the Panamanian evidently had a hard contract to fulfill and might take insane chances, including a collision in public. Hakim wrenched the wheel hard, whirling through a market parking lot. A grizzled pickup truck avoided him by centimeters and stalled directly in Guerrero's path, and then Hakim was turning north, unable to see how much time he had gained.

The road steepened as Hakim learned from a

road sign that Lake Piru and Blue Point lay
ahead. He searched his rearviews but the road
was too serpentine for clear observation, and
Hakim began to scan every meter of roadside for
possible cover.

He took the second possible turnoff, a rutted
affair with warnings against trespassers, flanked
by brush and high grass. The van threw up a
momentary flag of dust, a small thing but sufficient for Guerrero who came thundering behind,
alert for just such a possibility.

Hakim topped a low ridge and did not see
Guerrero two turns back. Dropping toward a hollow, he tried to spin the van but succeeded only
in halting it broadside to the road. He hurtled
from his bucket seat, threw open the toolbox,
and withdrew the stockless Uzi with flashing
precision. Two forty-round clips went into his
jacket and then he was scrambling from the
cargo door which thunked shut behind him. If
Guerrero were near, let him assault the empty
van while Hakim, on his flank, would cut him
down from cover.

But he had not reached cover when the van of
Bernal Guerrero appeared, daylight showing
under all four tires as it crested the rise before the
mighty whump of contact. Hakim stopped in the
open, taking a splayed automatic-weapons
stance, and fitted a clip in the Uzi.

Almost.

It may have been dirt from the jouncing ride,
or a whisker of tempered steel projecting like a
worrisome hangnail; whatever it was, it altered
many futures.

Hakim dropped the clip and snatched at its

twin, missed his footing, and sprawled in the dust. The van of Guerrero impended, crashing around Hakim's wheeled roadblock into the grassy verge, a great beast rushing upon him. Guerrero set the hand brake and exited running as Hakim, his weapon hoary with dirt, essayed a multiple side roll. He was mystified when Guerrero merely kicked him in the head instead of triggering the automatic.

Hakim waited for death as he gazed into the murky nine-millimeter eye of the Browning. "Daoudist," he surmised bitterly.

"I am Fat'ah," Guerrero mimicked, breathing deeply. His face shone with sweat and elation. "And in Panama, a *Torrijista*, and everywhere, always, KGB." The Soviet agent wiped dust from his mouth, the gun muzzle absolutely unwavering and much too distant for a foot sweep by Hakim. "Rise, turn, hands on your head." Hakim obeyed.

Guerrero marched him back to his own van and forced him to lie prone in the pungent dust. While Guerrero ransacked the toolbox, Hakim listened for distant engines, voices, a siren. In the primeval mountain stillness he could even hear ticks from his cooling engine, but nothing remotely suggested deliverance.

Presently, standing above the little Iraqi, Guerrero ordered his hands crossed behind him. Hakim recognized his garrotte wire by its bite and was briefly thankful it was not about his neck. At further orders, Hakim stalked to Guerrero's own vehicle and lay on his face beside it as he tried to identify a succession of odd sounds.

"Had you the wit to take a four-wheel-drive

path," Guerrero spoke pleasantly as he worked, "you might have escaped. Since the day before yesterday my front differential housing has been full of transceiver gear." Guerrero leaned into his van, arranged the controls, flicked the engine on and stood back. "You wanted coverage, Hakim Arif? Well, turn and stand—and smile, you are live on Soviet television."

The camera in Guerrero's hand looked very like a ballpoint pen but, unlike the unit he had left in the torture room, it did not store audiovisual data. It merely fed its impressions to the transceiver equipment packed into the van's dummy differential case. Hakim considered the possibility of a hoax until he heard the fierce whine of a multikilowatt generator over the engine, and then saw the great inflated meterbroad balloon, spidery metallic film covering its lower segment, that sat on Guerrero's horizontal rear cargo door. Almost certainly a dish antenna, he marveled, for a Soviet Molniya satellite in clarkeian orbit.

Hakim did not show his relief but remained docile as Guerrero shoved him down at the base of a manzanita shrub. Such equipment was fiendishly expensive and tallied well with Guerrero's claim to be a KGB infiltrator. Hakim was limp with gratification; at least his captor represented law and order, not capricious revenge by some gang of charlies.

"There was no American blockade," Hakim accused, and drew a hissing breath as the wire tugged at his wrists.

"What does it matter to whom I turned them? It was neatly done except for the girl, and a bent

mount on the differential housing," Guerrero
replied, slitting Hakim's sleeves, tearing away
the fifty-dollar shirt. "Chaim Mardor is entertaining the KGB—as you would be, had we
known your idiotic choice of sites in advance.
We opted against a motorcade; even you might
have been alerted by that in Moorpark. And later,
they could not bring equipment from Long
Beach in time to pinpoint our location while you
slept. Take credit, Hakim, for preventing us a
regular transmission schedule." Pride forbade
him to add that he had not been furnished with
sophisticated receiving gear, so that feedback to
Guerrero was relatively primitive.

"You are a fool, Guerrero; they could have
homed in on your unit, had you only kept it
going."

"And so might you, with the noise and microwave interference." Hakim took a stinging
slap. "That was for the lecture." Another slap,
with an effect that shocked Hakim. "And that
was for making it necessary to interrogate you
here where the terrain impedes local transmission. I dare not pass that village again before
dark."

Hakim swallowed hard. It was not Guerrero's
brawn that bred such terror with each small suc-
cessive violence. Hakim and pain were dearer
friends than that. Yet he felt a rising sense of
dread, and of something else; a betrayal of faith.
And how could this be so, when Hakim's only
faith was in Hakim?

Guerrero stepped away and laid the pencil-
slim camera on an outcrop of weathered basalt.
"You have seen these before," he chided. "A

similar device recorded your last tender sessions with the comedian. Later I will retrieve the microcorder and feed those scenes to the Molniya. Ravine or no ravine, the Molniya will receive me then, as it receives us now."

As he spoke, Guerrero took a slender case from an inside pocket. Hakim feared the hypodermic but, far worse, dreaded the fact that he was bathed in sweat. He prepared to flail his body, hoping to destroy the injector or waste its unknown contents.

Guerrero was far too battle-wise. He chose a nearby stick of the iron-hard Manzanita and, with a by-your-leave gesture to the camera, suddenly deluged Hakim with blows. It became a flood, a torrent, a sea of torment, and Hakim realized that the thin shrieking was his own. He, Hakim Arif, mewling like any craven Berber? He invoked his paladin's wisdom, ". . . no longer actor, but spectator, thought not to care how my body jerked and squealed."

Jerking and squealing, Hakim cared too much to feel the prick of the needle in his hip.

Hakim rallied with great shuddering gasps, rolled onto his back, and fought down a horror he had expected never to meet. His emissary, pain, had turned against him.

Guerrero leaned easily against a boulder, tossing and catching a drycell battery of respectable voltage. "You have long been a subject of KGB study at Lubianka in Moscow," he glowered, "and I am impressed by our psychologists. You built a legend with your vain volunteer anguish, Hakim, and never knew that the operative word was volunteer." His face changed to something still uglier. "You will divulge two items. The first, Fat'ah accounts. The second is your new Damascus site." He raised the stick and Hakim cowered, but the things that touched his naked flesh were merely the drycell terminals.

Merely an onslaught of unbearable suffering. Hakim needed no verbal assurance to learn that the drug made each joint in his body a locus of gruesome response to even the mildest electrical stimulus. When his spasm had passed he had fouled himself, to the syncopation of Guerrero's laughter.

"Your funds," Guerrero said, extending the drycell, and Hakim bleated out a stream of information. Squinting into the overcast as if to confirm the satellite link thirty-six thousand kilometers away in its unchanging position overhead, Guerrero grinned. "Coding, I am told, is automatic, and gracias a Dios for small favors. But it may take minutes to check your figures. Perhaps in Los Angeles, perhaps Berne or at Lubianka. But if you lie, you must understand that I will quickly know it. Lie to me, Hakim. Please. It justifies me."

Raging at himself, Hakim hurriedly amended crucial figures. The pain in his joints did not linger but its memory overhung him like a cliff. Through it all, degrading, enervating, the sinuous path of Guerrero's amusement followed each of Hakim's capitulations.

When Hakim fell silent, Guerrero pressed his demand. "You are learning, I see. Now: the Damascus site, the new one. The Americans would like to know it, too, but they tend to impose order slowly. We shall be more efficient

even without Pentothal." Hakim squeezed his
eyes tight-shut, breathing quickly, wondering if
it were really possible to swallow one's
tongue—and then the drycell raked his bicep
and jawline.

Hakim was transfixed, skewered on a billion
lances that spun in his body, growing to fiery
pinwheels that consumed him, drove all else
from his being. Hakim was a synonym of appalling agony. Guerrero, who had previously
laughed for the necessary effect, punished his
lower lip between his teeth and looked away. He
wished he were back soldiering under Torrijos,
hauling garrison garbage, anything but this
filthy duty.

Yet appearances were everything and,
"Again? I hope you resist," he lied, and had to
caution Hakim to answer more slowly. Under
torture, the answers came in a fitful rhythm; a
phrase, shallow breathing, another strangled
phrase, a sob, and still another phrase. Hakim
was finished so soon that Guerrero knew embar-
rassment. He had hurried, and now he needed
only wait. The military, he shrugged to himself,
must be the same everywhere.

Waiting for his van's radio speaker to verify or
deny, Guerrero viewed his keening captive with
glum distaste. "The girl was more man than
you," he said in innocent chauvinism. "Chaim
accepted capture, but not she. Another agent
took her knife. She fought. When he pointed the
knife at her belly, she embraced him. I never
heard the sound of a knife like that before, it—"

"Kill me," he heard Hakim plead.

"Before I know how truly you betray Fat'ah? For shame."

"Yes, for shame. Kill me!"

"Because you were so quick to surrender? Because you are not your beloved Lawrence, but only a small puppeteer? Absurd, Hakim. Think yourself lucky to know what you are, at last: a primitive little executive, a controller—even of yourself as victim. Is it so much more glorious to be a masochist pure and simple, than what you really are?"

"Enough! End it," Hakim begged.

"As you ended it for the comedian, perhaps. Let me tell you the greatest joke you will ever hear, Hakim, you snot-gobbling little coward. It is on both of us, but chiefly on you. The big blond one, Kenton, is neither a blond nor a Kenton. I dusted his fingerprints and transmitted them while you sought your damned newspapers. Something about him disturbed me.

"Last night I received a message which I deciphered twice to be certain—and still I wonder how it can be true: *Kenton is your Jewish target, Maurice Everett.*" Guerrero laughed aloud, slapped his belly in a gesture more violent than pleasant. "I hoped you would learn it for yourself so that I could record more of your butchery. But it was unnecessary. As it was, I waited for days on orders to record your disposal of Charlie George. Without those orders, my work would have been simpler." Guerrero spat in irritation.

Hakim stared. The Soviet security organ had waited only to obtain audiovisual records of Fat'ah killing the comedian? He fathomed the

KGB logic gradually, and concluded that they could use such evidence to justify reprisals in Syria, when and if it suited them.

Another thought brought a measure of calm: he still had control over Guerrero's future. Hakim exercised it. "It was not my intent to kill Charlie George," he said distinctly. "*And we left him alive.*"

Guerrero said nothing for ten seconds. "The video record will show that he died," he asserted, licking lips that were suddenly dry.

"It will show his breathing tube, and also what we both already know: that he is an actor." Their eyes met in angry silence.

Guerrero insisted, "The record will vindicate me," and Hakim knew that Guerrero too was posturing for the benefit of the camera pickup. His own effectiveness contaminated by haste, Guerrero would be forced to return—to kill Charlie George himself. And Everett as well, eliminating the last witness.

Guerrero approached again with the drycell and locked his gaze to Hakim's for the last time. Torture would prove nothing more, and Guerrero feared what it might seem to prove. The crowning irony was that under further torture, Hakim might only further compromise his torturer. Hakim trembled in tears, but did not drop his eyes. Guerrero laid the drycell on a stone.

Hakim did not recognize the coded sequence from the van but saw Guerrero register relief at a musical signal. In any case, Hakim in his weakness had told the truth. Guerrero was lashing Hakim's feet with wire at the time, and resumed the job until his prisoner was positioned; feet spread, knees bent, face up. Enraged at Hakim's revelation, Guerrero had chosen a vengeance option. He enjoyed that choice but did not realize its full expense to himself as he stalked to his van and returned.

Guerrero tore a strip of tape, placed it dangling from a branch before Hakim's eyes, and stuck a capsule to the tape within range of Hakim's mouth. "Before I knew you, Arif, I would not do what I do now. Let us say it is for Rashid, whom I hated to sacrifice. Did you think the bomb shackles jammed themselves?" He read the surge of anger that raced across Hakim's face. "So: no, I will not end your life—but *you will*. I wonder if you are devout, and if your followers in Damascus are. In any event, the capsule acts quickly. Exercise your control, Hakim; take one last life on television." With that, he whisked Hakim's van keys away. He brought the drycell near Hakim's side and the Iraqi arched away as well as he might, lashed to bushes by lengths of his garrotte wire.

The drycell went beneath Hakim's naked back, centimeters from contact. Guerrero trotted away with one backward look and Hakim strained fitfully to hold his arch. Weeping, laughing, Hakim knew that Guerrero had left his own van to permit transmission of Hakim's death option. Presumably Guerrero intended to return for his van later.

But Guerrero did not know of the toggle beneath Hakim's dash panel, which reduced the Panamanian's own options to zero.

There was no sound of starter engagement, only the slam of a door before, a moment later, the heavy concussion wave. The earth bucked and Hakim, muscles already past endurance, fell back. He cared nothing for the rain of metal and flesh that showered around him but, deafened and half stunned by the five kilos of explosive he had buried in the van, Hakim could still exult. The drycell had been turned on its side.

Hakim spent many minutes scrabbling at debris before he managed to grasp a stone that would abrade the garrotte wire. He kept enough tension on the wire to satisfy his hunger for torment, all the while glaring at the Soviet camera. He could perhaps make use of the van equipment. He might find most of the money in the wreckage of his own van.

And after that, what? His exploitation of media finally smothered, he had known for weeks that his enemy and erstwhile ally, television, had found an offense that could destroy him. Even before ransacking by the KGB, his coffers were too empty to maintain Fat'ah. The Soviet videotapes would produce hatred and scorn in the people who had previously financed him as easily as they bought English country estates and huge limousines. Hakim would find respect nowhere—not even within himself. There was no more Fat'ah, and Hakim was Fat'ah. Therefore there could be no Hakim.

The wire parted and Hakim rolled away. Eventually he freed his feet, then sat squatting by the drycell. He had triumphed over Guerrero, but that triumph was his last. The proof was that he could not bring himself to touch the drycell.

Hakim took the capsule from the tape with

gentle fingers, smashed the camera. "Forgive, El Aurans," he whispered, and swallowed.

It was minutes before he realized that the capsule was a harmless antihistamine, Guerrero's malignant joke. And an hour before he found that the injection, as Guerrero had known from the first, was the slow killer. But by that time Hakim had stumbled twitching into a stream far from the smouldering wreckage and was past caring. The body, a source of concern in some shadowy circles, was never found.

THURSDAY, 22 JANUARY, 1981:

Guerrero had been right about Chaim Mardor, in the letter if not in spirit: the wiry Israeli was a compelling entertainment. He had first entertained two field agents of the Komitet Gosudarstvennoy Besopasnostiy when he went into clinically certifiable shock at the suicide of Leah Talith. In that condition he was so far beyond reach with drugs, they found it necessary to feed him intravenously for two days, locked with his clothes in a windowless room of a safe house in Pasadena. The door was sturdy. No one but the physician, who had a key, could go through it.

Chaim went over it on Thursday morning, battering a hole in the ceiling with his head and shoulders, the minute he returned to his mortal coil and found his clothes. While Maurice Everett had splashed water on his face, fighting his internal panic over Guerrero's broad hints about double identity, the KGB had a full-scale panic in its safe house.

Chaim Mardor stormed out of the attic that morning, dispatched a balding cipher clerk with a hatrack and kicked the perimeter guard into jelly before taking the guard's cash and pocketing his short-barreled .44 magnum revolver. He had walked several blocks to Colorado Boulevard before he thought to set the red-smeared hatrack down.

The mind of Chaim Mardor was aflame with one concept that burned its way down into his belly: Fat'ah was dead. He had seen her self-sacrifice while Bernal Guerrero, the arm of Hakim Arif, stood by to gloat. And Chaim knew where the Iraqi had taken the hostages, to the frame house Chaim himself had furnished in the orchard past Fillmore. Hakim, Guerrero, even the hostages Chaim had never seen, all were culpable. Anyone in the farmhouse or near it would be equally culpable. Chaim Mardor was a death sentence in tennis shoes.

Chaim hitched a ride with a man in a Volkswagen bus who was virtually his external twin, discounting Chaim's abrasions; dark shoulder-length hair, jeans, and pullover. The driver took his passenger's catatonic silence for simple dejection, but his profound mistake was in patting Chaim on the knee. The single .44 slug passed a hand's breadth from the driver's nose, momentarily blinding him, precipitating his exit without even tapping the brakes.

Chaim took the wheel as the little bus sped up the Ventura Freeway. He slid into the vacated driver's seat and took the next turnoff, oblivious

to the traffic snarl behind him as cars avoided the
man trying to hobble off the freeway with flash
burns, lacerations, and a fractured tibia.

Chaim pawed through area maps in the glove
compartment, throwing those he did not want
over his shoulder into the cargo section. He
found the San Fernando Valley map, located his
position on it, and drove for his destination at a
pace relinquished to the insane. This was perfect
camouflage; everybody in Los Angeles drives
exactly like that.

Had Chaim found the turnoff toward the orchard ten minutes earlier, he might have passed
Hakim and Guerrero driving in the other direction toward mutual destruction. More likely, if at
all possible, Chaim would have smashed head-
on into whichever of them he saw first. El-
Hamma and Hakim had created in Chaim Mardor the ideal arm of Fat'ah; an arm that could
reach out even after the head was severed, re-
morseless, selfless, irrational. But Chaim had the
road to himself as he neared the orchard surrounding the frame house that contained
Maurice Everett and Charlie George.

Everett had torn at his tape in a frenzy the
moment Guerrero kicked the door open to hurl
himself cursing after Hakim. The glass fibers in
the tape resisted him until he managed to roll to
the splintered chair near the comedian. "Hang
on, Charlie," he said, repeating the recitation
like a prayer. He frayed the fibers away, bit by bit,
calming his own harsh respiration, listening
with hope to the whistled breathing of Charlie
George.

Everett did not wait to peel the tape from his

wrists when he had separated them. He ignored
the tape around his ankles as well, springing up
to attack the bindings that held Charlie George.

Charlie's feet were nearest. Everett did not
think to rip the plastic bag from Charlie's head;
perhaps in some way he was reluctant to spill
Charlie's blood. It was an absurdly stupid error
with bizarre consequences.

Peeling the tape from Charlie's ankles, Everett
spotted the knife Hakim had thrown. It lay open
near the doorway and in a moment Everett was
slicing through the stuff at his ankles, then at
Charlie's. He heard the Volkswagen engine then
and rushed to the next room, fearing Hakim's
return.

From the window he saw Chaim Mardor stalk
from the little bus. He had seen the man somewhere, could not place him, but had no difficulty
in identifying the snub-nosed handgun. He
whirled, struck the stump of his finger against a
chair, and dropped the knife as pain bludgeoned
him.

Everett stooped to retrieve the knife, moving protectively toward the front door. Chaim
stepped through.

Chaim was no one. There was no tomorrow;
there was not even a now. But there was a big
man with frightened eyes, and he held a knife,
and a knife had caused the death of Fat'ah. He
raised the handgun and fired as Everett ducked
behind Hakim's media center.

The report was a cannonade in the confined
space, blowing a tape machine into plastic con-
fetti. Chaim needed an instant to recover from
the recoil and to cock the single-action revolver,

holding it in both hands, and in that instant
Everett grabbed the handle of a portable television set. Both men shifted simultaneously,
Chaim squeezing another round off, Everett
swinging the portable set overhand. Everett had
not released the set when the slug plowed into
its steel chassis.

Chaim's handgun was one of a family of
weapons designed to stop the headlong charge
of a madman. At close range, the energy of one
slug from a .44 magnum is such that its impact
against any part of an onrushing enemy will
literally stop him dead. Everett was hurled spin-
ning away, stunned, his arm nearly dislocated at
the shoulder as the television set absorbed the
slug in its guts.

Charlie George concluded from the first explosion that Hakim Arif had returned. Only his
ankles were free, his waist and wrists still taped
to the table. Charlie, his feet facing the door,
could not see Chaim or Everett but he knew
mortal combat when he heard it. He brought his
legs up, then flung them down again. The table
tipped for an instant, almost brought him erect.
Charlie hooked his heels over the lip of the table,
levered his body along the table. This brought
his head up. It was then that he lost his breathing
tube. Frantically, Charlie folded his legs again,
bringing them back nearly over his head, and
gathered his strength.

Satisfied that he had blown the knife-wielder
away, Chaim Mardor turned toward the doorway
and looked into the gloom toward the noise,
cocking the revolver again. He saw buttocks and
widespread arms, Charlie's legs poised for an

instant, and Chaim did not understand what he saw. It did not look like a human form from his view and his finger paused on the trigger.

Charlie's legs came crashing down, the table tipping him up as it fell, and Charlie stabilized himself to stagger upright, arms still pinioned horizontally, the table strapped to his waist. He faced Chaim, strangling.

Chaim Mardor stood rigid, facing the apparition that had appeared before him like every butchered victim of every war in history. Its arms carried no weapon, could carry none in their imitation of the crucified orthodox martyrs of Neturay Karta liturgy. Its head was an almost featureless filmy horror, eyes staring through a shining red slickness. To Chaim Mardor it was victim, retribution, and golem combined in one flesh. He brought the revolver up with great deliberation and fired. Through the roof of his mouth.

Everett was only half aware of the report, strangely muffled, that removed the top half of Chaim Mardor's head. He swung himself to a sitting position against the wall, saw Charlie George reel against the doorway before collapsing.

Everett needed an interminable ten seconds to clear the mist from his brain, to stumble forward and tear the plastic bag from the head of Charlie George. He found the knife, stepping over things he did not want to see, and separated his friend from the table top. Coughing, gasping, Charlie gulped free air, then relaxed with closed eyes.

"Come on, pal," Everett croaked, "don't go to sleep on me now." He saw the unspoken question as Charlie looked at him, chest still heaving. "Those other two cock-wallopers; which one will be coming back?"

The keys were still in the Volkswagen bus. Somehow, weaving like a drunk, Everett drove it to Moorpark.

SATURDAY, 24 JANUARY, 1981:

Everett did not attend the private cremation service for Charlie George in Pasadena, convinced by physicians, the eloquent threats of David Engels, and telephone pleas of Gina Vercours. Instead, he waited at a Beverly Hills rendezvous for Rhone Althouse, who did attend.

Althouse gained entry by way of a conduit tunnel with its own guarded entrace. The only identification procedure was a handprint analysis, but its brevity was deceptive. Gas chromatography assured that the whorls were not synthetic while standard optical matching techniques pronounced Althouse's hands to be the genuine articles.

"Somehow I never thought of you as a redhead," was Everett's first remark as Althouse entered the waiting room.

"Life is a puttynose factory," Althouse returned, taking the big hand. "I wouldn't have recognized you at all except for the newspaper shots of Simon Kenton."

"That's one photographer I'd like to get my hands on," Everett growled. "For those of us bent on nudging it, a free society can get awfully expensive."

"You'll slide off the back pages of the papers in a few days," Althouse predicted, "now that Charlie is dead."

Everett, frowning: "Helluva loss to NBN."

"We have to think of it that way: ol' Charlie is defunct, expired, gone to his reward. And that's okay, so long as my old friend Byron Krause is still sniffin' the breeze," Althouse waved a gleeful finger.

Everett glanced at the wall clock. "Visiting hours are a sham in here, Rhone; let's jump the gun a few minutes."

"Don't say 'gun'," Althouse grumbled, following Everett to the elevator. Moments later they submitted to another print-check before entering the private room of Byron Krause. The attendant who opened the door never spoke but he did a lot of watching. Instinctively the visitors made every gesture slow and cautious.

The face behind the bandages must have tried to smile, to judge from the crinkles around the mouth and eyes. "Ow, dammit," said the familiar voice. "Maury, do you live here? I saw you this morning." The slurring was not any lack of alertness, but implied the constraints of the tiny anchors that kept the facial planes properly positioned.

"You were just whacked out this morning, Charlie. Sure I live here, until they get me patched. They're going to make me a new fingertip, too; guess where the skin is coming from," he smiled sadly, laying a hand on his hip.

"Pain in the ass, I expect," from Althouse.

From the bed: "Listen Rhone, glad as I am to see you, first good one-liner out of you and my silent partner here will cut you down."

"Don't say 'cut'," Althouse muttered, then slapped his own mouth. "Look: I'm a compulsive. Change the subject. What really happened at that farmhouse?"

Everett found a chair, Althouse another. Federal agents had pieced much of the story together, aided by tire tracks, reports of a high-speed chase, and fingerprints linking the destroyed van to the Iraqi, Hakim Arif. Everett supplied some of the information as he had it from Engels. "But I guess the biggest surprise, after all, was your opting for the identity change," Everett finished, nodding toward the comedian.

"I had a lot of time to think, before the media people got tipped off to who and where I was," was the reply. "I decided I'd rather be a live Krause than dead with all those other charlies. Funny thing is, that sadistic little shit Hakim messed me up so much, cosmetic surgery was necessary anyhow."

"How about the ear?"

"They can make me a new one. Some agent found my ear; stepped on it. Boy, some of the apologies I get," he shook the bandaged head ruefully.

Althouse brightened. "I gather from the news that Fat'ah's home base in Syria got creamed by

some other bunch there—and that should write
'em all off, now that Hakim Arif is feeding flies
all over Los Padres National Forest."

"No, he isn't," the big Commissioner said, and
shrugged into the silence he had created. "This
is for your ears only, God knows it's little
enough. Seems that the Soviets get nervous
when anybody but themselves begins to panic
the American public. They leaked the word—
don't ask me why, a quid pro quo maybe—that
the Iraqi turned his whole fanatical gang under
interrogation."

"Probably the kind we don't like to do," Althouse put in.

"I expect so. But Arif got away into the mountains afoot after that explosion. They think it was
the other guy, Guerrero, who's the flies's breakfast. But the Soviets think Arif was dying."

"They think; they don't know," Althouse
whispered.

"Disinformation at all levels," Everett replied.
"It's inevitable. Our people hope they've con-
vinced the KGB that they were wrong about an
FCC Commissioner hiding behind the face of
Simon Kenton."

"I'm resigned to being part of it," said the
comedian. "But if they can alter my larynx properly along with the rest of it, I may show up as a
retreaded top banana on TV again, one of these
days. You can't beat the money."

Althouse: "And if they can't alter you
enough?"

"Oh—I don't have to work. We'll get together
again and gin up something for the three of us,

maybe after the Commissioner's seven-year term is over."

"Could happen sooner than you think," Althouse said quickly. "I keep fingers into ABC surveys. It'd be easy to include a few items to find out who the public sees as enemies of terrorism. If the names vary widely or change quickly, I could see that the data gets published. Maybe an article in *TV Guide*."

"The point, Rhone, the point," said Everett.

"Isn't it clear? The point is, every charlie on earth should learn in time that it's the idea, and not the man, they're up against."

Everett cleared his throat. "And if you're wrong? If the same few names keep cropping up?"

"He'll falsify the data," chuckled the bandaged head.

"The hell I will," said Althouse with asperity. "I have some ethics. Nope, but I wouldn't publish the data, either. My ethics are, uh, flexible," he admitted.

"That's a relief," said the ex-Charlie George. "Your media theories have cost us all the parts we can spare. Oh, quit looking at me like that, Rhone, I'm not blaming you. You were right about the solution."

"And Everett was right about the odds against us," Althouse sighed.

"They ran out on D'Este," Everett agreed, adding, "and I'll miss the Charlie George Show."

"Just remind yourself it was all a lot of hype," Rhone Althouse said, grinning at the bandaged face for understanding. "When you think of the

odds this funnyman beat, you realize he was
never a very proper charlie."

Everett glanced at his watch. "Time for my
ultraviolet treatment," he said, getting up.

"I'll see you here again, then?" said Althouse

"For a few more days. Then I've got a date up
in the high lonesome with a one-room cabin."
He did not add, *and a blonde I'm very fond of,
who likes to ski when she isn't near a bed or a
tennis court.*

"In January? You're wacko, sire," Althouse
laughed.

"There is that," said Everett, and sauntered
out.

FRIDAY, 13 FEBRUARY, 1981:

Nearly three weeks crawled by before Everett's skin grafts satisfied the surgeons in Beverly Hills. The new finger would always be numb and stiff at the tip, and it would never leave a print. Fingerprints could be fashioned, but the technique was an outrage in time and money.

Maurice Everett gained almost no weight while in the clinic because the food all seemed to be vaseline in various disguises so the hell with it, and also because he daily performed all of the calisthenics he hated.

On a Friday evening, hair bleached afresh, implanted follicles flourishing in the graft at his temple, Everett bade his friend Byron Krause a brief farewell. "I'm going shopping," he crowed.

"Those are mighty domestic noises you're making," the ex-comedian called after him.

"Get your ear rebored," Everett called back, and walked on. He considered lingering to admit the truth; that he was feeling a call to upholster his cave, to ask a leggy lady bear to share it permanently, and intended to do so when he got the chance. No one knew his plans for the next week—except for Gina, of course. If he kept it that way there could be no slips, no vulnerability.

Engels had found him another superskate, a white virgin Mini-Cooper wearing Pennsylvania plates and sporty British car club badges as big as its hubcaps. It was, thought Everett, like pinning rhinestones on a gyrfalcon, but it would never be connected with Maurice Everett.

At an outfitter's store he found a down-filled bag that would zip onto his, laughing as he paid the ionospheric tab with Simon Kenton's charge card. He was remembering the night before his kidnapping, the first time he had found a grassy nook with Gina in the balm of a Southern California winter evening. ("Don't take off yuh coat, stranguh," she had deadpanned; "we could wind up half a mile from heah . . .")

Browsing among the freeze-dried foods, he had no trouble choosing those Gina liked best. At three-kilometer altitudes above the ski lift near Tahoe, they would eat with the abandon of starving weasels.

At a bookstore he chose volumes they would both devour: Muir, Renault, Steinbeck, Sturgeon. The Lovecraft, he thought with a lewd grin, was for nights when the wind ululated in the eaves of the cabin, when she would nestle against him for more than physical warmth. Given enough books and dehydrated stroganoff, they might not come down for years.

Stroganoff. The Russian word provoked a thought-chain ending with David Engels. He stowed the packages in the Mini, using only the surface of his mind to begin the drive up Interstate Five where, at Sacramento, he would sleep.

Engels had visited him twice in the clinic. The first time there was only good news: Gina, railing against the rules of the game to Engels, who did not have enough clout with physicians to get her into Everett's room. The Commission, which accepted Everett's participation via tapes and proxies, though Engels had caught some meditative glances in conference. The press, which had gone baying off after false musks when it determined that Simon Kenton was not worth a great deal of investigative reportage.

On his last visit, Engels had been more subdued, with good news and other news. The good news was that Gina had not stopped demanding to see her man. Everett knew that much; they spent too much money on scrambler-equipped telephone calls for him not to know. After one plaintive call from Phoenix, Everett had threatened to send her a vibrator. At the time, she had questioned his taste in coarse humor.

And two days later she had sent him the most startling dirty greeting card he had ever seen. As usual, some yahoo had already opened it as a routine precaution. But when he first picked it up, Everett thought he was empathizing a facet of Gina Vercours he had not felt before. It was a thin buckram volume filigreed with silver, restrained and elegant. It should have been the poetry of Keats, but its title was *Apotheosis of Tissues*. Inside was one page of onionskin with the couplet:

Could silk or satin aspire to moa'
Than sepulchre for spermatazoa?

And behind that page were fifty more pages—all of facial tissue. He had cursed because his left hand was strapped to his hip, and he tended to kick his legs when he laughed.

The other news from David Engels was passing strange. A middleman from the Central Intelligence Agency had learned of some subtle backtracking into NBN visitors and consultants by a private-investigating firm. The firm's only mistake was in failing to realize early that its client was a foreign agency which they never did manage to identify.

Among the persons of interest was a big husky specimen named Simon Kenton. That was all Engels had. It might mean nothing. On the other hand, it suggested that Everett might be well-advised to pack a Browning parabellum and, Engels had tapped a stiletto forefinger on Everett's breastbone, to get goddam good with it.

Everett thought about that, off and on, all the way to Sacramento.

SATURDAY, 14 FEBRUARY, 1981:

Gina Vercours rubbed her hands together as she watched the blaze spread under seasoned wood. She had found the cabin exactly where he had said it would be, a few kilometers above the top of the chairlift, just north of the saddleback behind which lay the very nascence of the turbulent American River. She was supposed to meet him at the foot of the chairlift at Sunday noon but, knowing Maury, she didn't trust the canny bastard. He'd come sneaking up to the cabin a day early, more than likely, to lay out some fey greeting as a surprise. Well, she could play that game too.

She smiled. Who would ever expect black satin sheets and a down comforter in a one-room cabin? After this, Maury Everett would.

A shadow crossed her mind. Everett would, she amended, if he lived. She stared into the flames as they grew, feeling the heat on her face, thinking it was how the sun might feel on a beach in Baia, thinking how it must feel when you are unextraditable on that beach in Brazil with the equivalent of a million dollars in Brazilian cruzeiros. That option was squarely in her lap, thanks to the KGB.

And all she had to do was show up there and claim it. That and one other detail, really the simplest detail of all. Because Maurice Everett trusted her.

It was a hell of a world, she reflected: you search until you are tired of searching for a man who has the virtues of machismo without its vices, and then they won't let you alone with him. They tangle him up in flags and finance, play political hockey using him as the puck, hound him finally into becoming something and someone he never wanted to be. And even that wasn't enough.

Better for her if she had never heard of Everett. She could have come to terms with a lower-middle-class life eventually, when the special jobs ran out. Everett, she was certain, had no intention of marrying. It hadn't been too late to leave Everett as he was when she'd met Charlie George, not even when she'd received the call, the only time she ever passed out from a telephone message, saying Everett was alive and en route from Moorpark to Beverly Hills in an unmarked FBI vehicle. It was not too late until the KGB, by some means she might never discover, connected her with Kenton, and Kenton with Everett. That was when the offer had come. All she had to do was kill Simon Kenton.

Why? No answer. Perhaps he had information

connecting Fat'ah with the Soviets. Perhaps they only thought he might have it. Perhaps, after all, Maurice Everett was only a symbol to them; a flag the KGB would like to see at half-mast.

It wasn't fair. The act would be so simple with his trust, so unspeakably complex because of that trust. She still had not decided, could not decide without Maury's unwitting help. There was plenty of time, weeks of it, and several directions to go across the high country if she should choose Baia over snowshoes.

Then she looked out the single window and saw him, standing tall in his leathers, staring across, probably at her tracks and the smoke from the chimney. He leaned back on the snowshoes, jogging down in his easy lope, the skis still high on his back. He could easily have switched to skis, she knew, sweeping down and around to impress her. And of course he would never dream of such a display, and this impressed her. She would ski better than he did, beat him six-oh in a million consecutive sets, and he would still be ready to take up the challenge. She would kill him, but she could not defeat him.

She had decided. She threw open the cabin door, squinting in the dazzle, smiling as he approached.

"I knew it, I goddam knew it," he puffed, grinning back, shaking his head as he removed the snowshoes. "Boy, did I have a surprise for you." Well, he still had a surprise for her, unless she expected his proposal already.

"What a coincidence," she said, the laugh throaty as she knew he liked it.

He stamped snow from his heavy shoes, swung the door shut behind him and lowered his pack to the floor. "Hey," he said, as she unsnapped his down jacket to run her hands inside.

She kissed him hungrily. "You'll run out of those one day," she murmured. "I'm gettin' it while it's good."

"Better than Kleenex," he grinned, "you randy bitch, you."

She persisted. "Another one, lover. The second thing you do is take off your coat."

He enjoyed her hunger; it matched his own. "Sorry I haven't shaved," he said into her ear. "I'll get handsome for you later."

She pulled back, the fire shining in her hair, amusement in her face. "You look," she said, "like a million dollars."

AFTERWORD

It's not always a joy to murmur, "I told you so." For the record, the trade edition of *Soft Targets* was on bookshelves before Iranian extremists stormed our embassy in November, 1979. A few people have asked whether the book may have even taught Middle-East militants to hold Americans hostage so that they could use our own media against us. It's a fair question.

Thank God I can live with the answer: trained political extremists *already knew*. The Soviets gleefully focus on any facet of our way of life that lends itself to our destruction—and carefully explain those facets to 'students' recruited to Moscow's Patrice Lumumba University for graduate work in subversion and terrorism. For nonfictional details on Lumumba Tech, I refer you to John Barron's *KGB*, and Ovid Demaris's *Brothers in Blood*.

Not that our enemies have to attend Muscovite seminars for their tactics; the KGB opened branch schools in other countries a long time ago. It's an ill-trained extremist who hasn't already learned that our *laissez faire* media— when their decisions are short-sighted—are ripe for his exploitation.

I first chewed on the problem during post-graduate work in media theory in the early 1970's. Terrorists were already gaining world-wide media forums by brutalizing innocents; it seemed to me only a matter of time before they'd do it to Americans. I didn't write about it then. I didn't have a remedy that would work in a free society.

Yes, I knew Orwell had written his future vision of 1984 without offering detailed remedies. I also knew that some critics deny that Orwell's book is science fiction, although it contained stunningly original work in the psychology of language, not to mention political science. I felt that, if psycholinguistics theory and media theory are sciences, then speculative fiction in those disciplines must be science fiction.

Well, I was already a writer of sf. I was also frustrated at my own terrorism/media scenarios because, at first, I kept cobbling up government control remedies in my head; and none of them were exactly models of free enterprise. Gradually, seeking alternative controls, I contrived the 'media war' thesis that was woven into *Soft Targets*. But nobody wants to be harangued in a piece of entertainment (sorry, Ayn Rand); so the book is only five per cent media theory. If I've done my job, the rest is entertainment.

Some of my colleagues in communication theory warned me, "It's hopeless, Ing. You can't succeed in commercial media, grabbing it by the short hairs. You're biting the hand before it feeds you."

I said, "You're forgetting science fiction." Few of my scholar friends believe there are commercial media people like Jim Baen and Ben Bova, *agents provocateurs* of speculation.

And almost everyone said, "For God's sake

don't admit you wrote *Soft Targets* with intent to commit message!" Well, the hell with lying about it. But my implied charter was to write an sf thriller and, if I failed in that, I was (at most) only five per cent successful. You judge.

Dean Ing, February 1980